It's *(mostly)*
Good
to be
Martha

ISBN: 978-0-9743076-6-4

Library of Congress Control Number: 2025908164

Cover and layout design by Lance Buckley

It's (mostly) Good to be Martha

a novel

MERSHON NIESNER

In loving memory of my BFF

Margaret Hoefle

7/9/34 – 2/20/24

Chapter One

The plaque on the office desk informed anyone who was paying attention that this was the office of Agnes Duly, RN, Assisted Living Director, Martyn Manor. The room felt overly warm and cramped with Agnes, Harold Lancaster, and me in close proximity. An overhead fluorescent light flickered; my chair was hard and straight-backed.

Harold had already been reprimanded, so it was my turn. As requested, I stood with some effort, my new hip stiff from sitting too long. "My name is Martha Anderson and I've broken the rules," I said. Under my breath I whispered, "Again." I knew I was taking a chance by asking a question at this stage of the game, but I was dying to know the answer. "Before you begin your interrogation—" Agnes frowned at the word, "may I ask how you discovered that my friends and I were out for the evening?"

"Your neighbor, Ethyl Haggerty, was walking the halls when she heard strange noises coming from certain apartments. She feared it was another plumbing issue and kindly notified the staff," replied Agnes sternly, her face a mask of pseudo-authority. "Given the apartment numbers, I guessed it was you and your cronies leaving the facility after hours and without giving proper notification to the staff. Now, may I continue?"

"Yes, ma'am," I said as contritely as possible. I should have known Ethyl was the snitch. She was always glaring at us from across the dining room. What was her problem anyway?

"Would you please repeat the question?" I asked, my mind returning to the present.

Agnes frowned and increased her volume. "I said, what do you have to say for yourself, Martha?" Although nurses gave up wearing starched white uniforms years ago, Agnes made wrinkled surgical scrubs look imposing.

"I'm sorry?" I looked at her and smiled, showing off my super-white veneers. At eighty-nine, I was like the family troublemaker. Since I'd been a goody-two-shoes for most of my life, I rather liked my new persona.

She shook her head and pursed her lips. "That won't do. You need to be more specific. What are you sorry for and how do you intend to make amends?"

My dad would have said Agnes was built like a fire plug. Since I'd recently become a football fan, she reminded me of Zach Tom, a three-hundred pound offensive tackle for the Green Bay Packers. She was endowed with a body that would be convenient if you were in the habit of slinging hay bales or maneuvering old folks in and out of beds and off of toilets. She gave me a most intense 'I'm going to get you at the snap' stare down.

When Agnes tapped her pen on the desk, reminding me that I was wasting her precious time, I shifted from one foot to the other. This wasn't due to nervousness but rather because it still felt like one leg was longer than the other even though my orthopedic surgeon (his PA, really; who sees their surgeon?) assured me this wasn't the case.

"I was the ringleader in a recent escapade. My friends are completely innocent, by the way. In the future, I will not order an Uber and go to Sam's Place after hours without informing the staff."

"And?" prompted Agnes.

"And that's all. What more do you want me to say?" I tried not to sound perturbed, but this was getting ridiculous.

"I asked how you'll make amends," Agnes said in a flinty voice.

"Oh yes. Well…" I had no idea how I'd make amends. Good grief, I wasn't in kindergarten. Did she want me to say I'd stand in the corner? Wear a dunce hat? Perhaps she wanted me to hand over my electronic devices, a tactic that seemed to work as a disciplinary measure with kids these days. Tap, tap, tap. The pen again. I had to think of something quick. "For the next seven days I'll go to my apartment immediately after dinner and stay there until breakfast. Even," I paused, racking my brain for the week's entertainment schedule, "even if outside entertainment comes to Martyn Manor." I used the full name of the facility in a show of respect.

Agnes made a note on her iPad. "Very well, Martha. But what about the staff who frantically searched for you and your friends? How will you make it up to them?"

This was the only part of my shenanigans that troubled me. I felt bad that my friends and I caused the staff anxiety. By and large, they were a good bunch, especially the night crew.

Who in the world wanted to babysit a bunch of old folks while they slept? B-O-R-I-N-G! I hoped they got extra pay.

Tap, tap, tap.

I sat down. My body didn't tolerate standing well; it much preferred sitting or walking. Storm clouds gathered across Agnes' broad face, but I didn't care.

"I'll apologize to each of them and invite them to come by my apartment for a can of soda. How's that?" Most evenings they came by around eight o'clock for soda and a chat anyway, but Agnes didn't know that. She was home alone, slumped down in front of her television by then.

"Forget the soda. It distracts them from their work. However, I will follow up on your apologies by asking them to email me after they've heard from you."

"Are we done now? I'm late for dinner and I hate to keep my friends waiting," I said with a phony smile.

"Yes, you're both dismissed." Agnes looked at me, then at Harold, who had also committed a "crime." My dad would have called us rascals.

Harold got up slowly, walked to the door, and held it open for me. "After you, Martha," he said in his deep baritone voice.

"Why, thank you, Harold. Are you going to the dining room?"

"Indeed I am. May I escort you?"

"I'd be delighted," I replied as I sashayed out the door in front of him. While walking down the hall, we talked about the unfairness of being called on the carpet.

"I had no idea that having my great-granddaughter for a sleepover would cause such a commotion," Harold said.

"I agree. It seems that this place is going to take some getting used to," I replied.

When we reached the dining room, we went our separate ways. Tables were unofficially reserved for groups who sat together at dinner. I sat at a round table for six. Madge, Molly, Margaret, Sally (we called her Missy so she'd be an M), and Anna (she didn't give a damn) were already seated at our table. Conversation stopped, and all eyes turned toward me as I eased into my usual chair. My co-conspirators in the late night (by Manor standards) escapade eagerly leaned in, waiting to hear what had happened at my disciplinary meeting with Agnes.

Madge, impatient as always, spoke first. "Well? Don't keep us waiting. What did she say? Are we all going to be locked up in the clink?" If she were standing, her hands would have been on her ample hips. A retired banker of some sort with gray hair drawn back into a tight bun, Madge wore no makeup or jewelry. She was normally our voice of reason but apparently, she was off her game last night. Either that or prior to dinner, she'd had more vodka than usual.

I unfurled my cloth napkin and carefully placed it in my lap. The dining room was formally set at dinner. Walls painted a soft aqua gave the place a fresh, coastal vibe. White and gray faux marble floors were for the convenience of those residents who used walkers. During the day, the room was flooded with an abundance of light from the bank of windows running along the outside wall. Tonight, there was a bud vase with three pink carnations adorning the middle of each table. We ordered our meals individually from a menu featuring two or three choices. Our dinners were served by uniformed waiters and waitresses, usually college students.

"None of you are going anywhere. You're all in the clear." There were audible sighs of relief around the table.

"What about you?" Missy asked, her brows drawn together.

"I'm definitely not going anywhere. For the next seven days, I'll be returning to my apartment immediately after dinner and staying there until breakfast." I looked around at the serious faces. "There's nothing exciting going on this week, is there?"

Molly, our "sweet young thing" at seventy-six who was always dressed to the nines, sported jet black hair, and executed a perfect eye-wing, answered. "I think the guitar guy is coming on Wednesday, but that's about it." She coquettishly cocked her head to one side and gave me a sweet smile. "I propose we assemble later than usual for dinner so your evening won't be quite so long. Perhaps 5:30?" Molly looked around the table for a reaction.

"You'd be willing to meet that late?" I asked, surprised by the kind offer. All heads nodded in the affirmative and the matter was settled.

After dinner, my friends left the table and headed toward the social room where Charmaine, our resident pianist, was playing jazz. Most nights, we sang along or simply sat and enjoyed the music. I reluctantly made my way to the unwelcome solitude of my cozy, in other words small, apartment. As I turned the corner to my hallway, I saw Harold leaning against the wall a few feet from my door. Seeing him again so soon was a pleasant surprise, but his presence also made me wonder what was going on. He was holding a brown paper bag.

"Hello, Martha. I see you're marching to Agnes' orders and making it an early evening."

I nodded. Whatever he was up to, I wasn't going to make it easy for him.

He put his free hand behind him and pushed off the wall. "Since you're confined to quarters this evening, I was wondering if you'd like company?" He held up the bag. "Perhaps share a bottle of wine?"

I carefully considered the offer. It was Monday night, but since the Packers weren't playing, there wasn't much on TV. Besides, a little male companionship wouldn't hurt. I wondered if he was a football fan. "Thank you, Harold. That's very considerate of you." I unlocked my door and he followed me inside. I dutifully put my key on the hook so I'd know where to find it in the morning. "I'll enjoy the company but not the wine. In the last couple of years, I've become more of a beer drinker."

Harold raised his eyebrows then pointed to the couch. "Go make yourself comfortable while I hustle down to Fred's apartment. He keeps a supply of beer in his mini fridge." Harold set the bag with the wine in it on my small, oval dining table. "I'll be back in a jiffy."

For a man up in years, he made good on his promise to hustle. I watched through my open door as he briskly walked down the hall. I considered whether or not I was attracted to him. I had noticed Harold before, of course; it's hard not to notice the few men in our facility, but I knew nothing of his character so at that moment, all I had to go on was his appearance. He had thinning white hair (at least there was hair), broad shoulders that were a little stooped, and alert blue eyes looking out from trendy, metallic-gray rimmed glasses.

One thing I considered a little odd was Harold's choice of attire. He wore jumpsuits, a one-piece outfit I'd call a onesie if I put it on a baby. I was aware that grown men occasionally wore them to do woodworking or handy-man tasks but it was unusual to see them worn to dinner. Harold's jumpsuit had short sleeves and covered his legs (thank goodness). They were colorful (tonight he was sport-ing burgundy), clean and, I had to admit, looked quite com-fortable. Also, the one-piece suit mitigated Harold's slight paunch. All in all, he wasn't too bad for an old guy.

According to what I'd learned in our joint meeting with Agnes, he was disciplined for allowing his nine-year-old great-granddaughter to sleep over in his apartment with-out the staff's knowledge or permission. She was discovered when Ada, Harold's cleaning lady, let herself in on her usual day and found the child asleep on the couch. Harold had gone to the dining room for an early breakfast. When Ada gave a start, the suddenly awakened little girl screamed, which according to Agnes, caused the staff to run from all directions thinking something dire had happened to a resi-dent. After the poor girl, I think her name was Marcella (another M), calmed down, the supervisor went in search of Harold to sort things out. All this didn't sound very serious to me. In fact, I thought it was rather sweet that he had a sleepover with his great-grand.

I placed two glasses on the table. I considered it unlady-like to drink from a can or a bottle. When Harold returned, he carefully poured my beer, then poured himself something red, perhaps a burgundy. At least he wouldn't have to worry if he dribbled down the front of his jumpsuit. After settling himself in my recliner, which I'd kindly left for him, Harold immediately launched into the story of his wife of sixty-five years dying and how her demise precipitated the displacement from his home to the Manor.

"I wouldn't be here if I'd learned to cook and do other household chores in my more formative years." He turned a shade of pink then looked away.

Harold may have been embarrassed, but I appreciated his honesty. In some ways, he was a victim of his generation—a time when men went to work and women stayed home and did all the cooking and cleaning.

"Also, my ticker isn't working quite right, so sometimes I need urgent medical attention. Otherwise, I'm as fit as a fiddle." He patted his chest. "Basically, I'm here for the three squares and clean sheets. What about you?"

I took a minute to think about how much to reveal before I answered. "My past is slightly more complicated than yours, but that's not why I'm here." I knew I had piqued Harold's curiosity, but I decided to save the more sordid details of my life for later. At this stage of our friendship, I intended to simply answer the main question. "I burnt a pot."

"And that's how you ended up here?" Harold asked with incredulity.

"Yes, I—-"

There was a loud knock on the door. "Martha, are you in there?"

The night crew had come for their soda and chat. "Yes," I hollered. "Come on in."

"Your door is usually open a crack and—" Judy, the RN on night duty, stopped in mid-sentence when she saw Harold sitting in my usual chair with a glass of wine pressed to his lips. The other two staff members, who had trooped in behind her, stopped in their tracks. "We're sorry to have interrupted your evening, Martha. We had no idea you were entertaining a guest."

Judy's face turned red, which only added to her fresh-as-a-daisy, schoolgirl charm. She had lovely skin, big brown eyes, and a pink rosebud mouth. She was a little skinny for my taste, but I knew it was the trend. I motioned for them to come forward. "You're not interrupting. Harold stopped by for a visit since I'm restricted to my apartment…" I looked at each of them, "as you've probably heard."

They stood awkwardly in the middle of my sitting room, and I could tell they were trying to decide whether to stay or leave. "Before you go—" I said, solving the issue for them, "I'd like to apologize for causing you distress last night. Truthfully, I thought our absence would go undetected, but you're a diligent group and I appreciate your concern. Will you accept my apology?" I looked at the sweet faces of Judy, Josh, and Kate. All three were under thirty—children, really—and they seemed eager to please the old lady who had become their friend and confidante.

Judy, who seemed to be the unofficial spokesperson for the night, responded. "Even though you scared the daylights out of us, we accept your apology."

After I said thank you, she continued. "We thought you all might have been abducted," she took a breath, "or worse."

"Now, Judy," I said in my best no-nonsense voice, "you know nothing as exciting as that ever happens here. Actually, the thought of putting a little excitement into our lives is why I came up with the idea of going to Sam's Place. I read on the Internet that it's a popular place for college kids and they have live music on Sundays." My voice rose as I relived the evening. "The hype was all true. The pop hits they played were a bit lively for us oldsters, but we enjoyed the atmosphere. I made a rule that we could only have one alcoholic drink each to negate the chance of falling."

"Good idea," Judy said with a deadpan expression.

"I have to let things cool down for a while but if we decide to go again, I'll let you know the night before so you won't worry. How's that?"

The other two smiled, but not Judy. "We'll pretend we didn't hear that," she said in her most grown-up voice.

To diffuse the chilly atmosphere, I pointed to the mini fridge. "Go collect your sodas," I nodded toward Harold so there was no doubt that he was invited to stay, "and leave us to our old-timer stories."

Judy handed out the half-size cans of soda my son kept in stock for me. If I regularly gave the team full cans they would stay too long and I could only listen to so many dramatic stories at a time. I did, however, try to give them good advice gleaned from my many years of living. Listening to their troubles gave me the feeling that I could still make a difference.

On their way out, Judy gave Harold a look that said, "Be a gentleman!" Apparently chastened by the earnest young lady, he quickly looked down into the ruby red of his wine.

After the door closed, I picked up the thread of our conversation. "Yes, all it took for me to take up residence here was a burnt pot and a retired lawyer, always-looking-at-the-worst-case-scenario son who spoke with my two daughters. The trio unanimously declared that I should no longer live alone in a space with a stove at my disposal." I looked at Harold who was still listening intensely.

"I might have had a few prior slip-ups but the burnt pot and subsequent visit by the fire department was the final straw for my children. As the oldest, my son has always been the leader of the pack, so he immediately hired a team to load up my few belongings that would fit into this minuscule space, engaged Got Junk? to pick up the rest, then whisked me away to Martyn Manor so fast it made my head spin."

I saw empathy bloom in Harold's eyes. "Are you mad or sad about having to move here so abruptly?"

I appreciated his introspective question. Was I mad or sad? I wasn't sure. I tended to live in the present, and at that moment, I was happy sitting there having an interesting conversation with a cold one in my hand. "I don't believe I'm mad or sad. Moving here was a big change but this is a lovely new establishment and since my son is footing the hefty bill, I have no complaints. I suppose moving to a facility like this was my destiny sooner or later."

Harold encouraged me to go on. He was such a good listener.

"I'm not as spry as I once was, although I'm doing much better now that I have a new hip. My memory isn't great but truth be told, it never was very good so it's hard to tell if dementia has set in or people are just noticing my forgetfulness now that I'm pushing ninety."

I turned and saw that the clock on my wall was coming up to eight-thirty. Although it wasn't late, I suddenly felt like a wrung out rag doll. I needed to wrap up this conversation and call it a night. So, without preamble, I said, "It's been a lovely evening, Harold. Thank you for stopping by."

I got up and took my beer glass to the alcove that's my half-kitchen. You could hardly call a mini fridge, sink, and cupboard a kitchen, but it negated the possibility of another fire. Harold came up beside me, rinsed out his glass, and placed it on the drainer.

"Perhaps we can do this another time?" he offered.

"Perhaps." I wasn't committing to anything. One never knew; maybe a better offer might come along. I had the feeling it was going to be an interesting week.

When I opened the door, Harold picked up his wine bottle, returned it to the brown paper bag, then stepped out. "Have a good rest of the evening, Martha."

"You too, Harold."

Chapter Two

The late night outing on Sunday, the stress of the disciplinary meeting, Harold's surprise visit intersecting with staff dropping by, and the lovely beer resulted in a particularly restful night's sleep. It helped that I only had to get up twice to go to the bathroom. Upon arising, I showered, dressed in my workout clothes, then exited my apartment and headed to the dining room for breakfast. Feeling as chipper as a sixty-something, I walked along the corridor at a faster clip than usual.

Breakfast was cafeteria-style. Our group only sat together for dinner. After taking a tray, I poured Grape-Nuts cereal into my bowl. I'd been eating the cereal since I read *The Magnificent Lives of Marjorie Post* by Allison Pataki, where I learned that she and her father were the originators of the crunchy little nuggets. I added fresh red raspberries and almond milk to the cereal, grabbed a green tea with lemon teabag, filled my mug with hot water then looked around for an empty table.

I had just started eating when Harold showed up. "May I join you?"

Even after a good night's sleep, socializing during breakfast was a stretch. "I'd like to enjoy a solitary breakfast if you don't mind, Harold," I said this pleasantly so he wouldn't be too offended, but I learned a long time ago to say what I mean and mean what I say.

His ears grew pink but he didn't back away. "May I come by again tonight?"

"*The Equalizer* is on tonight," I replied.

"The what?"

"You know, the television show starring Queen Latifah. It's one of my favorites, so I'll be quite content serving out my confinement in solitude."

This time, he looked miffed and backed away. "Perhaps another time then."

"Perhaps."

After breakfast, I returned to my apartment, read *The Morning*, a *New York Times* newsletter on my iPhone, then tackled their mini-crossword and spelling bee game. I did pretty well on the crossword but utterly failed the other. Oh well, there was always tomorrow.

My breakfast mostly digested, I proceeded to the lower level, which housed a small workout room. I watched HGTV while riding the stationary bicycle. The ride warmed me up for the arm and leg strengthening machines. My arms looked like crepe paper, but I wasn't ready to give up on them.

The rest of the day was spent embroidering a picture for my daughter, Ruth, reading, checking my email, scrolling through Facebook, and tidying up my apartment. I liked things to be neat, and I wouldn't think of leaving my bed unmade even if I never had another visitor. I was aware that social media was a time-waster but it wasn't like I was missing out on tea with the queen this afternoon.

At five o'clock, I dressed for dinner. It seemed odd to be going so late. Normally, we assembled at four-thirty, if not earlier. I slipped on my magenta blouse with the black polka dots, black slacks, and my black flats, which were actually tennis shoes in disguise. I had a closet full of cute shoes but as I'd grown older, I sported the practical footwear I vowed never to wear.

I applied face cream, filled in my gray eyebrows with brown powder on a little brush, added a dash of gray eye shadow, carefully lined my eyes, applied mascara, and finished up with red lipstick. I didn't use foundation because it felt too heavy. I told myself that age spots gave my face character.

Dinner was uneventful except for Madge, who wasn't looking or acting at all like herself. Her hair was in the usual bun, but she'd added light pink lipstick and a swipe of blush. She'd abandoned her usual too-long slacks and baggy sweater and was dressed in an attractive, though rather severe, black pantsuit. All I'd learned in the six months I'd known Madge, other than the fact that she was a retired banker, was that she'd never married and hailed from Canada; I couldn't remember how she happened to end up here. She liked a good vodka tonic, jazz, and we shared a love of books. She preferred historical fiction and fantasy. It seemed like a weird combination but each to their own. She kept looking at me from across the table. It was a look that seemed to be saying something, but I had no idea what. I smiled back at her, not knowing how else to respond.

Our meal was punctuated by our usual lively conversation. Our topic tonight was Taylor Swift and whether or not we considered ourselves Swifties. I tried to keep up with music trends so I could communicate with my young nightly visitors but I had to admit, I rarely listened to the top hits. We concluded that, indeed, we were Swifties simply because we admired her accomplishments and her philanthropy if not her music.

When I returned to my apartment after dinner, eager to settle in and watch my show, I found a note stuck to the door. I ripped the tape off and read the few words written in block letters with a heart drawn at the bottom. *You were the prettiest lady in the dining room tonight. M*

Hmmm… The letter "M" opened the door to the note being from any of my friends, with the exception of Anna, of course. It obviously wasn't from Harold, so who else could it be? Good grief, had I entered into an altered state of being? I hadn't had anyone show romantic interest in me for decades, and now two candidates were vying for my attention.

I dismissed the mystery and threw the note on the table before going to my bedroom to change into my soft clothes, which consisted of faded leggings, an oversized sweatshirt, and no bra. While I was undressing, I gazed into the mirror. Even in my prime, I was never considered beautiful. Cute perhaps, but not beautiful. Although not bad for eighty-nine, I was no longer cute. Well-preserved perhaps. For Pete's sake, that sounded like an antique couch. Distinguished? Naw. Pert. That was it! I was a pert old lady; lively, with a bit of fun left in me and a face that showed it.

I wasn't totally wizened up. After all, I was mobile, upright, and as always, chubby. I preferred the term chubby to fat. Ample thighs, a tummy but still a hint of a waist. I leaned into the mirror. The boobs were still perky because they were small. Actually, I was about right from the waist up, it was the area from the waist down that had caused me consternation for most of my adult life.

I ran my fingers through my short brown hair. I said I'd go gray at eighty but when I'd missed the deadline, I continued to have it colored. Hazel eyes, my dad's pudgy nose, pink cheeks that came from a skin condition called rosacea, but it kept me from having to apply rouge, or was it blush, and ears that wouldn't stop growing. They used to be shell-like, but recently the lobes hung down like I'd been wearing monstrous earrings all my life, which I hadn't.

Even though I'd not attracted attention from suitors in recent years, I had my share once upon a time. I was in my mid-forties when, Kevin, the father of my three children, and I were divorced. In the ten years that followed, I went a little nuts. I referred to that time as my "international years" when I dated men from eight different countries. I was pretty cute back then. I even attracted two husbands, Marvin who died suddenly of a heart attack not long after we were married, then Peter who stuck around for nearly thirty years before he died from congestive heart failure. Ironically, all three husbands were American born.

Nowadays, I was content to be unattached. In my experience, serious romantic relationships often led to stress, and that was the last thing I needed at my age.

I removed my makeup, dismissed the old lady in the mirror, then ambled over to my recliner, looking forward to a quiet evening in front of the television. Before I sat down,

I remembered to put a note on the door asking the staff to seek refuge elsewhere.

The next morning, after another night of reasonably good sleep, I woke up remembering that Wednesday was my day to take the Manor's complimentary minivan to the library. This interrupted my exercise routine but I'd go crazy if I never ventured into the outside world. I wasn't a shopper, so going to stores wasn't on my radar. Anything I needed, I ordered from Amazon. I found that it was much easier to let my fingers do the walking.

After a solitary (thank goodness) breakfast, I walked out the front door and stood in the designated spot to await my transportation. I took a deep breath. This was my first outing since the fateful evening at Sam's Place, and the fresh air smelled good. It was a pleasant January morning with sunshine, no wind, and according to my weather app, a mild forty-two degrees.

I'd been a Midwest girl all my life, but at eighty-eight, my son, Richard, (with approval from my daughters, Elizabeth and Ruth) transplanted me to Poughkeepsie, New York so he could keep an eye on me. "And just how's that working out?" I whispered to myself, then smiled. I hoped Agnes hadn't reported my misdeeds to Richard; he'd have a fit.

I wasn't resistant to the move and I appreciated the concern of my adult children, but the swift transition came as a bit of a shock. To entice me to move to Poughkeepsie, Richard told me that the town was called "The Queen City of the Hudson" and was settled in the 17th century by the Dutch. It was New York State's second capital shortly after the American Revolution. The name, he told me, was of

Wappinger Indian origin and meant "reed-covered lodge by the little water place." Did I care? Not particularly.

My footprint was the Manor, my hair salon, and the public library. I didn't even attend a brick-and-mortar church anymore. Every Sunday, I "attended" my old church back in Iowa via Facebook. It was convenient, but I missed the camaraderie of an in-person congregation.

When my transportation arrived, I carefully stepped off the curb and into the minivan. "The library as usual, Mrs. A?" asked Jake, the driver.

"Yes, thank you." I took a vacant seat toward the front and settled my purse and book bag on the space beside me. At one time, my eyesight had diminished but after my cataracts were removed, reading was a pleasure again. I was a multi-faceted reader enjoying Kindle, hardcover, and audio. Today, I was on a mission to check out a good romance book since that area of my life had picked up lately. I ordered my Kindle and Audible books from Amazon, so I thought I'd ask the librarian to suggest a new hardcover release.

The bus bumped along a road in need of repair. Looking out the grimy window, I saw nothing that held any significance to me. I was a transplant that hadn't taken root. Oh well, at least Jake was a careful driver. I was thankful I didn't have to rely on my son for transportation. I wanted to keep my book selections private.

Each time I entered a library I thought, *so many books, so little time.* I took a moment to look around. I was like a kid in a candy shop who wanted to sample everything on the shelves.

I slipped the return book out of my bag. I was a little embarrassed that the middle pages were slightly damaged by the beer I spilled while watching a particularly exciting playoff game. I'd gotten a bit rambunctious when Green Bay won. I hoped the person who re-shelved books wouldn't notice the malty smell and the library didn't have a disciplinarian like Agnes on staff. After discreetly depositing my book in the designated slot, I approached the checkout desk. There was a new girl standing at the counter, and I wondered what had happened to the very helpful Mrs. Fayerweather.

Politely enough, the new girl asked, "How may I help you?"

Two ladies, I couldn't remember their names, were seated to the left, diligently typing on keyboards. They looked over at me. "Good morning, Martha," they said practically in unison. Their greeting made me feel like I was on the TV show *Cheers,* where "everyone knows your name." I returned their greeting.

"I'm looking for a romance," I said to the young lady. I tried not to smile or blush. "Steamy but not too steamy. I want the story to hold my interest but not give me a heart attack."

"MMF, JP, CNC, MFM, BWWM, FTB, RH, or FMC?" When I gave her an 'I-have-no-idea-what-you're-talking-about' look, she helpfully added, "There are many varieties of romance books these days. However, we're not allowed to carry some of these categories at this particular library."

It was just my luck to be helped by a twenty-something who had an over-the-top knowledge of romantic literature. I was quite sure I didn't want to know what the letters meant so I didn't ask. "A simple romance will do."

The young lady leaned over the desk and whispered, "Boy on girl or girl on girl?"

I whispered back, "Either one is fine." I stepped back and put my hand over my mouth, amazed at what I'd just said. "But absolutely no violence," I added.

Winter (she wore a name tag, thank goodness) had a ring in her nose and one through the corner of each eyebrow framing her lovely green eyes. The hair on her partially shaved head was pink and she was wearing a short (above her belly button) sweater to match. When she stepped out from behind the desk, I noticed her black combat boots and denim bell bottoms. Good grief! When did bell bottoms make a comeback? I looked down at my skinny pull-on jeans. Was I totally out of style and didn't know it?

"Follow me. I'll take you to the stack where my favorite author's books are located," Winter said in a husky voice.

I wondered if I was brave enough to read what she read. To make conversation as we walked, I commented on her bell bottoms.

She gave me a quizzical look. "My what?"

I pointed. "You know, your pants."

"Oh, you mean my flares."

"In my day, we called them bell bottoms."

She gave me a "how quaint" smile and continued on. I hurried to keep up; Winter was all business and a fast walker. We stopped in front of a shelf filled with books by Samantha Young. I wondered how many books this author wrote in a year. I perused the shelf, noting that there were over forty books not counting the duplicates. Winter pulled one out. "I'd suggest you start with the first in this series."

"Thank you." I took the book and quickly shoved it into my bag.

"One more stop," she said before I could intervene. We walked to the M shelf, and she pulled out a book by Sarah Thankam Matthews. "One of each," she said as she handed me the book.

I wasn't quite sure what she meant by 'one of each,' but I added it to my bag. "Two's enough. Thank you, Winter."

"You're welcome. Let me know if I can help in any other way," she said before briskly walking back to her station.

Before proceeding to the checkout counter, I moved to a chair to examine the books' back covers and author bios. The author of the first book, *Beyond the Thistles,* lived in Scotland, which was the setting for many of her books. I wondered if this was like the *Outlander* series. I'd read those books and watched the television adaptations. They were a little steamy but not over-the-top. The book sounded promising so I slipped it back into my bag.

I pulled out the second book, *All This Could Be Different* by Sarah Thankam Mathews, and read that it was named one of the "BEST BOOKS OF 2022" by various known entities. The main character developed a crush on a lovely dancer, which gave me the impression that this one was a lesbian romance. I was glad to see that the book was about young people. Surrounded as I was by oldsters, I could use a shot of youthful intrigue.

This time, I was glad Mrs. Fayerweather wasn't at the desk when I checked out my two racy books. Winter didn't bat an eye. If she had, I would have noticed as her eyelashes were double the usual length.

After dinner that evening, just as I was getting acquainted with Sneha, her new friend Tig, and her college buddy,

Thom, in *All This Could Be Different,* there was a knock on my door. Too lazy to get out of my comfy chair, I called out, "Door's open. Come on in." I wasn't worried about abductors or murderers roaming the halls.

Harold stuck his face in. "Thought I'd drop by for a minute. I promise I won't stay long."

I tried not to sigh. "Come on in and have a seat." I closed and set my book down on the end table. I didn't offer him a drink. It was inhospitable of me but I wanted to keep this visit on the short side.

"I did much of the talking on Monday, so tonight, why don't you tell me about your family?" I suggested.

Harold didn't seem to mind that I wasn't emulating Martha Stewart. Martha Anderson seemed to be fine with him since he quickly made himself at home on my loveseat. He frowned as if he was thinking of something unpleasant, then began.

"You know about my wife. For the most part, we were happy. In fact, I'd say we were happier than most married couples." He nodded to himself as if affirming the fact. "We had two children, a boy and a girl. My daughter, Jennifer, takes after my wife. She's a wonderful mother and now grandmother. It was her granddaughter who was sleeping on my couch. Jennifer's a retired accountant, married, and lives nearby. She's the one who found this place and helped me move in."

When Harold's pause became abnormally long, I asked, "And your son?"

Harold frowned. "My son is another story entirely. He was a difficult child and grew up to be a difficult man.

He's been divorced twice, has no children, at least none that I know of, and has been unemployed off and on for most of his life. Now that he's too old for manual labor like construction and carpentry work, he's barely getting by." Harold looked at me as though he was weighing whether or not to continue. "Actually, he's mostly biding his time waiting for me to die."

I was appalled. "You can't be serious?"

"Oh, I'm serious, all right. He even asked me why I was living so long. He thinks I'm doing it just to punish him. Can you imagine?"

"No, Harold, I can't."

"John's an angry person, especially when he's drinking. He's almost seventy years old and still thinks the world owes him. We raised both kids the same way, so how did one turn out so good and the other one so bad?"

I knew it was a rhetorical question, but I responded by asking another. "Nurture versus nature is always a quandary, don't you think?" When Harold pulled his eyebrows together and tilted his head to the side, I explained. "I believe we think we have more control over how our children will turn out than is the reality. In my experience, children show their true nature early on, even as infants. We give them boundaries and a moral compass, of course, but sometimes nature takes over and they choose a path different from the one we hoped they'd follow."

Harold leaned forward. "Did this happen to you?"

"Not exactly. My son and two daughters all have similar values, but their personalities are very different. When I look at them as aging adults, I can still see the two-year-old in each of them. How they were all those years ago is pretty much how they are now." I looked over at Harold. "I hope you don't blame yourself for your son's behavior?"

"I try not to, but it's difficult. I also try to love him in spite of the fact that he wants me dead so he can have my money."

When I glanced at my wall clock, Harold took the cue, and even though the conversation was so personal and somewhat unfinished, he got up from the couch. "Oh dear. I've stayed more than my few minutes. It's time for me to go and let you get on with your reading," he said, pointing to my book. "Thanks for listening to the tale of my children, Martha. I've never told anyone about my son. Most people would judge me, but I had a feeling you'd understand."

"I appreciate your willingness to share. You can count on me to keep your story strictly confidential."

Harold walked to my chair, pulled a wallet out of his back pocket, and removed a small piece of paper. "May I give you my son's address and phone number? I'm not sure this is his most recent abode, but if something happens to me at least one person in my life will have his information."

I reluctantly took the offered note and tucked it inside my book. "If it will make you feel better."

"It will. Thank you." Harold turned toward the door. He looked tired and old. Telling me about his son had taken a lot out of him. "Don't get up. I'll let myself out." He stepped through the doorway. "Good night, Martha. I hope you sleep well."

"Good night, Harold."

I didn't feel like returning to my book after Harold left, so I asked Alexa to play some music and checked my Facebook feed. Scrolling was mindless but my mind couldn't handle anything else. The sad story of Harold's son kept coming to mind, and I wondered if John would ever try to hurry things along by doing something terrible to his father. The thought continued to haunt me as I slipped into my nightie.

Chapter Three

On the last night of my detention, I decided to throw a party to celebrate my freedom. I texted the girls, inviting them to come by my apartment after dinner. Only Missy, Anna, and Madge could come. Molly and Margaret had previous commitments. I also taped a note to my door inviting the night staff to join us.

Before going to breakfast, I got on my computer and ordered two bottles of Prosecco, a can of mixed nuts, a small chocolate cake, a bag of Skinny Pop popcorn (for those who were watching their waistlines), plastic champagne flutes, paper plates, plastic forks, and napkins. I scheduled the Instacart delivery for after lunch.

Later, I dressed for dinner with a party in mind, including my black slacks with a row of rhinestones running down the side, the new pink sweater I'd gotten for Christmas from my daughter Elizabeth, and earrings with pink stones an old boyfriend gifted me decades ago. Because the dining room was always chilly, I added the beautifully embroidered shawl my other daughter, Ruth, brought back from a business trip to India.

Most of my friends were also decked out. Even though she wasn't coming to my party, Molly had on a black frilly blouse with matching silk pants. I was confident Molly would eventually snag a man. Not only was she lovely and stood out in the crowd of older women, she had a pleasing personality that included a vibrant smile that lit up her eyes. The partygoers declined dessert which was apple pie a la mode. They were holding out for whatever I offered later.

Earlier that day, I'd asked the maintenance man, Jerry, to deliver folding chairs to my apartment. My living room decor featured gray walls, a navy blue recliner, and a love-seat with a modern blue and gray floral design. The brown folding chairs would stand out like sore thumbs but, along with my two kitchen chairs, there would be enough seats for everyone, including the Manor crew when they arrived. I didn't invite Harold. I thought about it but decided his presence would be a distraction from the celebratory nature of my party. In a facility where less than thirty percent of the inhabitants were male, they quickly became the center of attention at any gathering.

After dinner, my party-going friends followed me to my apartment. Madge opened and poured the drinks while Missy cut the cake. Only Anna and I had cake, but I knew it wouldn't be wasted once the youngsters showed up. Before they arrived, Missy proposed we return to Sam's Place when we deemed it safe for another outing. Speaking in her retired schoolteacher voice, Anna countered Missy's suggestion. "I heard about a place that has a Chippendale, Broadway-style burlesque show. Now, wouldn't that be a hoot?"

"I thought the Chippendales disappeared years ago," said Madge. Even though she tended to be a know-it-all, I appreciated her directness.

"I said—" Anna cleared her throat and spoke louder, "a Chippendale STYLE show. In other words, sexy hunks putting on a stage show. I don't think this is the kind of entertainment where the audience gets up-close and personal with the performers, but it could still be fun." When there was no discussion, Anna simply shrugged.

To revive the positive energy that had suddenly evaporated from the room, I asked, "What if I set up another outing to Sam's Place in a couple of weeks? This time, we'll let the night staff know about our plans so they won't become alarmed if they find us absent from our apartments. We can assemble here, then when the coast is clear, aka no Ethyl, we'll depart together. I'll order two Ubers as before and we'll maintain the rule of one alcoholic drink each."

I looked around the room. "Agreed?"

"That will certainly give us something to look forward to," said Anna, who had apparently given up on the Chippendales. Even though she sounded happy, she looked uncomfortable and overheated in her heavy turtleneck sweater. Her cheeks were flushed and her forehead was glistening. A heavyset eighty-something, Anna wasn't in the best of health. She had gastrointestinal issues, heart problems, high cholesterol, high blood pressure, and diabetes. I knew this because whenever I talked with her, she gave me a litany of her ills. This recitation was the opposite of Missy who had a rule to never speak of her "conditions." I liked Missy's approach, and I tried to do the same. It was easy, however, to lapse into an "ain't it awful" conversation when one old lady was upping the other on how many ailments she had.

Soon after our plans were finalized, Judy boldly walked through the door with my note in her hand as if it were an engraved invitation. Her cohorts, Josh and Kate, followed in her wake. When they looked around the room, I could tell they felt uncomfortable seeing "their residents" holding champagne flutes. "Would you all like a piece of chocolate cake?" I offered to get them in the swing of things.

"Yes, thank you," Judy replied. The other two nodded.

"I'm sure you're not allowed to drink alcohol while on duty, so help yourselves to sodas. You know where they are," I added. The trio made their way to the mini fridge then took the three remaining seats before Missy handed them plates of cake.

About ten minutes later, just as I was gathering empty dishes from my guests, there was a disturbance behind me. I turned in time to see Anna toppling out of her chair and landing face down on my area rug.

Judy rushed to her side. As the night shift RN, she was accustomed to handling medical emergencies. "Get my stethoscope and blood pressure cuff," she hollered at Josh. She kneeled beside Anna, rolled her over, and took her pulse. "Help me get this sweater off her," she said to Kate, who was kneeling next to her. "Will someone get me a cold washcloth and a glass of water?"

I quickly walked to the bathroom for a washcloth while Missy rushed to the sink and filled a glass with water. As soon as the sweater was removed and a cold compress was applied to Anna's forehead, she revived and struggled to sit up. "Stay right where you are," ordered Judy. "I need to get your vitals before we get you on your feet." Right on cue, Josh rushed through the door with the cuff and scope. Judy listened to Anna's heart then took her blood pressure. "Your blood pressure is sky-high. Have you been taking your pills?"

"I…I think so," Anna replied.

"I'm going to put you on the medication-assist program right away. Then we can be sure you're taking all of your prescriptions."

Embarrassed and chastened, Anna nodded.

"You definitely should not, I repeat, should not be drinking alcohol with all the medications you take. Do you understand?" Judy admonished.

Anna nodded again. I'd never seen Judy in full-out medic-in-charge mode. She sounded fierce, but her face showed how much she genuinely cared. After getting Anna stabilized, Judy turned to me. "I highly recommend that the next time you throw a party, you only serve sodas."

"I will. I promise," I said shamefacedly. I felt bad that Anna had this incident on my watch. I wondered if Agnes would get a full report. Good grief, I might be back in detention.

After a big drink of cold water, Anna was helped up. I offered her my summer dressing gown. Now that she had cooled down, she seemed all right, and there was a general sigh of relief around the room. Then Madge said, "Well, I guess it's time to go."

"I'll see that Anna gets safely back to her apartment," Judy said as she motioned for her colleagues to proceed her out the door.

Missy came up behind me and whispered in my ear. She smelled amazing. "I'll stay and help you clean up."

Before I could reply, she was on her way to my kitchen nook. I closed the door on my visitors and silence returned to my domain. "There's no need for you to stay, Missy. Everything goes into the trash except that little bit of left-over popcorn and nuts."

"I know." When she smiled, I couldn't help but notice how attractive she was. Not too girly, not too masculine, she had good bone structure, even teeth, sparkly brown eyes that had a bit of devilishness in them, and naturally curly gray hair that always appeared a bit untamed. When we both reached for the nut can and our hands touched, I felt a zing. I wondered if my involuntary reaction had been brought on by the book I was reading. I could tell she felt it too because she didn't pull her hand away but lingered a beat longer than necessary.

When the kitchen was spotless, the folding chairs were stacked against the wall, and the garbage was tied up ready to be removed in the morning, Missy said, "I best be going." But instead of walking out the door, she walked over to where I stood and gave me a peck on the cheek. She acted as cool as a cucumber as if we did this all the time. Damn, she smelled good!

"See you tomorrow. Have a good sleep, Martha."

"Thanks, you too," I muttered. After the door closed, I fell into my recliner and took a deep breath, wondering what had just happened and if anything HAD happened. When I took another breath, I realized that Missy's perfume had attached itself to my sweater. I wondered what the fragrance was. It was definitely something that stirred the senses.

The following night, after listening to the piano for nearly an hour, I returned to my apartment and this time, Missy was lounging against the wall by the door. I remembered seeing her leave the social room early but I had no idea of her destination.

"May I come in?" she asked.

I'd been dead tired a minute ago but upon seeing her, I miraculously perked up. "Of course." I unlocked my door and we both walked in.

"Go put your soft clothes on, Martha. I know you like to do that in the evening."

On my way to the bedroom, I whisked my book off the table. Missy gave me a knowing smile, which made me wonder if she recognized the title or knew the author. I returned to the living room and found Missy sitting on the loveseat with her shoes off. She patted the seat next to her, and I dutifully sat down. The space was small so we were sitting close enough that I could smell her delightful scent and feel heat coming from her body. "I hope you don't mind if I stay for a few minutes," she said.

Where had I heard that before?

"You're welcome to stay as long as you like."

"I happened to notice the book you're reading. I've read a few of Mathew's books. Are you enjoying the story?"

Trying to be as nonchalant as Missy, I replied, "I'm only about halfway through, but yes, I'm enjoying it."

Missy moved an inch or two closer to me. "In my opinion, only women authors can really do justice to romantic scenes involving women. What's your opinion?"

"I haven't thought about it. I normally read historical fiction," I replied with a nervous giggle which made me sound like I was in junior high.

Missy reached over and took my hand. "But—-"

Just then, there was a quick knock followed by the door flying open and Judy entering the room. Her mouth formed a big O and her eyes went wide. She turned and pushed the two behind her back into the hall.

I sat up straight. "It's all right, guys. Come on in."

"No, no," Judy said, backing out the door. "I didn't know you had company. Why wasn't there a note on the door?"

"Missy's visit was impromptu." I looked at Missy and smiled so she wouldn't be offended.

Judy called out, "Have a good evening," then decisively closed the door with a loud click. With the romantic mood interrupted, Missy put her shoes back on, said good night, and exited my apartment. I was left wondering what might have happened if Judy hadn't appeared.

Chapter Four

arely a week after Missy's visit, I was still in bed when I was jolted awake by loud knocking on my door. It took me a minute to get my bearings. "Hold your horses, I'm coming!" I hollered as I threw on my bathrobe and stepped into my slippers.

I opened the door to a very large man in a dark suit with squinty eyes and a hard set to his mouth. He was followed by a small Asian woman in similar attire and Agnes in her ever-present scrubs. "What do I owe the honor of this EARLY—" I emphasized the word, "morning visit?" I didn't invite them in.

The man spoke first. "I'm Detective Warren," he motioned toward his apparent partner, "and this is Detective Niles. May we come in?"

Agnes stepped forward. "The detectives need to ask you some questions, Martha. Let them in."

"Some questions? What about?" Even though I had no idea what was going on, fear fluttered in my stomach. I felt as though I'd just stepped onto the set of a *Law & Order* rerun, and I was annoyed that Agnes thought she could dictate who was allowed into my apartment.

When I hesitated, Detective Warren flipped open his badge as if this automatically allowed him entry and stepped inside. The others followed. "Please be seated, Mrs. Anderson. We'd like to ask you some questions about Harold Lancaster."

After I sat down, Detective Niles stepped over and held a piece of paper in front of me.

"What's that?" I asked.

Warren's deep voice dripped with authority. "That's a warrant giving Detective Niles permission to search your apartment while we chat."

I tried to match the authority in my voice to Warren's. "Chat? At seven-thirty on a Monday morning? Give me a break."

Since I was occupying my recliner, Warren sat on the loveseat, Agnes brought a straight-backed chair from my dinette, and Detective Niles disappeared into the bedroom where my unmade bed was still warm.

"When was the last time you spoke with Mr. Lancaster?" Warren asked.

"Why? Has something happened to Harold? What's this all about?" I repeated, irritated that they hadn't revealed the reason for their inopportune visit.

Warren leaned forward. "Mr. Lancaster has been missing for seventy-two hours, and you haven't noticed his absence?"

"Harold and I are acquaintances." I tried to sit up straighter. "We're not married, nor do we live together, so no, I haven't noticed his absence." I paused, hoping for more information. When none was offered, I asked, "Have you checked with his daughter? They're quite close. Perhaps he went for a visit and neglected to inform anyone." I looked pointedly at Agnes.

The detective replied, "Yes, we've spoken to his daughter. She contacted our missing persons unit a day ago, but we couldn't open an official case until Mr. Lancaster was missing for the prerequisite amount of time."

"I see." They always warn people under investigation to only answer specific questions and to talk as little as possible, but I had questions that couldn't wait. "Do you think I had something to do with Harold's disappearance? On what grounds did you obtain a search warrant? Are you taking me into custody? Don't you need to read me my Miranda Rights?" I wasn't a complete idiot. I knew a thing or two about the law. After all, my son was an attorney and I'd watched law shows on television going all the way back to *Perry Mason.*

Agnes leaned forward before the detective had a chance to speak. "Now, Martha, don't get yourself all worked up. You and Harold have a history of troublemaking, so I suggested—"

Detective Warren interrupted. "Mrs. Anderson," he gave me a serious look, his black eyes boring into mine, "you're not under arrest. Therefore, at present, we won't be reading you your Miranda Rights." He looked to see if I understood before proceeding. "To answer your other questions, when we were searching Mr. Lancaster's apartment, we found a note he'd left near his computer."

From a backpack sitting on the floor next to him, the detective pulled out a small plastic evidence bag containing a piece of paper. "This note, written in Mr. Lancaster's handwriting, as confirmed by Ms. Duly, says, 'Talk to Martha

Anderson if anything happens to me.' Also, the night staff told us that the gentleman in question has visited you in the evenings. With some arm twisting, they also told us they observed a Miss Susan Wellesley paying you evening visits and surmised that you may be more than just friends."

The detective returned the plastic bag to his backpack then looked at Agnes. She sat up straighter and gave him her full attention. "Ms. Duly told us about your penchant for breaking the rules so taking these circumstances into account, there was enough evidence to obtain a warrant to search your apartment and take you in for questioning. Due to the early hour and your age, we determined that questioning you here would be preferable."

Although my nerves were jingling, I spoke in an even, calm voice. "Just so I understand you correctly, Detective Warren, Harold disappeared three days ago, and you think I had something to do with it."

"Yes, we think there is a possibility—"

Niles returned from the bedroom and interrupted. "Sir, I think you need to see this." She held another small plastic bag in one hand and my library book by Sarah Mathews in the other. She put the new evidence into the detective's outstretched hand. He read the note encased in the plastic bag, examined the book, then looked at me. "My partner found this name and address on a piece of paper that was being used as a marker in a book," the detective held up the book, "by a well-known author of, shall we say, spicy lesbian romance. Can you identify the note?"

Warren gave the evidence bag back to Niles, who handed it to me. I didn't need to read the note; I knew what it said. "Yes, this is the name, address, and phone number for Harold's son."

"And why is it in your possession?"

"Harold gave it to me."

"And why did he give it to you? Have you met his son?"

"No, I've never met him. He gave it to me in case anything ever happened to him. Harold, that is."

"Did Mr. Lancaster suggest that his son was a dangerous person?"

"Not exactly. However, Harold did tell me that his son was quote, waiting for me to die, unquote." I hated to break my promise to keep Harold's story confidential, but what choice did I have?

Warren got up and paced about the room—a very unnerving exercise. He stopped in front of me. My arthritic neck hurt when I looked up at him. "Now, getting back to your situation, Mrs. Anderson. It sounds like you have two romances going on here."

When I ignored his comment, he asked another question. "Did you need to get one romantic partner out of the way to make room for the other? Most men would be angry if they knew they were competing with a woman."

I didn't dignify this with an answer, but the detective pursued his line of questioning anyway.

"Perhaps you obtained some ideas from your current book?"

I struggled up from my chair and stood in front of the detective. "I have nothing more to say without my lawyer present." I held out my arms, offering to be cuffed. "Are you going to arrest me?"

"No, I'm not going to arrest you, but don't leave town."

He walked to the door and the two women followed. He looked back at me. "I'll be in touch."

Chapter Five

After I closed and locked the door, I stumbled into the kitchen for a glass of water, then returned to my recliner and wondered if I should call Richard and ask him for legal advice. I decided against the call, gradually calmed down, and got dressed. But by nine o'clock, I still felt unsettled. I needed to talk with someone, so I texted Missy. Since she was part of the story, I thought I'd better alert her to what was going on.

CAN YOU PICK UP PASTRY AND FRUIT FROM THE DINING ROOM AND COME BY MY APARTMENT?

I figured the caps would alert her that my request was urgent.

Barely thirty seconds later I had a response.

Of course!

I put water in my electric kettle. Thank goodness I was allowed this plug-in. Not ten minutes later, Missy arrived with two Styrofoam boxes. I pulled leftover paper plates from the cupboard, forks from the drawer, and poured hot water over my special peach and ginger tea blend.

Lovely as ever in jeans and a fluffy blue sweater, Missy seemed unruffled by my strange request. "What's wrong, Martha? You look distraught." She took my hand, led me to the table, told me to sit down, and poured the tea into mugs.

"I've had a rough morning."

"Tell me." Missy leaned in.

After I recounted the details of the detectives' early morning visit, Missy's face showed the shock I was feeling. "I can't believe it! You must have been terrified."

"More annoyed than anything else. I wish I had asked Detective Warren how he thought I pulled off the abduction. Did I drug Harold, throw him over my shoulder, and haul him away to some clandestine location? Did I call an Uber or did I steal a car? Maybe he thinks I hired some muscle to do the deed." Missy smiled faintly. My what-ifs were pretty comical.

"Don't you hate it when you think of the perfect thing to say after the fact?" she asked.

"Yes. It happens to me all the time." I sipped my tea and took a bite of the warm and flakey chocolate croissant. "What do you think I should do?"

"We. What should WE do?" Missy replied.

"I hate getting you mixed up in this."

"I'm your friend, Martha. That's what friends do. They get involved in the messy parts of their friend's lives. And this is pretty damn messy!"

"So, where do we start? I'm not calling my lawyer son yet. He's likely to blow everything out of proportion. Plus, there are several details in what the detective is likely to tell him that I'd rather he not know."

"I understand." Missy looked into her half-empty mug like she was reading tea leaves. "So, were you, or are you, having an affair with Harold?"

"No! Absolutely not! He might be in pursuit but so far, I'm not buying. I allowed him to visit me in my apartment a few evenings, but all we did was chat about our past lives. That's when he told me about his son. That story, by the way, needs to remain completely confidential. I promised Harold I wouldn't tell anyone and now four people know."

Missy leaned on her elbow. "What if we look up this son? Do you have a copy of the paper the detective took from your book?"

"Yes. I figured I'd misplace the scrap of paper so to be prudent, I added it to my phone contacts for safekeeping. But" I paused, "don't you think the police are talking with him?"

"I'm sure they are but that doesn't mean they'll find out anything. Don't you think two innocent-looking, grandmotherly ladies can weasel out a hell of a lot more particulars than some dude in a uniform?"

I chuckled in spite of myself. "You're probably right, but how do we set up a visit? I think he could be dangerous. Especially if he's done something terrible to his father." Once the dam of what-ifs was opened, I couldn't stop them from flowing out. "Has he harmed Harold? Is he hiding him or keeping him away long enough to declare him dead?" I was breathless thinking of all the possibilities.

"Not to sound like Duly, but you need to calm down, Martha. We must approach this like professionals. Think of us as part of the team on *The Equalizer*. You know how calm

Queen Latifah's character Robyn is. Just like her, we need to be logical, use our technology wisely, and take advantage of our age. In other words, sneak up on this guy and find out if he's the perpetrator."

I took Missy's words into consideration. She was a wise woman. Then I asked, "Who else can it be? Harold definitely isn't the type who would simply take off without telling anyone. Even if he were, I'm pretty confident he would have confided in me if he was leaving."

Missy raised her eyebrows but didn't say anything.

I dug my phone out of my pocket. "Ok, let's start by looking up the son's address on Google Maps."

After I clicked on the address, we learned that John lived in the Town of Poughkeepsie, adjacent to the City of Poughkeepsie where we lived. "Says here it's five miles by car to his address. That's not far. We could take an Uber. What do you think?"

Missy crunched up her forehead. She really was cute. "I think we should wait and go tomorrow. Give the cops a chance at him. If they solve the mystery, then we won't have to waste an Uber fare."

"Good idea. Thanks for partnering up on this with me, Missy. If necessary, I think we'll make a great pair out there in the," I lowered my voice, "Concrete Jungle." I laughed at myself. I could be overly dramatic.

"I have a feeling John lives in a dump of an apartment, but maybe there's a concrete driveway nearby," Missy said.

"Should we call first?" I held up my phone for emphasis.

"You said he's mostly unemployed, so let's take a chance and just show up. If he's already been interviewed by the police, he'll have his guard down thinking that he's pulled one off—if he indeed has pulled something off. Once we get into his apartment, you can ask to use the bathroom and snoop around."

"That sounds like a plan." Relief washed over me.

Missy cleared away the containers and tea things. When she returned to the table, she had a small plastic bag in her hand. I'd seen enough of those for one day and wasn't eager to see another.

"I think you need a little something to calm your nerves," Missy said. "I don't believe I've ever seen you so worked up."

I shook my head. "No meds. I've never taken Xanax or anything like that. In fact, the only time I took a sleeping pill was the night my husband suddenly dropped dead of a heart attack. My daughter gave it to me."

"It's not a pill," Missy said, pulling something out of the bag that looked like a thin cigarette. "Have you ever smoked marijuana?"

"You have marijuana? How did you get it?" I was shocked but relieved she didn't have something else in mind. I wasn't ready for anything physical happening between us. At least, not yet.

"My doctor prescribes medical marijuana to help ease the pain of my rheumatoid arthritis. Some medical marijuana provides relief without the intoxicating effects associated with recreational marijuana. My prescription, however, is for regular weed. Recently, I've not needed as much as usual, so I have a couple of extra joints. Would you like to share one?"

I considered it, then wondered why not. It seemed to me that there couldn't be a better place to smoke my first pot than in my own apartment with someone I trusted. "If not now, then when? Right?" I finally said.

Missy smiled. "Right."

She lit the end of the joint, took a drag, then offered it to me. I inhaled just a bit and coughed.

"Let's go sit on your bed. That way, if we conk over, we won't hit our heads."

She laughed like this was a joke, but it made me nervous. We went to my bedroom, sat on my bed, and leaned our backs against the headboard. Then out of nowhere, Missy asked, "So, what's the theme of your life?" She handed me the joint.

This was such an unexpected question that it took me a minute to consider the answer. Fortunately, my mind was still functioning normally, at least what was normal for a well-used brain. "What an interesting question. I've never thought of my life having a theme." I passed the joint back. "Threes! My theme is threes," I declared a bit too joyfully. I was beginning to feel a little wonky.

"Explain."

"Well, I grew up with two sisters, Audrey and Betty. I was the youngest so unfortunately, they're both dead, but the three of us were very close. I have three children. I pray to God that none of them precede me in death." I paused to say a little prayer in my head. "I had three husbands. They, too, are all dead."

"Clever. Any threes in your life now?"

I smiled to myself, leaned my head on her shoulder, and closed my eyes. The marijuana was taking effect, but I understood what she was cleverly suggesting. "I'm definitely not in a three-way relationship as the brazen detective suggested." I raised my head and looked into Missy's eyes. "If that's what you're wondering." I giggled.

"I can attest to that. Unless—" Missy took the joint between her thumb and index finger. "Madge seems to be flirting with you lately. What about…"

Missy left the sentence unfinished and I jumped in. "Absolutely not! No, nada." When I shook my head for emphasis, I was suddenly dizzy.

Abruptly changing the subject, Missy asked another unusual question. "What about a nickname? Martha seems formal. You must have been called something else when you were growing up."

"My dad called me Spike. I have no idea why. My college friends called me Martre, as in the Paris neighborhood of Montmartre. I lived there for a year and loved the bohemian way of life, the art, the French men…." my mind returned to Paris.

"Did you ever go back, Martre?" Missy's smile looked a little crooked.

Hearing my old nickname seemed apropos as I sat there like a college girl smoking weed. "I returned to Montmartre to celebrate my seventy-fifth birthday. A friend and I rented an Airbnb for two amazing weeks."

Just as Missy opened her mouth to comment, there were three knocks on the door and my heart flew into overdrive. "Not again! Who could it be this time?" I shout-whispered as I considered what someone would assume if they saw us sitting on my bed sharing a joint.

Missy calmly got up. "You stay here. I'll handle this." She left the room, closing the door behind her. The words coming from the other room were muffled but I could tell it was Agnes. Even in my "out there" state, I could imagine another detention looming on the horizon. Several minutes later, Missy nonchalantly reentered the bedroom.

"What happened?" I still felt loopy but Duly's visit had jarred me awake. So much for the medicinal relaxation.

Missy sat back down on the bed. "Agnes said someone, we can only imagine that it was Ethyl, reported a strange smell coming from your apartment. When she asked for you, I told her you were in the shower. I explained about my medicinal marijuana and that today, I had chosen to partake of it in your apartment. She knows about my prescription because it's in my record. She looked around like she expected a rat to jump out of the woodwork but what could she do? I know she left with unanswered questions in her mouth but at least she's gone."

Feeling incredibly relieved, I said, "Wow, what a partner! Thanks for covering up for me. I know I'd have another detention if she found out I was high on your weed."

"You know, Martha, weed is legal now in New York so you aren't committing a crime. It may be against the rules here at the Manor but it seems to me that what you do in your apartment is your business."

I slowly nodded in agreement. Now that the adrenaline rush was over, I was so tired I could barely keep my eyes open.

Missy patted my arm. "You have a little nap. I promise you'll feel better when you wake up." Missy got up from my bed. "I'll see myself out." Before she left, she gently pulled the covers up around me and kissed me on the forehead.

What had I just done? Something my former self would have never considered—that's for sure! Smoking pot…with a female admirer… "You're never too old, Martha," I said to myself as I drifted off to sleep.

Chapter Six

The next morning, I stopped at Agnes' desk on my way to breakfast. In my most innocent voice, I asked, "Have you heard anything from Detective Warren?"

Agnes glared at me.

"I'm really worried about Harold." I gave her my best sad-eye look, a trick I'd learned from my granddaughter.

Her face softened. "All I know is the police talked with his son to no avail." Agnes looked down at her desk. "Unfortunately, Harold is still missing, his daughter is driving me crazy with her constant texting, and I'm behind on my reports." She looked back up at me. "Is that all?"

"Yes, thank you." I left, glad that she didn't mention the marijuana incident. Perhaps she was so overwhelmed with paperwork she forgot. Why was I kidding myself? Of course, she hadn't forgotten. She just hadn't figured out what to do with me yet.

I texted Missy after going through my morning routine. No caps this time.

Want to take a little trip after lunch?

I was confident that she'd know what I was referring to. I didn't want to leave an electronic trail.

Absolutely. I'll come to your apartment.

Feeling like a private investigator, I arranged for an Uber to pick us up at one-thirty.

Missy arrived dressed head to toe in black. We looked like twins. "We've been watching too many crime shows," I observed. Missy just smiled and adjusted her turtleneck. "Are you sure about this trip to the son's house? It could be dangerous," I said, wanting to give Missy a chance to back out.

"Are you kidding? I haven't had this much of a rush since…." she paused, turned pink, then added, "Never mind. Not for a long time."

A text notified me that our Uber had arrived and we hurried out the front door and into the car. On the way, I saw a Dollar General and asked the driver to pull over.

"What are you doing, Martre?"

When I heard my old knickname, I felt like a college coed for the second time in two days. "I'm going to pick up some cookies. Who could turn away two old ladies with cookies?" I chuckled. The Uber driver looked at me in his rearview mirror and I gave him a finger wave "Wait here. I'll just be a minute."

I quickly returned with two plastic bags and settled myself in the car.

"Show me," Missy said.

I pulled out a plate, a box of chocolate chip cookies, and a roll of aluminum foil. "Help me put these cookies on the plate. Covered with the foil, they'll pass for homemade."

As we made our way through town, the view became more and more depressing with dilapidated buildings, rusted-out cars, and a few stray cats. I pointed out the window. "We sure aren't in Kansas anymore."

Missy gave me a puzzled look but, before I could explain, our driver pulled up to a small house seriously in need of repair with a deserted lot to one side. The paint on the house had once been blue but had turned a dirty gray, the two front steps were broken, and the door looked a little wonky (my new favorite word). This escapade reminded me of my days as a social worker. I'd entered a lot of houses that looked like this one; some were even worse.

"You sure this is the right address, lady?" the driver asked.

I read the address out loud from the contacts on my phone.

The driver looked at his GPS. "This is it. But are you sure you want to go inside?"

Missy and I looked at each other. "We're sure!" we said in unison.

I opened the car door. "If we're admitted inside, you don't need to wait for us. If we don't go inside, we'll return to the car and you can take us back to the Manor."

"Whatever you say, lady." He looked back through the mirror again. "Even if you get inside, I'll wait at least ten minutes. No charge."

Missy opened the door on her side. We were too old for sliding across the seat. "That would be very kind," she responded sweetly. She walked to my side of the car, took the plate of cookies from me, and I got out. We squared our shoulders, confidently walked up a sidewalk with dead weeds in the cracks and slowly climbed the two steps with no railing. Missy knocked. The doorbell was hanging by its cords. When no one came, she knocked louder.

A man opened the door. "What do you want?" he gruffly asked. He was tall, broad- shouldered, had gray hair seriously in need of a cut, and a three-day beard. His blue plaid flannel shirt had the sleeves rolled up, and his jeans had holes in the knees.

He looked at the foil-covered plate. "I ain't buying nothin' either." He started to close the door.

"We're not here to sell you anything, Mr. Lancaster. We're here for a visit," I said. "We brought you cookies."

Missy held out the plate. "You do like cookies, don't you?"

"How do you know my name?" he barked.

Missy said, "Your father is a friend of ours. We thought you might be worried about his disappearance and in need of comforting. We, too, are feeling quite distraught about the matter. May we come in and chat for a moment?"

In his apparent shock at this pronouncement, John stepped back from the door. We seized the opportunity and entered the house. The hall smelled of stale tobacco, greasy food, and cats. I was, once again, reminded of homes I'd visited as a social worker. I was just twenty-one and had no inkling of danger.

Assuming that long ago persona, I briskly walked down the hall with Missy close at my heels. We entered the kitchen and Missy set the plate of cookies on the cluttered countertop. John, obviously stupefied by what was happening under his nose and in his own house, helplessly followed.

What was he going to do? Rough us up as he escorted us out the door? I hoped not. He was Harold's son after all so he couldn't be all bad. Could he?

"Where's your tea kettle?" Missy asked.

John pointed to a cabinet. Missy pulled it open, took down the well-used kettle, filled it with water, and set it on the stove while I removed the foil from the cookies.

Missy looked around. "And the cups?"

John pointed to the drainer. Missy retrieved two mugs and then washed out a third that was sitting nearby.

"You can't just come in here and…" John blustered, then seemed to be at a loss for words.

"Don't worry, John. May I call you John?" When he didn't respond, I continued. "We're only here to help you sort out the disappearance of your beloved father." I smiled at him. "We're quite harmless."

Missy, who somehow found three tea bags, poured hot water into the mugs and handed one to our host. "Now, if you'll direct us to the living room, we'll have a nice cup of tea and a chat," she said.

John removed old newspapers and junk mail from the coffee table, and Missy sat the cookie plate down. She and I sat on the worn couch, the arms shredded by a cat's claws, and John sat across from us on a lop-sided recliner.

"How did you get my address?" John asked as he took a cookie. Apparently, he'd given up on trying to get rid of us.

I gave him my best grandmotherly look. "Well, dear, your father talked of you often and gave me your address in case I ever needed to reach you."

"He talked about me?" John's eyes widened.

"Why, yes. He told me you've had a rough time of late and that he's worried about you."

"He did?"

"Of course he did. You're his only son, after all."

John leaned forward and set his mug down. "I can't imagine him ever saying that he was worried about me. My sister is the one who always gets his attention. She's the perfect one. Do you know about her, too?"

"He mentioned her but it's you he's been thinking about these days."

John slumped back in his chair. "But…" John hesitated then continued, "I told him I wanted him to die. How can a father care about a son who's that terrible?" He put his face in his hands.

"There, there, John," Missy soothed. "When we locate your father, we'll straighten this all out. I'm sure you don't really want him dead." Missy gave him a sad look. "Do you?"

When he didn't answer, Missy and I quietly sipped our tea while John sobbed into his hands. When he regained control, he wiped his face on his sleeve then said, "No, I don't really want him to die, but I'm struggling to survive and desperate times call for desperate measures."

"I'm sure they do," I agreed. "But just exactly how desperate are you? What have you done in your desperation?" Sensing that we were getting down to the nitty-gritty, I worked hard to keep my voice even.

John grabbed a tissue from the box sitting on the table and blew his nose. "I…I forced my father to come here. I threatened him by saying I'd do something to scare his great- granddaughter."

"Marcella?" I asked.

He gave a slight nod. "Once I got him here, I thought I could force him to give me my inheritance ahead of time."

"And?" I prompted.

"And I found out that all of his money is in an irrevocable trust. A trustee pays his bills and basically gives him pocket money once a month. He has no control over his estate."

I looked around. Perhaps Harold was close by. "I see."

John's voice sped up. "He gave me what he had on him, which wasn't much. He also offered to help me fix up this place. He's real handy, you know."

"No, I didn't know."

There was a lull in the conversation, so I asked THE question. "Where is your father now?"

John looked from Missy to me with the expression of a kid caught with his hand in the cookie jar. "He's out back trying to get my old Chevy to start," he muttered.

I put my hand over my heart. I was so relieved I could have cried and for once, I was literally speechless. Missy took over. "Well then, I think you should go out back and invite him in for cookies and tea. I'll go rustle up another mug."

John obediently got up, went to the back door, and hollered, "Hey Pops, come inside and get warmed up."

And, just like that, the mystery was solved. No one was hurt and John got to maintain a shred of his dignity. In a couple of minutes, Harold banged through the back door, entered the living room, and immediately dropped into a nearby chair when he recognized the two old ladies dressed in black ops outfits with mugs on their knees. The look on his face was priceless.

There was a bit of chit-chat about us being in John's house, then I said, "Call your daughter, Harold. She's worried sick about you."

John quickly left the room, returned with a cell phone, and handed it to his father.

"While you're making that call, I'm sure your son will kindly pack up your things while I retrieve our Uber." I gave John a don't-give-me-any-sass look.

"Yes, ma'am," he said as he left the room.

Missy and I took the tea things into the kitchen. While she was washing the mugs and doing some general tidying up, I called our Uber driver. When Harold walked into the kitchen, I said, "Let's get you home."

With tears in his eyes, he nodded, apparently too choked up to speak. That was all right. There was plenty of time for us to swap stories later.

Chapter Seven

No one, not even Agnes and the two detectives, came to apologize or congratulate us on locating and returning Harold to his apartment unscathed. The one exception was Harold's daughter, Jennifer, who graciously sent a lovely bouquet of flowers with a note thanking Missy and me. Also, I wasn't called on the carpet for my marijuana escapade so that was something.

We learned later that the detectives had paid a visit to John's house but because he politely kept them from going inside and they didn't have a search warrant, nothing came of the visit.

Robyn, Queen Latifah's character, doesn't get paid for her heroic acts so I was okay with no recognition and little thanks. I was just glad my friend was back home safe and sound.

The next day, Harold told me that his son had locked his cell phone in a gun safe. Since he didn't have a workable car and stores were too far for him to walk to, he had no way to let anyone know his whereabouts. He apologized for the disturbance he caused everyone.

It turned out that Missy knew a thing or two about Veterans' benefits and, since John was a vet, she helped him access several services including part-time employment, better housing, and medical benefits. She was so smart!

With the "Missing Harold Case" behind us, Missy and I were open to other investigative opportunities but, alas, nothing showed up. Feeling a little let down from the high of our adventure, I planned our next trip to Sam's Place. To negate Ethyl's prying eyes, this time we met in my apartment and exited together when we confirmed that the coast was clear. The night before our outing, I gave the night staff a heads-up so we weren't breaking the rules.

As before, Sam's Place was busy but after a few minutes' wait, the hostess was able to show us to a booth for six. The agile filed into the booth first, the most feeble among us sat on the ends. There was no discussion about the arrangement; we simply used our common sense.

Sam's was a Cheers-like neighborhood bar with sticky floors and smoke-stained walls from the years before smoking indoors was banned. Maroon leather booths took up space along three walls, small tables with wooden chairs stood in the center of the room, and a belly-up bar spanned the far wall. Unfortunately, the place smelled like Lysol. Since Covid, it seemed that restaurants had a disinfectant smell. I missed the malty, spilled beer fragrance from when bars smelled like bars.

There was a small stage in the corner of the room. Tonight, the entertainment consisted of a young man with tattoo sleeves playing an electric guitar and a middle-aged woman in a fancy sequined jumpsuit singing. Her outfit reminded me of Harold's attire.

After we were greeted by the waitress as if we were regulars, I reminded the girls of their one-drink limit. I gave Anna a stern look and she promptly ordered a Diet Coke. Madge ordered her usual vodka tonic, Missy ordered a martini with extra olives, and I ordered a Coors Lite. I couldn't hear the other orders. The entertainment had started, and along with the patrons' talking and laughing, the noise level in the room rivaled the touchdown cheering on Monday Night Football.

I looked at the faces around me and saw ear-to-ear smiles. I doubted if the amazing atmosphere or fabulous entertainment was causing this much delight. I think it was the sense of freedom and doing something slightly outside of the lines that had perked up six old ladies.

Before our drinks arrived, the waitress returned and asked if we'd like anything else. She apologized for our order being slow and explained that the bar was short-staffed. I took the opportunity to order two baskets of onion rings. It had been a while since dinner, and I didn't want anyone to suffer the repercussions of too much alcohol and too little food. I was reminded of Judy telling me to act responsibly when it came to my friends. She was right, of course. If I insisted on crossing the line, I had to be careful not to go too far. The food appeared before the drinks, and the onion rings were scarfed down as if we hadn't eaten in days. Nothing tastes better than salt and grease!

We didn't stay long once we imbibed our drinks. It was after nine, and everyone was ready to get back to their apartments and go to bed. I noticed Margaret looking particularly tired and pale. My Spidey Sense told me something was wrong. I made a mental note to talk with her after dinner the next day. Since my mental notes often disappeared, once I got settled in the Uber, I sent myself an email reminder.

I tip-toed past Agnes' desk the next morning, hoping she hadn't gotten wind of last night's outing. Even though it was on the up and up, she probably would have disapproved. When she didn't look up, I gave a sigh of relief.

The feeling of joy from our outing carried me through the day. I even rode an extra two miles on the stationary bicycle.

Heeding the email to myself, I approached Margaret after dinner. "Let's talk a minute before we join the others." She looked only mildly surprised and held back as the rest exited the dining room.

Margaret was about my age, a retired elementary school teacher, wickedly smart, funny, and kind. She was taller than me (I was short and getting shorter all the time), had thinning white hair that used to be red (she had stories of riding her pony to school with red pigtails flying out behind her), eyes that looked into your soul without judgment, and a mouth that was usually smiling. She was one of my favorite people in the world and another reason I wasn't sad or mad about being relocated to the Manor.

We found a couple of chairs along the wall and took a seat. All the residents had vacated the dining room, and the servers were busy cleaning up, so no one looked our way. I took her hand in mine. It wasn't a romantic gesture and I was certain she didn't perceive it as one. It was a friendly gesture, and we were both comfortable with it. "My instincts are telling me you're not well, Margaret. I hope I'm wrong."

She gave me her knowing smile. "I had a feeling you were on to me."

"So, tell me what's happening." I gave her hand a gentle squeeze. It felt cold and bony.

"My pancreatic cancer is back. Stage four." She looked at me, probably deciding on how much more to say.

I nodded. She wasn't looking for a dramatic response. Margaret was a pragmatic person.

"I've declined treatment. Once is enough. Eventually, they'll bring hospice in to keep me comfortable."

"I'm so sorry to hear this."

"Thank you. I appreciate your concern but as long as I don't have to suffer, I'm all right with coming to the end of my life. I've been blessed with almost ninety years of living and it's been a great ride." She gave me a wan smile.

There wasn't much else to say so we sat in companionable silence. When it was my turn, I hoped that I'd face death with Margaret's calm demeanor. When the staff turned off the lights, we took the cue and proceeded arm and arm to the social area. Thankfully, Charmaine was playing classical music on the piano. It was just the right antidote to a heartbreaking but soulful conversation.

Margaret kept popping into my mind, so the following afternoon, I texted her. *Anything left on your bucket list that you want to do? I'm up for whatever. Thinking of you.* (Heart emoji)

Thirty minutes later, my phone pinged. It was Margaret. *As a matter of fact, there is one thing left. Let's talk.*

After dinner, the staff was setting up for a special event, so Margaret and I moved to the quiet of my apartment. I offered her the recliner and I took the couch. She was looking better tonight. Perhaps the outing to Sam's had been too much for her. Because I was thinking along these lines, I was surprised by what Margaret said.

"I want to see a musical on Broadway one last time."

I didn't want to say "healthy enough," so instead, I asked, "Are you up for a trip to the city?"

"I am if we go soon."

"Soon as in next week?"

Margaret pulled a little notebook from her purse and perused it. "I looked up the train schedule. We can catch the 8:55 am and be back by 8:40 pm. That's ample time for lunch and a show. What do you say?"

"I say, absolutely! When?"

"There's a matinee at two o'clock next Wednesday."

"And the show?"

"What about *Moulin Rouge, The Musical*? I know you lived in Paris at one time so I thought this might be right up your alley. It's the new show at the Al Hirschfield Theater on 45th."

I was practically speechless. "Do you know that when I returned to Paris to celebrate my 75th birthday, my friend and I rented an Airbnb just blocks from the Moulin Rouge?"

Margaret's eyes lit up. "I had no idea, but I think this whole thing is meant to be. Don't you?"

"Like kismet."

"Yes. Kismet."

We were both quiet for a beat as we let this thought settle in. Then Margaret spoke. "My oldest daughter has lived in New York City for years and will arrange everything. She'll have a car meet us at the train station and drop us at a restaurant near the theater so we can have lunch before the show. She'll also arrange for accessible seating at the theater so we won't have to climb stairs or wait in line. After the show, she'll have a car waiting to take us back to the train station."

"Don't you want to attend the show with your daughter?" I asked, concerned that she might feel obligated to take me.

Margaret looked thoughtful for a minute. "I love Linda dearly, but she's my daughter, not my friend. I want to have this adventure with a friend who can share my excitement about seeing a Broadway show for the last time. She understands and is more than willing to make the arrangements for us. By the way, the trip and show are my treat."

When I started to protest, she held up her hand. "Please let me do this, Martha."

Margaret returned to her apartment and I circled February 5th on my calendar.

I woke up the following morning thinking of our trip. I had only visited New York City twice in my life; once to take my grandchildren to see *Lion King* and once to go to the Metropolitan Museum of Art. Both were side trips corresponding with a visit to Richard and his family. Although I was a small-town girl at heart, I did love the vibe of a city. There was nothing like standing on a street corner surrounded by a mob of people in midtown Manhattan.

Half an hour later, I was dressed for my workout and about to leave the apartment, when there was a knock on the door. I opened it to Missy's and Margaret's sad faces.

"What happened?" I asked with alarm.

"May we come in?" asked Missy.

"Of course." I stepped aside. "Just looking at your faces tells me something bad has happened."

They sat together on the loveseat and I impatiently sat on the edge of the recliner.

"Anna died last night," said Margaret. "She had a massive stroke and died within minutes."

"Tell me more."

Missy explained. "She pulled her emergency cord, and Judy arrived immediately and called 911, but our dear friend was gone by the time the EMTs arrived."

Although this news wasn't totally unexpected, it was still a shock.

Missy added, "We wanted to tell you before you heard it elsewhere. I ran into Judy as she was leaving her shift at six this morning."

"Six?" I asked.

"I couldn't sleep, so I went for a hall-walk," Missy explained. "I think Judy told me about Anna because she knew we were close friends. We'll let the others know when we see them tonight." My two friends got up from the couch and headed to the door.

"Thanks for coming by and letting me know. See you later," I said as they left.

I knew I was in shock because I had no tears. All I could think of was, "At least she got to enjoy one last fling at Sam's Place."

Chapter Eight

Anna's remembrance service was held on Saturday in the social room. Our group, a handful of other residents, and three staff members were in attendance. Anna's children had already whisked her body back to Ohio for a proper funeral and burial so none of them were present. And, just like that, our friend Anna was gone.

Although the brief service wasn't a funeral, it did offer closure for those of us who were her friends. Most of us shared a special memory. Madge joked about Anna reciting her litany of ailments to anyone who would listen, I talked about our meaningful book discussions, and Judy recalled her enthusiasm for life even though she was ill. Everyone agreed that Anna was a good-hearted soul and a light in our lives that had now been extinguished. Although we all shed tears, we felt grateful that Anna hadn't suffered.

After the service, Margaret confirmed that our trip to NYC was still on for the following Wednesday, so when I got back to my apartment, I booted up Amazon to shop for a new outfit. Pants seemed in order since February weather can be unpredictable. I researched the trends. I didn't want to look like a "down at the heels" elderly lady—especially not in The Big Apple.

One stylist wrote, "Rock a pair of silver metallic pants with a sleek black bodysuit for your next night out and watch heads turn." Maybe not. I looked further. "After a good, long run, it's time for skinny jeans to step aside and let a new trend take center stage. As a replacement, stylists recommend barrel, bootcut, and straight-leg silhouettes — all of which are having a moment right now."

I ordered a pair of black bootcut trousers. I also wanted to have "a moment right now."

Next, I read that lace was trending. I was reminded of Molly's lace blouse so I ordered a burgundy one which would work out nicely under my short, black, wool coat.

Tuesday night, I laid out my clothes and took a shower so I wouldn't have to do it in the morning. Per Margaret's request, I ordered an Uber to pick us up at eight-thirty sharp.

The trip to the station, the train ride, and locating the waiting car went smoothly, and we were dropped off in front of the restaurant where we had reservations. A few yards away, we saw a man in his tidy whities, another man with a beard dressed as a woman in a tutu, a woman on stilts, and a few people with placards predicting the end of the world. They were wandering around in a cordoned-off area. Tourists were going crazy taking photos with their phones. There was nothing like The Big Apple!

In keeping with our Parisian theme, our lunch was at a French restaurant. Even though we ate inside, the intimate dining room had a streets-of-Paris look with white cafe chairs, potted plants scattered about, and a trellis leaning against one wall.

I ordered my all-time favorite, Salade Nicoise. Margaret ordered jambon-beurre also called Le Parisien, which refers to the type of ham used in this traditional French sandwich. We each had a glass of wine. Even I wouldn't consider ordering a beer in a French restaurant at noon.

There was a long line in front of the theater but when we showed the passes on our phones, we were whisked into the lower level and escorted to seats on the aisle. When the lights flickered, my heart leaped. There was nothing like a Broadway show! The big gold curtain slowly rose and I patted Margaret's hand. "Here we go," I whispered. She turned to me and smiled.

The prelude, performed by a full orchestra, awakened all my senses. The beauty of the scenery was mesmerizing. When the first performer started to sing, his tenor voice penetrated my entire body. For over an hour, I was carried back to Paris on the wings of singers and actors who were the best in the business.

At intermission, I offered to bring Margaret a bottle of water which she graciously accepted. Knowing the line would be long, we were both thankful we didn't need to use the bathroom. When the action during the second half of the show slowed, I looked over at Margaret. The muscles in her face were relaxed, her eyes were shining, and there was a faint smile on her lips. Her pain, her diagnosis, and her impending death were momentarily forgotten. I could tell that she was totally immersed in what was taking place on stage. I mentally checked off the last item on her bucket list.

On our trip home after the long day, we both nodded off, and the porter had to shake us awake when we arrived at our station in Poughkeepsie.

The next morning, I noticed that Margaret was missing from the dining room, so a few hours later, I brought lunch to her apartment even though I knew she had the option to order in. Sometimes, when a person wasn't well, the last thing on their mind was food. She gave me a wan smile and thanked me for my kindness. I could tell that the trip had taken a lot out of her. "Was it worth it?" I asked after I put a sandwich on the TV tray in front of her and sat on her mauve couch.

"Absolutely! I'm completely spent, but in a good way." She looked at me and smiled. "You helped make my day, dear friend. It wouldn't have been the same without you."

"A memory to last us the rest of our lives." I sighed. "However long or short that may be. Right?"

"Right. Now, go away and let me eat my sandwich and take a nap. I'll make an effort to come down for dinner."

I saw myself out. Aware that we both were living on borrowed time, I felt ever so thankful for my Best Friend Forever and our amazing trip to Broadway.

Chapter Nine

Spring suddenly dropped in like a welcome friend from the past. I swapped out the stationary bike for walks around the property. The swans were back on our small, man-made pond; they kept the geese at bay. The purple grape hyacinths were in bloom with the budding daffodils close behind. Being in nature refreshed my soul and walking did a world of good for my hip. I wasn't fully recovered from my surgery, but I was hopeful that by the one-year anniversary, I'd be fit as a fiddle as my dad would say.

Hospice had installed a hospital bed in Margaret's apartment and, most days, she was on a morphine drip. I could hardly believe that only a month ago we were enjoying *Moulin Rouge! The Musical* on Broadway. I visited her every day just before lunch and sometimes later in the afternoon. She was busy with nursing procedures the first thing in the morning and tired out by dinnertime. Always her pleasant self, Margaret was a role model for how to die with dignity.

With only four remaining at dinner, we scaled down to a square table. We were a pretty somber group, and I was racking my brain for a new excursion we could take that would perk us up. After listening to some lively 50s tunes around the piano, I returned to my apartment, booted up my laptop, and searched the Internet for "things to do near me." I came up with a karaoke bar just three miles from the Manor. The description said, "Winner of the best karaoke and college bar in the Hudson Valley."

When I introduced the idea of going to a karaoke bar at dinner the following night, three heads nodded in the affirmative but without much enthusiasm. Nevertheless, after alerting Judy to our outing, we assembled at my apartment on Wednesday to Uber over to Maloney's Irish Pub and Steakhouse. After entering the establishment, we were directed to a booth for four. Although this was more restaurant than bar, the waitress didn't seem to mind when we ordered three Irish decaf coffees and a Guinness for me. Looking around, I noticed most patrons had drinks and fries, rather than steaks, in front of them.

Maloney's was classier than Sam's, with well-scrubbed wide plank wood floors, walls papered in green plaid with white wainscot below, and shamrock cut-outs strategically placed around the room. A karaoke booth stood at the front of the room with a small stage to the side. A young lad was at the mike singing off-key. When he garnered little applause, I used his lackluster performance to encourage Missy to sign up to sing. I knew she had a lovely voice because I frequently heard her at the piano sing-alongs. She agreed and signed up for "O Danny Boy." When her name was called, I squeezed her hand for encouragement as she exited our booth. It was meant to be both affectionate and friendly which reminded me of just how complicated relationships can be.

College kids, some probably with fake IDs, filled the place. Although our group of old ladies stuck out, I was confident Missy's singing would make the youngsters sit up and pay attention.

My heartbeat accelerated when I saw Missy, her unruly hair swirling around her head, step on stage in fashionable above-the-ankle gray slacks, a red boat-neck sweater, and gold hoop earrings. She confidently took the mike. Her beautiful rendition of "O Danny Boy" brought tears to my eyes. When the song ended, the crowd erupted into applause which brought on more tears. I was so proud of her. After she executed a little bow, one of the nearby college dudes offered his hand to help her off the stage. A basket of fries miraculously appeared at our table.

When the fries were eaten, we took our leave. Heads turned as we briskly walked toward the door. No longer were we invisible old ladies. I took Missy's hand just before slipping out into the night and our waiting Uber.

The four of us could travel in one car, with three in the back seat and one in the front. Riding shotgun was probably against the rules but, Ted, our usual driver, didn't mention it. We requested him specifically when we needed transportation. Madge sat up front. She was the widest and liked to be in a position of control. I think she imagined herself driving.

The following morning, Richard called inviting himself to lunch. I wondered why he didn't text; calling felt intrusive these days. He sounded calm so apparently, he hadn't learned of my recent escapades. I suggested we meet in the dining room. There was no sense taking a chance of running into Agnes in the hall. I had grown bored with the meal rotations by now and would have preferred to have lunch at a restaurant but my son probably wanted to make sure he was getting his money's worth and I was grateful for his attention.

I dressed in my "dutiful mother" clothes—a white, no-iron Chico's blouse and black skinny jeans (I couldn't seem to wean myself away from them). I applied pink lipstick, saving the red for party time, and stepped into my ever-present Sketcher slip-ons. I must say, I looked downright respectable and rule-abiding. I didn't resemble Queen Latifah in the least.

"How have you been?" Richard asked after we were seated.

"All right I guess," I replied noncommittally, careful not to give any hints about my recent karaoke escapade or memorable trip to Broadway. I might have shared my story of the trip to the city, but I knew Richard didn't approve of me going on treks too far beyond the confines of the Manor.

"Are you well looked after? How's the food?"

Looked after? Was I a horse in a stable? The food was pretty good, considering this was an institution, but the over-cooked veggies and stringy beef weren't my favorites. Setting these snarky responses aside, I politely responded. "The staff here is very diligent." I thought to myself, *If he only knew!*

"And the food?"

"The food is fine. Thanks for asking."

He looked around the room. When Missy spotted him, she gave him a little wave. "How are your friends?"

"Well, Anna recently died from a massive stroke, and my best friend, Margaret, is being cared for by hospice and on a morphine drip. Other than that, they're fine."

I could tell my response set him back on his heels. I knew I was being heartless and a little mean, but I wanted him to wake up to the fact that this wasn't a controlled atmosphere storage facility where people lived forever.

He cleared his throat and took a sip of his iced tea. "I'm sorry to hear about your friend dying and the other one in hospice. It must be difficult to be surrounded by elderly people in ill health."

I appreciated his kind response. He really didn't deserve my negative attitude. I think I was simply taking my helpless and sad feelings out on him. Trying to be more positive, I said, "We're not all on our last legs. Some of us are still rather hale and hearty for our ages." I smiled to reassure him that I was one of the "hale and hearty" ones.

I shifted gears. That was enough about me. It was too easy to end up on thin ice. "How's the family? How's retirement?" I asked.

He perked up. "The family is fine. Maria sends her love. We rarely see the kids. Samantha and Rich are busy with little David and Susan is immersed in her career."

I was reminded of the Cat's In the Cradle, silver spoon song where the dad worked all the time and the little boy kept saying, "I'm gonna be like you, Dad."

"And retirement?"

Richard looked down at his chicken salad and then back up at me. "Retirement isn't quite what I'd expected. I miss the camaraderie of the office staff and the challenge of being in the courtroom. I suppose I should have found an outside interest earlier on. I've never had an indoor hobby, and now that's a liability. There's only so many days of the week I can golf, especially here in New York."

I tried to be sympathetic toward Richard but for Heaven's sake, he had every opportunity to do whatever he wanted with his time. Blessed with good health and ample finances, the world was his oyster. Making an effort to shut down "Judgmental Martha," it occurred to me that something else might be going on in his life that I didn't know about.

"How's Maria adjusting to you being home more?" I asked.

I could tell from the look on his face that this was a touchy subject. Just as he was about to answer, the fire alarm went off. Richard jumped out of his seat, I calmly stayed in mine. I looked up at him. "Do you smell smoke?"

"No, but the voice on the recording is telling us to exit immediately. We should go!"

He pulled my chair (with me still in it) out from the table. "If you insist." I got up knowing that one of the residents probably pulled the alarm handle thinking it was a video game or something. It happened all the time. Now THAT was a reason to be called in for disciplinary action. While we were waiting for the fire department to arrive and turn off the alarm, Missy and Harold joined us. My up-tight son, my potential girlfriend (or GIRLFRIEND as my gay granddaughter once said), and my male admirer all standing together was just too much.

"There's obviously no fire," I hollered over the screech of the alarm. "I'm going back to lunch." Without a backward glance at the trio on the curb, I walked around the building, through an unlocked side door, and resumed sitting at our table in the dining room. My soup had gone cold but the ham sandwich was edible, so I finished eating. Soon after, the alarm went quiet.

My son returned, sat down, looked down at his chicken salad, then pushed it aside. "Good heavens, Mother. How frequently does the alarm go off?"

He sounded exasperated. I hoped he wouldn't make a big deal out of this. I smiled to reassure him. "Oh, perhaps twice a month. Usually during the day, thankfully. One of the things you get used to when you live here. There are locked covers on the alarms but whoever is setting them off is skilled at picking them. One of these days, they'll find out who it is."

He still looked aghast, so I went back to my last question. "And Maria, how's she handling your retirement?"

"Fine, I guess. She's frequently out with friends and going to her clubs but," he looked like a kid who had figured out the correct answer to a test question at the last minute, "we always have dinner together."

Richard folded his napkin and laid it on the table, my cue that the visit was over.

"Thank you for coming. Please give my love to the family," I said, getting up to give him a hug. He wasn't much of a hugger, but he responded.

"Stay well, Mother. Let me know if you need anything. See you next month."

Richard left the dining room, and I retreated to the sanctity of my apartment. Although I received weekly calls from my daughters, Richard was the one who consistently showed up for me and I knew I should feel more appreciation for his concern. Why was it so difficult for me to be kind to my son? There was no doubt that I loved him but if I was entirely honest with myself, I had to admit that I didn't always like him.

Chapter Ten

The Tuesday before Mother's Day, Margaret slipped into a coma and her daughter, Linda, arrived. The Manor provided a guest room for visiting family members which was convenient in circumstances like this. Madge, Molly, Missy, and I relieved Linda whenever we could so someone was with Margaret at all times. Of course, there were various hospice nurses and staff members who rotated in and out but they didn't love Margaret like we did.

I'd never watched someone die, and I was feeling anxious in case I happened to be present at the time of Margaret's passing. I knew that a person's hearing was the last to go so I read passages of poetry to her or recited words to songs I knew she liked. Sometimes, I sat quietly and simply held her hand.

On Sunday morning I received calls from my children wishing me Happy Mother's Day. I let each one go to voicemail. I quickly responded kindly by text, but I wasn't feeling celebratory as I dressed and made my way to Margaret's bedside, allowing her daughter time to freshen up and go to breakfast.

I was sitting by my friend's bed humming the familiar hymn, "It Is Well With My Soul," when her eyes popped open and she spoke in a voice so soft I had to put my ear near her mouth to hear.

"Anna, what are you doing here? You're supposed to be dead," she whispered.

I'd swear on a stack of Bibles that's exactly what she said before she closed her eyes and took a slow, shallow breath. When her breathing became labored, the nurse intervened and checked her pulse. I texted Linda.

Come back, I think the end is close.

Just before Linda arrived, Margaret took a raspy breath, her jaw went slack, and I could no longer see her bedcovers rise and fall. I looked at the nurse and mouthed, "Is she gone?" She nodded. I leaned over and kissed her on the forehead. "Goodbye, dear friend. I'll be seeing you soon."

When Linda entered the room, I gave her my condolences and left. Although I felt extremely sad, there were no tears, so I made my way to breakfast, ate my Grape-Nuts, drank my tea, then returned to my apartment. I sent a group text to the other three. I knew I should have visited them personally or at least called with the sad news, but I desperately wanted to be alone— alone with my memories of Margaret, few as they were in the scope of our long lives, alone with thoughts of my own impending death, and alone with my God, who had been a rock in times of grief or trouble for as long as I could remember.

Around one o'clock, I was watching the recording of my remote church service when I heard a soft knock. I pushed pause, padded across the room in my slippers, and opened the door to find Harold standing there with a take out box in his hands. "I thought you might be getting hungry since I didn't see you at lunch. I'll just set this up, then leave you to it."

I stepped aside and he went to my kitchen nook, pulled a paper plate, napkin, fork, and glass from my cupboard. While he was transferring the tuna salad sandwich (I could tell from the smell) and slaw onto a plate, he said, "I heard about Margaret. I know you two were very close. I'm so sorry for your loss."

Those simple words somehow broke the damn and I started to cry. Harold set my plate on the table and gathered me into his arms. I put my face into his chest and sobbed. I knew I was making ugly-cry noises, but I couldn't help it. Harold didn't say a word; just held me close and gently patted my back. When I came up for air, he grabbed the napkin off the table and handed it to me. I wiped my eyes and blew my nose. He opened his palm to collect the snot and tear-soaked napkin, then tossed it into the trash. Emotionally spent, I was suddenly hungry.

Harold pulled out the chair and I sat down at the table. Then, like a magician, he pulled a can of Bud from his pocket, opened it, carefully poured it into my glass, then took the seat across from me. "Do you have Alexa?" Harold asked.

"I do."

"Alexa, play classical music," he ordered.

Alexa obeyed, and Beethoven's "Ode to Joy" filled the room. I scarfed down my tuna sandwich, ate my slaw, and drank my beer. "Thanks, Harold, I needed that."

"Which?" he asked with a sly smile on his face.

"All of it. The food, the beer, the hug, the good cry, and the music. I was hungry for it all."

Harold picked up the dirty plate and empty glass. "I'm glad you're feeling better. Now, go sit." He pointed to my recliner.

Like a child unable to make clear-headed decisions, I was open to being told what to do. I remembered feeling exactly the same when, Marvin, my fifty-five-year-old second husband, suddenly dropped dead of a heart attack many years ago. I sat in my recliner, pulled the lever, and stuck my legs out. Harold took a seat on the couch. "What's your best memory of Margaret?"

The answer immediately popped into my head. "That's easy. Three months ago, we completed her bucket list and took the train to New York to see *Moulin Rouge,* a new Broadway musical. The day was magical and I'll never forget the look on Margaret's face as she was transported to Paris and away from her troubles."

Harold smiled as if he'd conjured up a vision of my memory. "I stopped by to see her a few times after hospice came in," he said. "She told me about your trip and how much it meant that you were willing to accompany her. Margaret thought the world of you."

This caused me to tear up again, but I was all out of boo-hoos.

Harold crossed his legs. "You've been through a lot recently. Losing two of your friends in just a few months is a big blow. Be gentle with yourself, Martha. You need to take time to heal."

"Don't forget the stress of losing you for a while. Believe me, that was a whopper also."

It was Harold's turn to tear up. "You and Missy were superheroes in that escapade. You changed my life and my son's." Harold plucked a tissue from the box on the end table and noisily blew his nose. "By the way, John's doing well. He's moved to a low-cost housing apartment, has part-time work in a bakery, and is volunteering at a shelter. I'm proud of him, and I take every opportunity to tell him so."

I felt a smile bubbling up. "It's surprising what two old ladies and a plate of cheap cookies can do."

Harold nodded, then he slowly got up from the couch, walked over and patted my hand. "Go take a nap."

After Harold left my apartment, I lowered my legs, dutifully walked to my bedroom, and laid down for a mid-afternoon nap.

I woke up an hour later feeling groggy and headachey. I'd never done well with naps. I took a shower, thinking it would refresh me and sure enough, I felt better when I emerged. I dressed for dinner and then finished watching my church service.

At four-thirty I trudged down to the dining room. Three sad faces greeted me at the table. After general chit-chat, I posed the question Harold had asked me. "What's your best memory of Margaret?" The question elicited a lively conversation and a great deal of loving reflection. I mentally thanked Harold for showing us a way to smile while remembering Margaret.

Chapter Eleven

Unlike Anna's brief in-house remembrance, Margaret's family arranged for a funeral that took place in the Poughkeepsie United Methodist Church. Since she had lived in Poughkeepsie most of her adult life, there were several rows of mourners. Harold sat with the four of us sporting a dark suit and shiny shoes. I barely recognized him out of his jumpsuit.

After the service, Margaret's daughter handed me a small gift bag. I pulled out one of her mother's favorite scarves and held it to my nose. Margaret's scent still clung to the scarf. "Thank you. I'll always treasure this remembrance of your mother."

Linda replied, "You helped make the last year or so of her life joy-filled, Martha. She spoke of you often."

June brought plenty of sunshine and lost keys. Somehow, I kept forgetting to deposit my apartment key on the hook by the door. Consequently, I had to scour my apartment three times in three weeks looking for it. I also lost the name of the minivan driver. I knew it was somewhere in the recesses of my brain, but when I couldn't retrieve it, I resorted to asking Missy.

"What's the name of the guy who drives the minivan for this place?" I asked as we were walking to the social room for a required program about STDs. I wondered if they could really require us to attend.

"Jake." Missy's eyes looked troubled. "Why?"

I tried to sound casual. "Just wondering. I seem to have forgotten."

"Did you, by any chance, also forget to return your latest library books? I happened to see them on the dinette table the other night. It seems like they've been there for a few weeks now."

"My goodness, I certainly hope not!" I said a bit too loudly. "I pride myself on never having an overdue book." Remembering the beer-spilling incident, I added, "A little well-used sometimes, but never late."

After we were seated, I pulled out my phone and went to "my books" on the library's website. Sure enough, three books were more than a week late. I looked over at Missy. "You're right, my books are late. Thanks for giving me a heads-up."

Agnes, standing at the front of the room, shushed us. "Ladies and gentlemen, thank you for coming. As part of Martyn Manor's accreditation, we're required to present this program on the dangers and prevalence of sexually transmitted diseases and illnesses within senior living environments."

Many of the residents looked down at their hands and some were swinging their crossed legs, but Agnes trudged onward despite the emotionally chilly temperature in the room. "Angelina Gangestad, a doctor specializing in Obstetrics and Gynecology, says that there are a number of reasons why older adults may be susceptible to contracting an STI, or sexually transmitted illness."

Agnes looked around to be sure no one had drifted off, then she continued. "Dr. Gangestad says that older people may underestimate their risk and not take precautions such as condom use and STI testing before having sex with a new partner. Lack of concern about pregnancy is also likely to diminish condom use."

I wasn't entirely surprised by this revelation. I'd read about The Villages in Florida and the prevalence of STDs there. As Agnes soldiered on, I made an effort to stay attentive. When the program was over, everyone avoided eye contact as they trooped out of the social room.

Agnes' presentation had piqued my curiosity about STDs and seniors so when I returned to my apartment, I Googled The Villages and read that it's one of the most well-known fifty-five-plus communities globally and one of the best places to retire in Florida. The hype continued, "The friendly atmosphere, endless activities, and nightly entertainment draw Active Adults." Just as I got to the juicy bits about how active can translate to wild, there was a knock. "Come in."

Harold walked through the door uncharacteristically empty-handed.

"Have a seat," I said, glancing up from my computer screen. "You'll never believe what I'm reading about The Villages." When Harold looked perplexed, I added, "I came back here and looked them up because I heard it's a swinging community for seniors." When he still looked blank, I impatiently added, "I'm following up on our program this afternoon."

Harold finally nodded and sat next to me at the table.

"Listen to this," I looked over at Harold to be sure he was tuned in, "and I quote, the retirement community has its own shops, bars, grocery stores, schools, and apparently its own sexual activity code using different colored loofahs."

"What's a loofah?" Harold asked.

At least he was listening. "You know, those round things made of nylon netting that one hangs in the shower. Apparently, there are videos of some residents displaying loofahs on their cars or golf carts, allegedly to identify their swinging sexual styles." I shook my head. "Good grief, who knew?"

"Yeah, who knew?"

Harold seemed to be a bit overwhelmed by all this, but I found it fascinating so I continued. "Want to know what the Loofah Code identifies?"

"I guess so."

"The Loofah Code identifies what each loofah color represents. It says, and I again quote, white is for beginners, black is for couples who want it all. Do you know what that means?" I looked over at Harold.

"Nope." Harold was a man of few words today.

"Neither do I. Anyway, teal means bisexual, purple is for those who like to watch, yellow is for couples that are down but still nervous, pink likes other people to watch them, and blue means they play well with others."

Harold looked a little pale. "What does 'down' mean?"

"It means whatever someone is interested in, they're all for it."

Harold shook his head. "This is too much information for me. Are you sure it's true?"

I scrolled down the screen. "Here's another article that says loofahs simply help residents find their golf carts since many look alike." It was my turn to shake my head. "I don't know. The golf cart identification story seems like a cover-up to me."

"All I can say is thank goodness we live here." Harold looked at me, obviously weighing my response. "You wouldn't want to live there, would you?" he asked.

"Absolutely not, but I do find all the hoopla fascinating in a voyeur sort of way. Of course, many of those folks are younger than we are." I considered my statement. "Way younger."

Harold got up and helped himself to a glass of water. I had to admit I enjoyed seeing this man of the world squirm. "Well, since I only had sex with one woman for over fifty years, I'm not worried about STDs or STIs or whatever," he said.

Knowing Harold was married for over sixty years, I couldn't help but ask, "What happened in the intervening years?" I gave him a mischievous smile.

"I did spend time overseas, you know. Being in the Army for over thirty years does put a person in some unusual circumstances."

Harold was certainly being cryptic. "Like?" I asked.

"Good grief, Martha, that was over sixty years ago. Must I go into detail?"

"Not if you don't want to. I'm just naturally a curious person." I smiled at him sweetly.

Harold carefully sat his glass on the table. "Anything else new we can talk about?"

I decided it was time to let him off the hook. "I have overdue library books. I've never missed a due date before. I'm a little worried about my memory."

Harold's eyebrows came together. They were hard to miss because of their bushiness. "You seem okay to me. As far as I know, nothing dire has happened since you burnt the pot. Has there been anything more serious than late library books that you haven't told me about?"

I thought about his question for a moment. "Just misplaced apartment keys and misplaced names. I guess you're right. I'll stop worrying. Thanks, Harold."

My friend nodded then got up and dutifully placed his glass in the sink. "Best be going. You sure gave me a lot to think about."

I smiled. "Always at your service, Harold. Come back whenever you get bored."

Chapter Twelve

On Wednesday, I waited for the minivan as usual. I had added the driver's name to the "notes" section of my iPhone just in case it slipped my mind again. I was checking the name when he pulled up. "Hi, Jake," I said a little too loudly.

"Good morning, Mrs. A. Mind if I make a stop at the 7-11 on our way to the library?"

"Of course not, Jake." Maybe if I said his name enough it would stick.

When I was finally dropped off at the library, I marched up to the desk with my delinquent books in tow. "Good morning, Winter." I was so thankful for name tags. I wished the whole world walked around wearing them. It would be so helpful! "How much do I owe?" I handed her my books just as Mrs. Fayerweather came around the corner.

"Good morning, Martha. It's so good to see you," she said.

"Where have you been? I've missed you," I replied.

"I had a bit of a health setback, but I've returned. Can I be of help here?"

Winter handed Mrs. Fayerweather my books. She typed something into the computer then looked at me. "These books are late, but since you've never had late books before, I believe we can wave the fine."

"Really? I'm more than happy to pay. I feel terrible that the return date slipped my mind."

Mrs. Fayerweather smiled. "No worries. It happens to the best of us from time to time."

I put my hand over my heart. "I promise to be more diligent in the future. Thank you for letting me off the hook."

Apparently realizing that the ball was back in her court, Winter asked, "Is there anything I can help you with today?"

"Not today. I heard *The Bucket List* by Rachael Hannah is good. I recently helped my friend fulfill her bucket list so I thought the book might be timely. I can find it on my own."

Winter turned her attention to the computer and I wandered off down the aisles.

When mid-June popped up on the calendar and it was officially summer, I pulled out my white capris which were a nice change from the skinny jeans. Then I headed to lunch.

The dining room was unusually crowded, so I needed to share a table. I spied a woman sitting alone and asked if I could join her.

"Please do. I'd love the company. I'm Maude, and you are?" she held out her bird-like, blue-veined hand.

I noted that she was another "M" name, gently shook her hand, and introduced myself. Maude was elderly, meaning older than me, frail with lots of wrinkles, and wearing a style of summer dress that was popular in the 70s.

Just as I was about to put a forkful of salad into my mouth, I noticed a bulletin sitting in the middle of the table. After reading it, I asked my tablemate if she'd like me to read it aloud. She wore thick eyeglasses and I doubted whether she could have read the smallish print.

"Yes, dear. That would be very kind. Thank you," she answered in a quiet, raspy voice.

I read, "BEWARE. According to the local police, there have been two purse snatching incidents in the vicinity of Martyn Manor in recent weeks. Be especially diligent if you walk off the premises. If you see anyone suspicious, immediately report them to the authorities."

Maude placed her hand over her heart. "Gracious me. What is this world coming to when we can't even go for a walk without worrying about our safety?"

Apparently, she didn't watch the national news. Frankly, this was the least of our worries in the scope of what was happening in the world. I didn't say this, of course. Instead, I said, "If someone tries to take my purse, I'll happily oblige and give it to them. Losing a purse is nothing compared to getting knocked down or worse."

Maude looked at me then down at the large, black purse sitting on the floor next to her chair. "You're right, of course. It's just that I use my purse as a sort of filing cabinet. It holds my bills, my pills, my recent correspondence, and a hefty amount of cash. I don't like using those plastic cards. They aren't safe, you know."

I could have said so many things in response to her remark but instead, I took the last bite of my salad. It had taken me a lifetime to learn to keep my opinions to myself when I knew they wouldn't make a twit of difference. "Just be careful," I warned her before I got up. "It was nice eating lunch with you, Maude."

"You too, ahh…" she paused. "What's your name again?"

"Martha."

"Oh, yes, Martha. Names slip my mind so easily these days."

Under my breath I said, "Tell me about it."

A couple of weeks later, I heard that two women from the Manor had been approached by a man and relieved of their purses. One woman apparently tried to fight back and was knocked to the ground. She wasn't hurt, thank goodness, but the situation sounded like it was getting worse, and the person who resisted her assailant sounded like Maude.

Three days after learning these details, I happened to see Detective Warren talking with Agnes outside of her office. After experiencing a bit of déjà vu, I stopped and asked him about the purse snatching incidents. I could tell from his expression that he was trying to place me. He was probably thinking that all the little old ladies in this building looked alike.

"It certainly is a growing problem…" he paused.

"Martha. My name is Martha Anderson."

"Oh yes, I remember." He fiddled with his keys. "You and your friend located Mr. Lancaster."

"Yes, that's me." I moved on, wanting him to stay focused on the issue at hand. "Was Maude the woman who resisted her assailant?" I asked, looking from the detective to Agnes.

A frown crossed Agnes' face. "How do you know her name? We haven't released any details."

I gave Agnes a little smile that said, "I'm not as dumb as you think." I looked toward the detective. "I happened to have lunch with Maude the day you distributed the warning flier. She told me that her purse is her filing cabinet where she stores all of her important papers. She also said that she keeps a good amount of cash in her wallet. She indicated that she'd be very reluctant to give it up."

Detective Warren shifted from one foot to the other. "We're very concerned about these incidents. I'm glad the latest victim…Maude, was it?"

Agnes nodded.

"It was fortunate that Maude wasn't injured."

On the spur of the moment I asked, "What if you used someone as bait? You know, like they do on the TV show *NCIS*." He frowned but didn't say anything, so I continued. "When the bad guy shows up to snatch the purse of the decoy victim, you'd have someone waiting to arrest him before he could get away." Just talking about the notion got my adrenalin going. "You'd catch him red-handed."

"That's actually a good idea." Warren looked at me with a bit more respect.

"Unfortunately, we don't have anyone in the precinct who matches the description of the recent victims. The perpetrator or perpetrators seem to only accost older women. It's his MO."

I knew about MO or modus operandi. It was a Latin term that described an individual's way of operating. "What if I satisfy his MO and become the bait? I fit the description quite nicely, don't you think?" I gave him my grandmotherly look.

"I'm afraid that would be too risky, Mrs. Anderson."

Duly, who obviously concurred, scrunched up her face at my suggestion.

Not wanting the detective to dismiss my suggestion, I added, "I thought you wanted to catch this guy before someone got hurt."

"We do. Of course, we do."

"Well, I'm offering you the perfect solution. I'll sign a waiver saying that I'm doing this of my own free will and I'll not sue the department if something goes sideways, which I'm sure it won't."

This time, Warren looked more convinced. "Let me talk to the captain and get back to you."

I held out my hand. "Give me your phone and I'll put my name and cell number in your contacts. That way you can easily reach me should the captain give you a green light."

He somewhat reluctantly unlocked then handed me his phone. I added my name and number to his contacts. After the detective left, Agnes asked me to come into her office. "Have a seat."

I gingerly sat on the edge of the chair.

"Won't you require permission from your son if Detective Warren's supervisor gives you the go-ahead? He pays your bill, so I expect he has power of attorney."

"You're correct, my son pays my bill here. However, I'm in complete control of my finances and my life. I don't need his permission for anything I do."

Agnes tapped her pen, a terribly annoying habit.

"Then I'll leave this matter between you and the detective."

I got up from my chair. "Thank you for your concern. I'll be returning to my apartment now. Good day."

Agnes waved me out.

That afternoon, I considered my offer and suddenly felt less confident. I decided to text Harold. It seemed to me that a retired Army Colonel was just the person to run this by.

Can you come by my apartment this afternoon? I have something I want to discuss with you.

Not a minute passed.

I'm on my way. (Smiley face emoji)

I had barely gotten settled in my chair before Harold knocked and stuck his head in the door. "What's up?"

He looked a little giddy. Apparently, this was a man who liked being asked for his opinion. "Have a seat. I want to run something by you."

After I explained my plan to Harold, he was quiet for a beat. "Let me get this straight. You offered yourself as bait in order to catch a purse snatcher?"

"That sums it up. Good idea, huh?"

Harold scratched his head. "If you weren't my friend, I'd say it was an excellent idea, but since I'm definitely biased toward your safety, it's hard to say."

"So, if I were a stranger, you'd say yes?"

"Maybe. Would Detective Warren be in charge of this operation?"

"I suppose so. He's going to run it by his supervisor."

"Well, he didn't do such a great job the last time he was in charge of a case involving a certain person," he tapped his chest, "from here."

I hadn't thought of that.

"Are you going to tell your son?"

Harold would have to ask that annoying question. "I wasn't planning on it. He'd raise Cain about it and claim he had some kind of authority to stop me."

"Does he?"

"No, he doesn't. I might owe him a certain amount of courtesy since he pays my Manor bill and he's my son but, as I explained to Agnes, I can decide what to do with my life. Why is there an assumption that a man most likely has control over my destiny?"

Harold squirmed a bit, then put his palms out in front of him. "No assumption. Just asking questions, that's all." He paused, then looked at me. "Would you consider allowing me to sit in on the planning if this thing goes through? Two heads might be better than one. I want to make sure Warren is more thorough this time than he was with his investigation into my disappearance."

I thought for a moment. Two heads were better than one, especially when one head was a little on the wonky side. "Thanks for the offer. I agree with your premise. I'll let you know if the captain gives a thumbs-up."

At dinner that night I made an effort to sit next to Molly. Given that she's always touching up her makeup with cosmetics she pulls from her cavernous purse, I figured she might have an extra one lying around. "Do you by chance have a large purse I can borrow?" I asked after the salad had been served.

"A what?"

I repeated the question a bit louder this time. Molly had a hearing problem but wouldn't consider getting hearing aids. She was very vain when it came to things like that.

She gave me a strange look. I wasn't about to reveal any details of my possible clandestine adventure but I did need to give her something. "Have you noticed that I always carry small purses?"

She nodded.

"Well, I may be going to my son's house in a few weeks. It would be just for the day but I want to be able to take a few more things than I usually carry in my small handbag. You know, extra makeup, a sweater, things like that, and I thought a larger purse would be just the ticket."

"Ticket? Ticket to what?" Molly asked.

I turned so I was looking directly at my friend and repeated what I'd just said. Molly looked convinced. The extra makeup example was a genius addition to my explanation.

"Of course. Any particular color?"

I raised my voice. "No. Whatever you have that you're not using will be fine."

Molly cocked her head in the way she sometimes did. "May I drop it off later this evening?" she asked.

"That would be very kind of you," I said with a little trepidation. She seemed a bit too eager but I was grateful for the prop. It would be good to have a big purse on standby in case I got the call.

Chapter Thirteen

After our evening entertainment featuring a singing quartet from a local high school, I returned to my apartment and slipped into my soft clothes. Before I had a chance to sit down, there was a knock on the door. Expecting the visitor to be Molly, I was surprised when Missy popped her head in. She was carrying a book. Was her visit a coincidence? Somehow, I thought not.

After entering, she handed me the book. "I haven't read this yet, but I thought you might be interested. I know you recently read a book about a bucket list."

I sat down and looked at the title. *Someone Else's Bucket List* by Amy Matthews. I turned the book over and read the blurb on the back. "It sounds interesting. Thanks for thinking of me. I'll bring it back when I'm done."

"No rush," Missy said as she nonchalantly sat on my love seat.

"Molly is coming by shortly. She's bringing a purse I asked to borrow." I thought it was a good idea to give Missy a heads-up in case this wasn't a coincidence. Before she had a chance to erase it, I observed a frown flash across her face.

"Well then, I best be going," she said rather curtly.

She started to get up and I waved her down. "Believe it or not, I'm capable of having more than one visitor at a time." I hoped I didn't sound too sarcastic, but this was ridiculous. The three of us, plus Madge had dinner together every night. What was so special about being in my apartment? I sighed. Who was I kidding? Apartment visiting was a whole other thing around the Manor.

We had barely started a conversation when there was another knock. Before I could respond, Molly burst through the door with two big purses in tow. "Oh!" She stopped short when she saw Missy. "Did I misunderstand about it being all right to drop a purse off tonight?"

Men can be frustrating but WOMEN—they were another story entirely. "No, Molly, you didn't misunderstand. Missy just came by to give me a book she thought I might enjoy." I held the book up. When she continued to stand just inside the door, I said, "For heaven's sake, come in and take a seat."

She dropped one purse on my small dining table, deposited the other on the floor next to the loveseat, and sat beside Missy. They looked at each other as though they hadn't just eaten dinner together less than two hours ago.

"Now, isn't this cozy," said Molly. It was a statement, not a question. I wondered what Detective Warren would say if he came in right now. Since his inclination was to imagine the bawdy and risqué, I figured that he'd have a field day.

The three of us chit-chatted but it felt forced, nothing like our usual banter at dinner. As if three wasn't already a crowd, there was a third knock on my door and Harold poked his head in. He had a bottle of beer in one hand and a bottle of wine in the other. "Oh dear. It looks like you're having a hen party. I won't interrupt." He turned to go.

"You might as well come in and join us, Harold." I pointed to a wooden chair. "Pull up a seat."

He squeezed the bottles in next to the purse and obediently sat down. The silence in the room was palatable. I racked my brain for a conversation starter.

Harold finally broke the ice. "Would either of you ladies like a glass of wine? It's a robust burgundy."

Harold was sporting his summer wardrobe which tonight featured a light blue, pinstriped jumpsuit. He'd added a splash of cologne which was very noticeable in the warm, crowded room.

Both ladies shook their heads from side to side.

"Thank you, Harold, but I was just leaving." Missy pointed to the book that was still in my lap. "I just stopped by to drop off a book."

Molly jumped up next. "I'll be on my way too. I came to give Martha that," she pointed, "purse she asked to borrow."

Both ladies exited in a rush as if a snake had just entered the room. Harold poured himself a glass of wine and held up the beer bottle. I shook my head no. "Thanks, but not tonight."

With glass in tow, Harold moved to the love seat. "That seemed awkward. How come?"

Since I wasn't sure of the answer to that question and, even if I was, I preferred not to discuss my potential female suitors with Harold, so I simply said, "Your guess is as good as mine."

He nodded, oblivious to any potential relationships brewing. "I came by to get an update on the Purse Snatcher Operation. Have you heard anything from Warren?"

"Not yet. I don't know what the hold-up is. I heard on the news that another woman was accosted. This time, the encounter was near the library." I pointed toward the purse on the table. "I borrowed Molly's handbag as a prop in case the detective contacts me. I figured the bigger the better because it will be easier to snag. What do you think?"

Harold looked over at the purse. "I guess so. I wonder if the police would consider filling that thing with the dye that bursts out when the object is opened. You know, like they do with a bag of money that's stolen from a bank."

"Interesting idea, but I hope the perpetrator never gets a chance to open the bag. Believe me, I'll let the purse go VERY easily."

Harold took a sip of wine. I hoped he wouldn't dribble on his light blue onesie. "Have you said anything to your son yet?"

"No, and I don't plan to."

Harold held up his free hand. "Got it."

I might have said that last bit a little vehemently but frankly, I was tired of discussing it. Even though the charged atmosphere had calmed down, Harold seemed nervous.

"Anything else on your mind?" I asked.

He cleared his throat, a sure sign that something uncomfortable was about to emerge.

"I was wondering if you'd like to go out to dinner sometime. You know, get out of this place and eat some REAL food. I read in the local paper that the Brasserie 292 is a…" Harold pulled a newspaper clipping from his pocket and read,

"Stylish French Brasserie in a restored storefront with a copper tin ceiling, cafe tables, and red booths. Whatcha say?"

I smiled. I couldn't help it. Harold had certainly done his homework. How could I possibly pass up going to a fancy French restaurant when I was starved for something other than institutional food and my all-time favorite cuisine was French? I was daydreaming about a starter of escargot followed by lamb shank in red wine when I heard Harold speaking.

"Excuse me? I missed that last bit."

Harold cleared his throat again. "We don't have to call it a date if you don't want to but I'll promise to put my suit back on if that will sway you." He grinned.

Harold could be quite charming when he set his mind to it. "How can I possibly say no? French food is my favorite. I spent a year in Paris when I wore a younger woman's clothes." I said that last bit in a sing-song voice. It was my favorite line from an old song.

"I might have heard something about your penchant for all things French," Harold said with a mischievous grin. "So, it's a date?"

"It's a date. Want me to arrange for an Uber?"

Harold tipped his glass up and finished his wine. "Sure. I also heard you have special talents in Uber arranging. Order the ride for tomorrow at five-thirty. I'll make dinner reservations for six. We'll eat at a grown-up hour." He took his glass to the sink and rinsed it.

"No need to wear a tie. Pants and a shirt would be nice, though." I smiled at Harold when he walked by my chair on his way to the door. He gave a thumbs-up.

"Good night, Martha."

"As my dad used to say, sleep tight and don't let the bed bugs bite," I responded.

Harold gave his head a little shake. I knew he was smiling. He appreciated my "dadisms."

Chapter Fourteen

I pulled out the lacy blouse and trendy slacks I wore when Margaret and I went to Broadway. I thought seeing them again would make me sad, but I experienced quite the opposite. Wonderful memories came flooding back, and I had the feeling that good new memories were about to be made.

Harold arrived right on time. He was wearing a blue button-down Oxford shirt, dark slacks, and loafers. "Ready?" he asked, looking me up and down. "You look beautiful."

I threw on my shawl. It was always cold in restaurants. "Thanks. You look pretty spiffy yourself." Harold grinned like a teenager, took my arm, and escorted me down the hall.

Our Uber was waiting at the curb. There was no need for clandestine arrangements tonight. Earlier in the day, Harold and I dutifully informed the staff of our outing. There were a few knowing smiles but what did I care? We weren't going to a sleazy, by-the-hour motel room; we were simply going to dinner, which was a perfectly normal thing for two adults to do.

After we were seated at the restaurant, Harold asked, "Might you forego a beer for some French wine or champagne?"

"Champagne would be lovely. I even prefer it to beer."

Harold placed an order for two pricey glasses of bubbly.

The decor was just as Harold had described. French elegance with brass, glass, and red leather banquettes. I settled back in my comfortable seat and took it all in.

When the waiter reappeared, I ordered an appetizer of the escargot I'd dreamed of earlier, and Harold ordered fried oysters. Warm bread was delivered to our table, and I used it to soak up the garlic butter left in the little indentations that once held the escargot. Some would call them snails and turn up their noses, but to me, they were exquisite.

It was nearly impossible to decide between the red wine braised lamb shank and the seared duck breast, but since I'd fantasized about the lamb, I ordered it. Harold ordered risotto with shrimp. Even though I wasn't much of a wine drinker these days, I felt compelled to ask the waiter for his suggestions of what to drink with my lamb.

"Cabernet sauvignon, grenache, and shiraz all make for a good start but, if you're feeling more adventurous, have a look at Carménère, Nero d'Avola or Primitivo," he offered with authority.

"I'm feeling adventurous. Bring me one of those you mentioned at the end. Whatever you think is best," I said. He nodded and backed away. I was enjoying this outing immensely.

Harold looked like he'd aged backward in the last hour. I could tell he felt as proud as a peacock for pulling off this lovely excursion. I held out my glass of something I couldn't pronounce. "To you, Harold, for making this a night to remember."

"À ta santé," he replied in French.

Well, well, it seemed there were many surprises lurking behind those bushy eyebrows.

For dessert, we shared a crème brûlée accompanied by decaf cappuccinos. A perfect ending to a perfect dinner.

After we Ubered back to the Manor, Harold insisted on walking me to my apartment. I unlocked the door and Harold took a step inside. "I know it's late and I won't stay. I won't even sit down," Harold offered. "But I would like to give you a proper good night kiss if that's permissible."

In answer, I held my face up to his. He wrapped his arms around me and placed his warm lips on mine. It was a very respectful but impressive first kiss. There was definitely no tongue involved. We parted and said good night.

Too late for my soft clothes, I went straight into my nightgown and robe but I was too wound up to go to bed right away. I needed to unpack the evening and relive all the "feelies" of a luxurious dinner with a gracious, surprisingly cosmopolitan gentleman who had just kissed me.

The following night at dinner, my friends inquired about my health. "You look particularly rosy tonight, Martha," observed Madge somewhat ruefully. "By the way," she asked, "where were you last night? I hope you weren't ill."

Did she think rosy was a good thing or did she think I had a fever? One could never tell when it came to Madge. "I'm feeling quite chipper, thanks," I replied. I was undecided about whether or not to confide in my friends about my dinner date with Harold. I couldn't deny that it was a date and even a casual observer could sense the new energy that had arisen between us. Maybe it was best to come clean.

Besides, the women in this place were like dogs with a bone when it came to gossip. They would get to the bottom of my dinnertime absence one way or the other. So, when the chatter died down, I came clean.

"Harold and I went out to dinner last night. The rosy cheeks may be a hold-over from the champagne."

"Champagne!" repeated Missy. "Ooh la la."

I saw that shadow of a frown cross her face again.

Madge intervened. "And just where did you imbibe this champagne?"

Couldn't she just ask where we went? I told them about Brasserie 292 and the delectable dinner. I left out the part about the kiss.

Molly placed her hand behind her ear. "Did you say Brasserie?" When the word was confirmed, Molly continued. "I'm jealous," she said with a little pout. "Broadway and now the Brasserie. I've read about that restaurant. It's one of the best in town."

Thank goodness dinner was over before more could be said, and we moved on to the social room where there was a special guest singer. She was good but I thought Missy could hold her own if they were in a competition. Ah, Missy. I guess my date with Harold had sealed the coffin on any possible romance with that charming lady. As my dad would say, "You can't have your cake and eat it too."

Chapter Fifteen

I had just returned to my apartment after working off the extra calories from the French feast, when my phone rang.

"Hello?"

"Mrs. Anderson?"

"Yes."

"This is Detective Warren. Are you still willing to participate in the purse snatcher sting?"

"Yes, of course. Did the captain give the ok?"

"Tentatively. He wants to meet you and go over some details. Can you come to the precinct tomorrow morning? Let's say ten o'clock?"

"Yes, I'll be there. I'm bringing a friend with me." I didn't pose it as a question. I learned that if you want a certain answer, you don't offer an alternative.

"That will be fine. I'll see you tomorrow. Ask for me at the front desk."

I texted Harold.

Mission is on. Can you accompany me in the morning?

My phone instantly pinged.

Call me.

I called Herald and filled him in on the particulars. I could tell he was like a kid who had the prospect of getting a pony. I cautioned him that it was still not a done deal. I didn't want this giddy old man to suffer too much disappointment. For someone who basically wished this operation wasn't happening, he was awfully excited to be a part of it.

When we arrived at the precinct the next morning, we were ushered into a windowless room with four chairs and a scuffed-up conference table. The atmosphere definitely felt more intimidating than our disciplinary meeting with Agnes. Detective Warren entered, followed by an even more imposing (if that was possible) gentleman close behind.

"This is Captain Rosado," Warren said.

Rosado shook our hands. He was younger than I'd imagined, probably late-forties. He had short, black hair and was built like a male version of Agnes. As tall as Warren but even broader, he looked like a full-back on steroids with a 'don't mess with me' attitude.

Warren nodded in my direction. "This is Mrs. Anderson and…"

I stepped in to help him out. "Mr. Lancaster. You remember him, don't you?" My slightly impertinent question caused Warren to frown. I wanted him to know that I might be the old lady in the room but I knew how to maintain the balance of power.

"Ah, yes, of course. Mr. Lancaster," said Warren, turning a shade of pink.

Rosado abruptly sat. "Let's proceed. Tell me in your own words, Mrs. Anderson, just what you proposed to Detective Warren concerning the purse snatcher."

I went over my suggestion of being bait. I didn't use that word, of course, but I made it clear that the idea was mine and I wouldn't sue the precinct if anything went wrong.

"And what do you have to say about this, Mr. Lancaster?" Rosado asked.

Harold put his elbows on the table. Once again, he was dressed in his blue shirt and slacks, which gave him a more authoritative look than his usual jumpsuit might have. "I have nothing to say at the moment. I'm simply here as another set of eyes and ears." He looked from officer to officer. "And, to make sure the plans for this operation are sound."

A military man through and through, one couldn't miss the authority in Harold's voice, even if it was a bit shaky.

The captain laid his hands flat on the table. "The public is becoming quite agitated over this purse snatching menace, and I'm getting flack from the mayor." He looked at me. "Therefore, I believe it's worth the risk to have you act as a potential victim, Mrs. Anderson. You do know it could take more than one try. Correct?"

"Yes, I'm aware."

"The perpetrator or perpetrators are extremely cagey and have eluded the best of our men on the streets."

"What kind of protection will you provide?" Harold asked.

Rosado redirected the question. "Detective Warren?"

"There will be two unmarked squad cars in position along the street. One on each side. In addition, there will be two plain clothes officers on foot nearby. Not so close as to cause suspicion but close enough to nab the guy if he shows."

It all seemed reasonable to me. I looked at Harold and he nodded. "When do you propose we do this?" I directed my question to Detective Warren since he seemed to be in charge of the details.

Rosado looked at Warren who continued. "Most of the incidents have happened on the weekend so we're assuming this person or persons works during the week," Warren said, drumming his fingers on the table. "Let's do this tomorrow since it's Saturday. I'll advise the team of their duties today. I'll text you when everyone is in place. Let's say about eleven o'clock in the morning."

I frowned. "Should I just walk out the front door and head down the street?" Before he could answer, I asked, "Which direction? Right or left?" I wasn't good with north or south, and I wanted to be sure I was going where the good guys were watching.

"Turn left when you leave the building. Don't look around, or he might get suspicious. Walk at your usual pace. Hold your handbag in your hand; don't put it on your shoulder. It will be easier for him to snag if it's in your hand, and there's less chance of you being knocked over."

Harold looked dubious. "How far does she need to walk?"

"Not more than ten minutes each way." Warren looked over at me and asked, "Is that too much walking for you?"

"That's about my max right now. I had my hip replaced less than a year ago."

Warren made a note on a pad he pulled from his vest pocket. "Return to Martyn Manor when you're ready. Don't overdo. We'll plan for no more than twenty minutes total. Less is fine."

Rosado spoke up. "If we don't apprehend him tomorrow, we'll repeat the operation on Sunday. Are two days in a row too much for you, Mrs. Anderson?"

"No. That's fine."

The two men got up. The planning meeting was apparently adjourned. Harold pulled out my chair and we exited together.

"I'll have an unmarked squad car drop you back at the Manor. Just wait here a minute," offered Rosado.

I had never ridden in the back of a squad car since it wasn't exactly on my bucket list. I must have looked a little nervous because Harold took my hand. "I think it's a sound plan, Martha. Not that I like the idea, but if you're determined to do it…" he trailed off.

"I'm determined. A little nervous but confident. It's part of my Equalizer persona."

Harold frowned. "You're what?"

"Do you remember the TV show I told you about? *The Equalizer*?"

"I remember. So, what does this operation have to do with your favorite show?"

"I'm inspired by the main character who solves crimes and does good in the world. She doesn't get paid and she gets involved with cases no one else will take. The only difference is," I paused to remember the details, "she's a retired, highly trained CIA operative."

Harold frowned. "And you're not. Don't forget that part."

"I won't. I promise."

Chapter Sixteen

I surveyed my closet for what to wear. I finally chose a frumpy floral blouse, my usual skinny jeans, and slip-on sneakers. Next, I considered what to put in my decoy purse. Left empty, it was too floppy to be worth snatching. I put in a big plastic cup, a paperback book, and an old tee shirt to fill it out. I put my apartment key on a chain around my neck. No sense taking a chance on losing it. I misplaced it enough on my own.

Standing in front of my tall mirror with the pocketbook in hand, I turned one way then another, finally coming to the conclusion that I looked like the ideal target for a purse snatcher. Just before leaving my apartment, I saw dark clouds forming to the east (or was it the west?) and decided to throw on my old trench coat in case it started raining.

Harold met me at the front door looking more nervous than I felt. I gave him a friendly pat on the chest. "Don't worry. I'll be all right."

He didn't seem convinced.

I did a little pirouette. "How do I look? Like a vulnerable old lady?"

Harold gave me a tiny smile. "You look adorable."

I blushed.

My phone pinged. I scanned the text and gave a thumbs-up. "It's go time," I said to Harold. "See you in twenty."

I wondered how women regularly carried purses this big. I felt like I was about to take a cross-country trip as I walked out the front door and turned left per Detective Warren's instructions. I looked at the sidewalk or straight ahead, being careful not to look from side to side.

I walked for ten minutes. Then, feeling disappointed that I had yet to be accosted, I was about to turn around when I heard footsteps behind me. I resisted the urge to look back, but I slowed my pace slightly. If this was the guy, I wanted to get the snatching over with pronto. The footsteps quickened, and before I knew it, a man jogged by, grabbed my purse and ran on. Just like in the movies, two men jumped out from behind a hedge, two others bolted out of cars. The person was fast, but with four in pursuit, he didn't have a chance. I stood perfectly still, mesmerized by the unfolding drama. It was one thing to watch a police sting on television, it was quite another to see it up close and personal.

An officer yelled, "Stop!" Another one lunged forward and tackled the man. Two more rushed up, hauled him up by his collar, and announced that he was under arrest. I couldn't hear the details, but I saw them place handcuffs on his wrists and escort him to an unmarked squad car parked nearby. When I turned to start my walk back to the Manor, a policewoman in uniform exited a car and walked toward me.

"Are you all right, Mrs. Anderson?" she asked when we were face to face.

"I'm fine."

"Are you sure?"

"Yes, I'm sure."

I didn't want to dilly dally. I wanted to get back to Harold before he had a heart attack.

The policewoman dutifully escorted me back to where my friend was waiting. He gave me a hug and walked me to my apartment while I filled him in on the details. "That went well, don't you think?" I asked Harold.

"Swimmingly. You were terrific," Harold said as he left me at my door to return to his apartment and, most likely, a nip of bourbon.

Now that the operation was over, my heart started pounding and my hands started shaking. I sat down in my chair to steady myself. I assumed that my delayed reaction wasn't unusual. When I finally calmed down, I changed my clothes, got out my embroidery, and wondered when they'd return Molly's purse to me.

That afternoon, I received a call from a local newspaper reporter. He'd heard about the sting, as he called it, and wanted to interview me. I agreed to meet him in the lobby a few hours later.

The reporter looked as I imagined he would. Shabby chic. Although the term is often used to describe decor, it was the perfect description of this thirty-something man wearing tennis shoes, a denim shirt with a tie whose knot was hanging low, jeans, a scuffed-up satchel over his shoulder, and shaggy brown hair.

"Mrs. Anderson?"

"Yes, that's me. You're the reporter from *The Poughkeepsie Journal*." I was so confident I didn't even make it a question. We shook hands.

"Before we start, do you mind if I get a photo? Stories without photos don't get much attention," said the serious young man who introduced himself as Blake, no last name.

I considered this for a moment. Did I really want my face spread about? Since I didn't know a soul in this town except those here at the Manor, I figured it didn't make much difference. I'd tell my friends about my adventure at dinner so they'd hear about it before seeing my photo in the morning paper. "Where do you want me to stand?" I asked.

Blake pointed toward a tall potted plant. I walked over and struck a pose. He took several photos before we returned to the chairs in the seating area near the door. He asked questions, and I related the story as succinctly as possible. I steered away from the line of questioning that made me out as a hero and emphasized my role as an ordinary citizen just doing my duty.

That night at dinner when I told my tablemates about my adventure, everyone was wide-eyed, but only Madge spoke. "Martha, what were you thinking?" she asked.

She said this loud enough that several heads turned in our direction. Apparently, she didn't approve but it was too late now. I was glad I hadn't spoken of this earlier. I explained my motivation and steered the conversation elsewhere.

After music, Harold dropped by to toast my success. "Thanks for supporting me," I said, taking a sip of my beer.

"Your presence at the meeting boosted my confidence. Thank goodness everything went as planned."

Harold sipped his wine. "I hope you don't have any future Equalizer Operations planned."

"Nope. Not yet." I reached over, punched him in the arm, and smiled.

He didn't smile back.

The next morning, I was about to leave for breakfast when there was a loud knock on my door. When I opened it, Richard rushed in and slammed the morning paper down on my table. "Mother, what in the world were you thinking?" he said in a loud, angry voice.

I picked up the paper, wondering what Blake had written. I scanned the article on the front page just below the fold. My photo was prominently positioned, and Blake had a by-line. Blake Black. His name had nice alliteration. In addition to a few quotes from me, there was a quote from Detective Warren, Chief Rosado, and (good grief) the mayor. The headline read, "Meet Martha, The Hero of a Recent Purse Snatching Sting." The article highlighted my advanced age.

"Well?" my son asked impatiently.

He was flushed and I was concerned about his blood pressure. "This article is a good explanation of the operation. I certainly don't consider myself a hero however, just an ordinary citizen doing my duty." I repeated this last bit from what I'd said in the interview.

"A sting operation to catch a thief is not the duty of an eighty-nine-year-old woman residing in assisted living!"

My son was definitely worked up. I should have thought of this consequence when I'd agreed to do the interview but I'd never dreamed he'd read a printed newspaper and certainly not a local edition. He was an online *New York Times* man all the way.

I took my key off the hook. "Well, what's done is done. I'm sorry to have upset you, but I don't see any point in discussing it further." I opened the door. "Would you like to join me for breakfast? I'm hungry."

Richard huffed and puffed. He wasn't accustomed to being summarily dismissed. Perhaps it was time he learned how to deal.

Chapter Seventeen

On Wednesday, four days after the sting, I woke up wondering about the young man who was arrested. Did he post bail or was he sitting in a jail cell? Assuming he was the only perpetrator, I wondered what the punishment was for multiple purse snatchings. What was his motivation? Was he desperately in need of money? Were his actions part of a gang initiation? I knew he deserved whatever the law threw at him, but somehow I felt partially responsible.

With questions still nagging me after lunch, I called Detective Warren. I decided I wouldn't go in with a "you owe me one" attitude. Instead, I'd ask questions from a "concerned grandmother" point of view. My call was referred to Detective Niles. She remembered me from the Lost Harold Incident, and of course, she was familiar with the Purse Snatcher Sting. I expected her to say, "I can't discuss an ongoing case," but she didn't. She answered my questions but gave me nothing beyond the basics.

She told me that the young man, Steve Billings, had posted bond and was released from jail. Since they only had clear evidence of the one event, he could receive a fine and anywhere from a year to five years in prison. The detectives believed he had no gang affiliations. Any personal questions about the young man went unanswered.

I asked two final questions. "When was he arraigned and does he have a court date?"

The detective was silent for a few seconds as she presumably looked at her computer. "He was arraigned yesterday and the judge appointed a public defender to handle his case. The court date was set for August 12th. Is there anything else I can help you with, Mrs. Anderson?"

"No, thank you. I appreciate your willingness to speak with me."

I Googled Steve Billings. There were two men with that name living in the Poughkeepsie area. One was a college professor, the other was a young man with an impressive Instagram following. The photo on his account matched what I remembered of my assailant. His Facebook feed didn't amount to much. I was aware that young people had abandoned this particular social media when their parents and grandparents took it over so I wasn't surprised. By checking various other accounts, I learned that Steve was only twenty, younger than I'd thought, and worked as a bagger and stock boy at a local supermarket. Photos indicated that he lived in an apartment with roommates. Did he lose his job after the arrest? Did he get kicked out of his apartment? Was he homeless?

A few minutes later, another crazy question came to mind. Could I talk my son into representing him? Not that I wanted to get him off - he obviously did the deed, but I did want him to have a fair trial or hearing or whatever the next step was.

Putting all this aside, I settled in to read my latest library book. I'd barely gotten through one chapter when a text came in.

Did you forget about our plans to be partners at Canasta today or are you avoiding me?

The text was from Missy and I could tell she was upset.

I'm so sorry! I forgot. I promise that I'm not avoiding you! How can I get back into your good graces?

A couple of minutes went by.

You can take me back to Murphy's. Just us this time. I'm dying to do karaoke again.

I paused to think about her request, then texted her back.

When do you want to go?

Short pause.

Tonight! It's Wednesday.

I considered this a minute. Why not? It sounded like fun.

Ok. Let's skip dinner and grab a bite there. Each of us can text the other two that we're under the weather. I am feeling a bit peckish. Probably a let down from my adrenalin rush on Saturday. Come by my place about six o'clock. Everyone should be in the social room by then. I'll set up the Uber.

See you then! (Heart emoji)

I guessed by her response that Missy hadn't given up on me entirely.

Daytime temperatures were on the high side for July, so I searched my closet for a summer dress. I didn't often wear dresses. My legs weren't what they used to be, but I found one that fell just below my knees.

After getting dressed, I went down the elevator and milled around the office waiting for Judy to come on duty. When she arrived, I told her about my plans with Missy. She noncommittally nodded then added, "Don't worry. I won't report you missing. Just be back by nine o'clock and, for heaven's sake, act responsibly."

She smiled to soften this last bit. I knew she was just looking out for me, but it was hard to accept the role reversal.

Apparently, karaoke always drew a crowd because even at six-fifteen, the place was swarming with college kids. Like my dad used to say, "You couldn't swing a cat by the tail without hitting one."

We were offered a booth in the corner. When I slid in, Missy slid in next to me. Our backs were to the wall. This seating arrangement felt a bit uncomfortable, but I went with it. After we ordered, Missy signed up to sing.

"What song did you pick?" I asked when she returned to our booth.

"You'll see, it's a surprise." She winked at me.

I felt a flutter in my stomach. I was very susceptible to winks.

We ordered burgers with fries. Grease and salt were always yummy. When we had finished eating, Missy reapplied her lipstick. She too was wearing a summer dress but hers fell just above the knees. It was yellow with little white flowers.

A few in the crowd obviously remembered Missy's last performance because there was light applause when she stepped up to the stage. The music started and I immediately recognized Andy Williams' "Moon River." The kids had probably never heard this popular song from the early sixties, but it brought fond memories back to me and I recognized the romantic gesture.

As before, Missy received a big round of applause. What an ego boost for an eighty-something residing in assisted living. I hoped the excitement wouldn't spike her blood sugar. I happened to know she was a fragile diabetic who needed constant monitoring, which was what led to her current living arrangement. She returned to our table a little breathless.

"That was fantastic!" I said, giving her a side hug.

"It was for you. I'm glad you liked it." Missy's rosy cheeks and wild curls made her look particularly adorable.

I checked my watch. It was only seven-forty-five, but playing the responsible adult, I thought it was prudent to leave. I was worried about Missy's coloring and the fact she'd just gone to the bathroom—again. I texted our Uber driver and learned that he was just around the corner.

Missy picked up the check and paid. I wondered if that was a signal of some sort. I must stop trying to figure out "lesbian protocol" and just go with the flow. After all, it's not unusual for friends to pick up checks for friends, no matter the relationship.

On the way to my apartment, I checked in with Judy. She gave me a "good girl" accommodation for returning early. It's no wonder older people start acting like children.

I put a "gone to bed early" note on my door. I was tired and not up to entertaining any male, female, or combo of visitors. I put on my nightgown and summer kimono which reminded me of Anna whenever I wore it. I missed her. I checked my email, text messages, and Facebook feed. There was nothing interesting, so I settled back for a good think.

There were lots of questions dancing around in my head. Did this new thing with Missy have any bearing on my relationship with Harold? What should I do, if anything, about Steve Billings? Was Richard still mad at me? I hadn't heard from him since the newspaper article incident. I felt no need to apologize but I did want to keep the lines of communication open with my son.

I decided it was best to give Richard a little more time to cool off and checked that one off my list. Just because Harold and I had kissed didn't mean we were in a committed relationship. I wasn't sure he'd agree, but I thought we were both free to explore other possibilities. Check. That took me to Mr. Billings. It was too soon to approach Richard about representation so I decided not to worry about that. I could, however, Uber over to where Steve worked and inquire about his employment. I'd say I was a friend of the family. If he was jobless and homeless I wanted to know. I'd consider the "why" later.

Enough think-time. I was ready to "hit the hay," as my dad would say.

Chapter Eighteen

The next day, I went through my usual morning routine while trying to keep the afternoon Bingo game on my mind. I didn't normally attend Bingo, but Missy invited me and I was still trying to get back into her good graces. I put a sticky note that said, "Bingo @ 2:00," just inside my door to help me remember.

Thanks to my note, I met Missy right on time. Winning five dollars early on motivated me enough that I was able to endure the rest of the afternoon with a semi-positive attitude. I vaguely listened to the outraged chatter all around me about someone hiding their Bingo cards so they could use the same ones every week. Apparently, the regulars were going to report the misdeed to Agnes. Once again, I thought that living here was like being in middle school.

After dinner, Harold approached me. "I heard from your tablemates that you and Missy were under the weather last night." He gave me a look that told me he was dubious. He was probably thinking it was very coincidental for us both to be gone. "I hope you don't have a bug of some sort," he added.

I pulled Harold over to a chair and we sat down. I told him about Missy and me going to Murphy's. I explained about making up for forgetting the Canasta game. If Harold and I were ever going to have a serious relationship, which I doubted, I didn't want the foundation to be lies. I had always been straight with him. Besides, he was too smart to fool.

"I hope you had a good time. I'm relieved to know that you're well." I wasn't entirely convinced that Harold hoped we had a good time, but I left it alone and got up from the chair.

"May I accompany you to the social room?" he asked, offering me his arm.

"Of course." This formal dialogue reminded me of when we first became acquainted in Agnes' office. Were we starting from scratch?

As we walked, Harold told me that his great-granddaughter, Marcella, and her friend, Tulsi, were coming for a visit the next day because her mother had an appointment. "I've been called upon to girl-sit. Would you like to meet them?" Harold pulled a handkerchief from his pocket and wiped his nose. "They'd like to meet you."

"Why on earth do they want to meet me?"

Harold pocketed his handkerchief and continued. "You may not know it, but you're quite a celebrity in this town. My granddaughter showed the girls your photo in the newspaper and told them what you did. She wants her daughter to have strong women role models. When they found out that you're my friend, they asked if they could meet you on their next visit."

"Of course! I'd love to meet them. How old are they again?"

"Marcella just turned nine, and her friend is nine and a half. Apparently, it's important to be exact at that age."

"I always say I'm pushing ninety. I think a year ahead so when I get there, the number won't surprise me."

The following morning after I returned from my work-out, I had a text from Harold.

The girls have arrived. Want to come over?

I opened my door then texted back.

Sure. Give me a minute to change.

While peeling off my workout clothes, I tried to think of something I could take with me to give to the two young ladies. I rummaged through my jewelry box and found two smallish, beaded bracelets. Although they were young, I imagined that they were also Swifties.

The girls were adorable in their sundresses and flip-flops. They were both brown as berries, from the sun and probably their heritage. I guessed that Marcella was Italian and Tulsi was Indian. Not at all shy, both chattered away from the moment I entered Harold's apartment. They wanted to know exactly what it was like to have my purse snatched, how I could have been so brave as to be a decoy, if I knew anything about the "bad guy" and what was going to happen to him. I patiently answered their questions, flattered that they were so interested in this old lady.

After a few minutes of their enthusiastic interrogation, I changed the subject and asked them what they liked about school, their favorite subject (since academics hadn't surfaced as part of their answers to the first question), and if they were Taylor Swift fans.

"We love Taylor Swift!" they said in unison as they bopped around the room singing, presumably, one of her songs. When I saw that they were wearing friendship bracelets made from plastic beads, I pulled out my little gifts and passed one to each girl.

"These are made from REAL rocks," said Marcella holding hers up to the light.

Tulsi corrected her—after all, she was a whole six months older. "Stones, Marcella. They're called stones."

I held out my arm, displaying my own bracelets. "I hope we can be friends."

The girls slipped their bracelets onto their wrists. "These are so fetch!" said Marcella. She looked up at me. I must have had a question mark on my face because she asked, "Do you know what that means?"

"I'm assuming fetch means cool. Right?"

"Right. And now the three of us are besties. Thank you, Mrs. Anderson." Tulsi also thanked me. Obviously, their parents had taught them good manners.

"Are you sleeping over tonight?" I asked Marcella.

"Oh no! That didn't work out so well. My mom is picking us up later this afternoon."

"Your sleeping over worked out well for me."

She did a whhhaatt?

"That's how I met your great-grandfather. We'd both been called into the equivalent of the principal's office for getting into trouble."

She looked at her GiGi, her name for Harold. "YOU got into trouble?"

Harold smiled. "Yep. Sometimes even old folks bend the rules. Like letting little girls stay over without asking for permission or telling anyone."

I could see the wheels turning in Marcella's head as she tried to decide if this was a good thing or not. Rule-bending was frowned upon in her world but she probably considered that perhaps in her GiGi's world, it may be all right.

Tulsi looked at me. "Do you bend the rules sometimes too, Mrs. Anderson?"

She looked so earnest, I tried not to smile. "Sometimes. Mr. Lancaster and I can be rascals but we never do anything that will hurt anyone."

"Rascals?" Marcella tipped her head.

Harold spoke up. "Someone who is mischievous once in a while. Like when you hid your big brother's iPhone but told him a few minutes later where it was."

Marcella nodded. "I get it."

After hugging each girl and assuring them that we would get together again, I left Harold's apartment with a bounce in my step. Being around the two youngsters had perked me up. However, I was closing in on my expiration date. I could only handle that kind of energy for so long before I was exhausted. I returned to my apartment, put my feet up, and read until dinnertime.

The next day, I decided to visit Steve Billings's last known place of employment. My strategy was to talk with a fellow bag boy. I took an Uber and, when we got there, I asked Ted to wait while I shopped.

"Sure, Mrs. Anderson, anything for you."

Apparently, I was one of his better customers. I tipped well.

The supermarket wasn't in the best neighborhood but not as bad as where Harold's son once lived. I walked in, grabbed a cart, and started throwing in bulky items. A six-pack of mini pop cans, a bag of Skinny Popcorn, a package of napkins big enough to last me a lifetime, and a package of toilet paper. When I checked out, I asked the bagger if he'd take my purchases out to the car and load them for me.

"Sure, Lady," said a pimply-faced kid about Steve's age.

After we exited the store, I turned to the young man and asked nonchalantly, "Do you happen to know Steve Billings?" I walked slower than usual so I'd have time to ask questions. The boy patiently walked beside me, pushing the cart.

"I knew him, but he doesn't work here anymore."

"Why not?"

"He got himself arrested and the boss fired him."

"Oh dear. How's he going to pay his share of the rent?"

"He can't. He's livin' in his car. Lucky it ain't been repossessed yet." The boy looked at me more closely. "Hey, ain't you the lady that caused him to get caught? I seen your picture in the newspaper."

I smiled. "Don't you know that all of us little old ladies look alike?"

This seemed to baffle him. He loaded the groceries into the waiting Uber's trunk and returned to the store.

Chapter Nineteen

I awoke on Monday feeling under the weather. My throat was sore, my nose was running, and I had a cough. I made myself a cup of tea for breakfast and ordered-in lunch. I didn't eat much from my lunch tray and I uncharacteristically took a long nap. It was already after six when I woke up. Even after the long nap, I felt exhausted. My cough was worse and my head ached. Knowing Judy was at the desk, I called her. "Can you come by?" I croaked into the phone.

In a few minutes, she knocked then opened my door.

"I'm in the bedroom," I called out in a loud whisper.

Judy couldn't hide her shocked expression. She'd never seen me sick enough to be in bed. "Martha, what's wrong?" she asked.

"I'm sick. Head, nose, throat, cough."

Judy placed her hand on my forehead. "You have a fever." She turned away from my bed. "I'll be right back."

She must have jogged all the way because she returned in the blink of an eye. She listened to my heart and lungs, took my temp, looked down my throat, and swabbed my nose.

This time, Judy took precautions and wore a mask.

"When did your symptoms start?" she asked.

"This morning."

"Why didn't you notify Agnes?"

"Thought I could sleep it off." It hurt to talk, so I kept it short.

Ding. Judy's timer on her Apple Watch went off and she checked the Covid testing strip.

"Bad news?" I croaked.

"I'm afraid so. The test shows you're positive. I'll call the doctor and get an order for Paxlovid."

I hated taking pills. In my experience, the side effects were often worse than the ailment.

"Necessary? Side effects?"

"At your age, you're a high risk for hospitalization so I highly recommend you take the drug."

I nodded and gave her a look that said, continue.

"Side effects might include impaired sense of taste, diarrhea, muscle aches, and nausea but you ought to feel better in a couple of days. Since we caught this at the onset, the drug will, hopefully, keep the duration of Covid to a minimum."

"All right. I'll take it."

Judy put a glass of water on the table beside my bed and fluffed up my pillow. "You rest. I'll talk with the doctor on call and get you started on the med as soon as possible."

At nine o'clock that evening, Judy arrived with a tray. There was applesauce, toast, and a small packet of peanut butter, which Judy knew I liked. After setting the tray down, she held out a card with pills in plastic bubbles. "Here's your five-day pack of Paxlovid. Take two tablets tonight after you eat something," she indicated the tray, "then continue in the morning. Do you want Agnes to dispense the meds tomorrow?"

I shook my head. "I can do it."

Judy's beeper went off and she looked at the message. "I'll be back shortly to take your tray and get you settled for the night," she said before rushing off.

I picked at the food, making an effort to eat as much as I could. I knew I needed to keep my strength up. I drank all of my water. I didn't want to get dehydrated because I knew they'd put me in skilled care if I required an IV, and I definitely wanted to stay in my apartment. After setting my tray aside, I struggled out of bed, went to the bathroom, then fell back onto the bed and into a restless sleep.

I sensed that Josh, Kate, and Judy checked on me in turns during the night. Sometimes I spoke to them; other times I simply acknowledged their presence and drifted back to sleep, knowing I was in good hands.

In the morning, Agnes, fully gowned, masked, and gloved, delivered my breakfast tray, checked my vitals, told me I was doing ok, asked if I had taken my meds, and exited. So much for bedside manner.

Despite Agnes' assurance that I'd live, I felt worse. I ached all over, my throat was killing me, and I was coughing so hard I felt like I might crack a rib. I finally sucked on a lozenge which abated my cough for a while. Although I was dreadfully tired, sleep eluded me as my mind went into overdrive.

What if I continued to go downhill and I had to be intubated? Not wanting to cash out with a tube down my throat, I asked God to let me beat this Covid demon and live long enough to have a heart attack on another day or die in my sleep after a wonderful evening enjoying family, friends, and good food. Thinking that I might be asking for too much, I decided I'd settle for a heart attack without the loved ones and food, but it needed to kill me right away. I didn't want to linger for days, and I definitely didn't want to be attached to machines.

As my mind wandered, I couldn't help remembering the televised images of intubated old people, their bony, blue-veined hands motionless on the white bedcovers. I could barely handle the swab they did to diagnose a strep throat. Eventually, I worried myself back to sleep.

I was barely aware of the comings and goings during the next twenty-four hours. Feeling a bit better on day three, I ate my breakfast. When an orderly came at noon with my lunch, there was a small envelope on the tray. After he left, I opened and read it.

Dear Martha. I'm worried sick about you. I wish I could see you but they tell me I can't. I tried to text but apparently, your phone is turned off or in need of a charge. Get well soon, dear friend. As always, Harold.

He was such a sweetie! The note perked me up enough that I moved to my recliner and turned on the television. I checked my cell phone. My dad would have declared it "dead as a doornail." I plugged it into the charger. I needed to let my family know of my ailment if they hadn't already heard from Agnes. Unable to reach me by phone, Richard was probably beside himself. He hated being out of control.

When my phone was charged, I sent two group texts, one to the three kids, and another to my three friends plus Harold.

I have Covid. On Paxlovid. Being well cared for. Miss you.

There was a flurry of responses. I acknowledged each one with a little heart emoji above the message. Emojis were such time savers.

When Agnes came to listen to my lungs and take my temp, she set my dinner tray on the table. I spied another little envelope and I opened it as soon as she was out the door. My dinner could wait.

Martha, where in the world did you pick up Covid? I hope it wasn't at Murphy's. I'd feel so guilty. I miss your sweet smile. Get well soon. Love, Missy.

I tucked the thoughtful message into my end table drawer along with Harold's.

By day four, I was feeling well enough to take a shower and dress in my soft clothes. All of my symptoms had lessened, but I was still exhausted. No matter how much sleep I got, I was tired. Also, all food tasted awful. I made an effort to eat as much as I could, but it nearly gagged me.

I received daily texts from my kids and friends and I kept them abreast of my progress. I knew that no matter how good I felt, I needed to stay in isolation at least until the following week. I'd be very strict with myself about this because I didn't want to pass Covid on to anyone, especially not to anyone at the Manor. We were all residing here because we were vulnerable in some way.

On Monday, a week after the onset of my symptoms, Agnes arrived with a doctor in tow. They were both gowned and masked. I felt like a leper but I understood the necessity of being cautious. The doctor took my vitals, Agnes retested me for Covid. "Your Covid test is negative, Martha," Agnes announced without fanfare.

I must have had a big grin on my face, because the doctor, whose name I don't remember, spoke in a cautionary tone. "You need to take it easy, Mrs. Anderson," he said with great gravity. "You don't want a relapse."

"I certainly don't. When can I rejoin the outside world?"

"Possibly tomorrow. We need to have one more negative test. One can't be too cautious in a place like this."

Agnes stepped forward. "I'll test you in the morning. Your breakfast and lunch will arrive on a tray as usual."

They left without further ado. The apartment was too quiet and I missed my friends. I was, however, immensely grateful that I'd recovered. I was aware that I was close to the end of life's rope but today was apparently not the day I was going to fall off.

Chapter Twenty

My first foray into the world of people beyond my caregivers was to dinner on Tuesday. Because I'd given my friends a heads-up, they had a red rose in a vase sitting at my usual spot.

"We're so happy to have you back," said Molly, her chic fall dress and false eyelashes all aflutter.

I looked around the table and suddenly became acutely aware of the two friends who were missing. I realized that this could have been a table for three tonight, but I couldn't remain somber surrounded by such smiling faces.

"I bet you got it from those two little girls who visited Harold. You talked with them, didn't you?" Madge asked.

"I could have gotten Covid from anywhere or from anyone. Jake, the minivan driver, Winter, the librarian, the mailman, my son. The CDC doesn't seem to be concerned about picking it up from surfaces anymore, but one never knows. I refuse to speculate."

With that discussion shut down, we moved on to what had been going on during my absence. Women at the Manor specialized in gossip.

I was told that one of the servers was pregnant and due in January. Maude, the lady who resisted her purse being snatched, had been moved to skilled care following a bad fall and our activities director, Maxine, would start offering chair yoga next week.

My friends each declared themselves "fit as fiddles," as my dad would say, although I seriously doubted if that was entirely accurate. Missy's face was flushed, Madge had put on enough weight to be noticeable, and Molly was struggling more than ever to hear the table conversation.

I retired early, prudently deciding not to stay for the social hour. I was taking my doctor's orders seriously. I was already in my soft clothes when there was a tap on the door. "Come in."

Harold entered with a big vase of bronze mums, purple asters, and dark red dahlias. "They told me you couldn't have flowers when you were sick, but I checked with Judy last night and she said you can have them now that you're cleared to reenter the world."

I pointed. "Put them on the table, Harold. They're beautiful! Fall flowers are my favorites. Thank you."

"I won't stay. I know you need to get plenty of rest. I just wanted to let you know I missed you and prayed for your full recovery."

When I raised my eyebrows, he said, "What? You don't believe I pray? How do you think I made it through a couple of wars with my body and mind mostly intact?"

I patted my chest. "Well, your prayers worked. I really didn't want to take the 'Covid-Exit'; definitely not the hill I wanted to die on, as my dad would say. I'm waiting around for a nice big heart attack in my sleep."

Harold rolled his eyes. I was aware that most people didn't like discussing death, especially theirs or that of someone they loved or liked, as the case may be. Harold didn't engage with my statement. "Good night, Martha. I'm glad you're back in circulation."

"Good night, Harold. Thanks again for the flowers, the sweet note, and your prayers."

The knowledge that I was living on borrowed time followed me throughout the week. I was considering what I could do to pay it forward when I remembered the girls telling me that Maude had been moved to skilled care while I was sick. I wondered if she would like a visit. I was also curious if Steve or someone else was her assailant.

After breakfast, I skipped my workout, knowing that the walk to the skilled care unit would be more than enough exercise for me in my still weakened state. The walk was along unfamiliar corridors. The only visit I'd made to this neck-of-the-woods was when Richard and I toured the entire facility over a year ago. I wished I could leave a trail of breadcrumbs. I had my cell phone with me, but I truly hoped I wouldn't have to call and ask someone to find me.

I finally arrived at my destination and learned that Maude was in room 202. I found her sitting in a recliner watching television. "Good morning, Maude. I'm Martha. We met at lunch a month or so ago."

Maude graciously muted the television. Her expression was blank at first then a slight smile dawned on her drawn face. She had aged considerably since I last saw her. "You're the lady who said she'd give up her purse."

"I am. And you're the lady who said you wouldn't. I'm glad you weren't injured in that altercation." I tried not to sound judgmental; it was my worst attribute. "By the way, can you remember what your assailant looked like?"

"Please sit down." Maude motioned for me to sit on the only other chair in the room. "Let's see, it all happened so quickly."

I waited patiently, hoping she could dredge up the memory.

"What I remember most is that the event caused me to stay inside from then on which wasn't good for my mental or physical health. I was afraid it would happen again."

"I understand."

"Now that I think about it, I believe the man was tall and heavy-set, like a football player. He was around my nephew's age."

"And that would be?" I asked.

"Middle-aged. Maybe forties. At the time, I couldn't come up with these details and the police never returned to question me. I probably should have gotten in touch with them when my mind cleared. Why do you ask?"

I leaned forward so I didn't have to speak too loudly and explained how I had acted as a decoy in order to catch the perpetrator. "The person who snatched my purse wasn't the same person who took yours, which means that Steve, the person who took mine, was telling the truth when he said he only took my purse, which was just a prop."

Maude said, "That was a brave thing for you to do. I'm glad you weren't hurt."

I sat back. "When I heard that you were knocked down, I didn't want that to happen to anyone else. But to learn more about the purse snatching incident isn't the main reason I came to visit you."

"It wasn't?"

I smiled. "No. I came because I'd heard that you'd moved out of assisted living, and I thought you might need a little cheering up."

"That's an understatement!" She looked thoughtful. "After my fall and broken arm," she pulled the afghan off her right arm, which was encased in a plaster cast, "I had no choice. They deemed me a serious fall risk. Even here, I have to call someone before I can move from my bed or chair. If I get up without calling for help, an alarm goes off. It's extremely confining, to say nothing of frustrating when I have to make an urgent trip to the bathroom."

I nodded empathetically. Having recently been in isolation for more than a week, I had a greater sense of what it was like to lose your independence. "Do you have family nearby?" I asked.

"Sadly, no. I only have one daughter who has never married. She lives in North Dakota, of all places. She helped me make this move but she probably won't be returning for at least six months." Maude looked down at her hands. "It can get pretty lonely." She looked toward the door. "I know it's hard to imagine since people are constantly coming and going."

My heart broke for this sweet lady. No family in the area and no way to make friends since she couldn't even get out of her chair to go to the bathroom without assistance. "If you'll have me, I'll be your friend."

Unexpectedly, tears flooded Maude's eyes. She grabbed a nearby tissue and wiped them away. "I'm sorry," she choked out.

I allowed her time to regain her composure.

"I'd love to have you as a friend. Remind me of your name again? I feel terrible that I can't remember it from one minute to the next."

I reached for yesterday's menu and wrote down my name and cell number. "Here you go. Do you have a cell phone? Do you know how to text?"

Maude reached under her afghan and pulled out her phone. "I do, and I do." She smiled proudly. "My daughter taught me when she was here. She wants me to text her every morning after I wake up. I guess she wants to know I'm still alive," Maude gave me a weak smile. "She'll be delighted to know I have a new friend. Most of my cronies from assisted living have passed on. That's why I was sitting alone the day we met at lunch."

I stood to leave. "Us old ladies have to watch out for each other."

"We do. Thanks for coming..." Maude glanced at her scrap of paper, "Martha. I'll be looking forward to your next visit."

"One other thing..." I was torn about whether or not to ask this of Maude.

"Yes?"

"Would you be willing to call Detective Warren and give him the description of your assailant? The call could mean that a young man spends less time in prison."

"Of course. Do you have his number?" Maude pulled her phone out again, and I reached for it.

"I'll put his name and number in your contacts. Just go to your phone app and type detective. His number will pop right up." I put the information into Maude's phone and handed it back to her.

"I'll do this right away before I forget," Maude assured me. "Thanks again for your visit."

"You're welcome. I'll come by again soon."

After I left Maude's room, I stopped to consider whether to turn right or left. I must have looked confused because a staff person approached me. "May I help you?"

"Can you point me in the direction of assisted living?" I asked, feeling embarrassed.

"Of course. Go down this hall," she pointed to the right, "then take the second corridor to the left. You'll see the elevator. When you exit the elevator, turn right, and you'll soon be in familiar territory."

"Thank you." I turned right and walked down the hall. I looked around and then asked myself, "Where do I turn left?" Good grief, I'd already forgotten. I continued walking, searching for familiar signposts. "Was that framed landscape on the wall I passed earlier?" I wasn't sure. I walked for several minutes without passing an elevator. Then, I suddenly felt tired all over. It was like I'd run into a brick wall. I contemplated what to do next. The distant memory of when I was lost in a giant forest in Wisconsin with zero water on a hot summer day and no one knowing where I was flitted through my mind.

Reminded that this time I had a cell phone, I pulled it out of my pocket. I would never hear the end of it if I called Agnes. She might even use it as an excuse to move me to skilled care. I decided to call Harold. He loved having a mission or a problem to solve. If he led men through the jungles of Vietnam, he could probably find me in the no man's land between assisted living and skilled care. I called his number.

"Martha. What a surprise."

"I'm lost, Harold."

"You're lost? Where?" he said with alarm.

"If I knew where I was, I wouldn't be lost." I chuckled into the phone. I couldn't help myself. "I'm in between assisted living and skilled care. I can't seem to locate the elevator that is supposed to take me back to familiar territory, or so some staff person told me. Do you think you can find me? I've run out of steam."

"What floor are you on?"

"I'm on the second floor. I visited a new friend in room 202. I haven't gone up or down. I turned left when I exited her room."

"How long have you been walking?"

"Ten minutes tops. Covid really took a toll. I'm completely pooped, Harold."

"You stay put and don't worry, I'll find you in a jiffy."

Harold sounded so confident. I hoped he was right because the hallway was deserted. At least I wasn't broiling in hundred-degree weather with no water. I did a lot of stupid things when I was in my forties.

In a few minutes I was relieved to see Harold briskly walking down the hall toward me. He waved. "You found me," I foolishly said before tearing up. Harold rushed forward and put his arms around me.

"You're going to be all right, Martha. Everything's going to be okay," he soothed.

"I know. I just feel so stupid. How could I have gotten lost under my own roof?"

"Well, your portion of the roof is quite a distance from this section. Don't worry about it." He took my hand. "Are you up to walking a bit further?"

I nodded.

"Then let's get you home."

Chapter Twenty-One

Except for my usual jaunts to meals and the workout room, I laid low for a couple of days. The getting lost episode took a physical toll; say nothing of what it did to my confidence and self-esteem. I concluded that it would be a while before I regained my pre-Covid strength. I hated to think it, but perhaps my more-than-occasional memory loss was the new normal for me. I wondered if I should make an appointment for an evaluation.

Four days before Steve Billings' hearing, I made another trip to the grocery store. Due to Covid, I hadn't followed up on his homelessness, and I wanted to know the latest before I saw him in court. As before, I requested my Uber driver to wait, threw a few things in a cart, then asked the bag boy to carry my purchases to the car. As we walked, I asked him about Billings' whereabouts.

"He's still living out of his car as far as I know." The boy looked me over. "Ain't you the same person who asked about him earlier?"

I nodded.

"Well, if you want my advice, I'd say forget about Billings. Why would you want to waste your time on a bum who steals purses from old ladies? If he had any decency, he'd steal from a 7-11 or a Walmart."

I considered the boy's statement. It seemed to me that stealing was bad no matter what the circumstances but I understood his point. At least his assertion showed that he had a shred of propriety. "Thanks, I'll take your advice under consideration." I handed him a twenty dollar bill.

He handed it back. "We ain't allowed to take tips."

"It's not a tip. It's a thank you for being considerate of old ladies." I gave him a nudge with my elbow. "Including me."

The boy gave me a weak smile then he pocketed the money.

The next day, Richard came for his monthly lunch. Thankfully, he'd calmed down from learning about the sting operation and me having Covid. Halfway through lunch, I decided to ask him a risky question. "Would you like to accompany me to a hearing at the courthouse on Tuesday?"

He choked on his iced tea. "A hearing? Who's hearing?"

"Steve Billings' hearing."

"Who?"

"You know, Steve Billings, the purse snatcher."

"Mother, why on earth do you want to go to his hearing?"

Aware that this was an unusual request, I took my time to think of just the right words to use. I patted my lips with my napkin. "I want to be certain he gets a fair shake. He has a court appointed attorney. You always said, and I quote, never allow yourself to get in a situation where you have to have a court appointed attorney, unquote."

Richard finished chewing his bite of sandwich. "If I don't go with you, will you go anyway?"

Honesty is usually the best policy. "Yes."

"In that case, I'll accompany you. What time?" He gave me a squinty look. "I'm assuming you know."

At least he gave me credit for doing my homework. "Tuesday, August 12th at two o'clock."

I saw a tiny spark light up in Richard's eyes. He had a reason to return to court and get brownie points for helping out his aged mother at the same time. "I'll pick you up out front at one-thirty."

"I'll be there."

Richard finished his lunch and took his leave. As he exited the dining room, I noticed a little more pep in his step.

That night, Harold showed up with wine and beer. I hadn't had a beer since going to Murphy's, so I welcomed the libation. When he attempted to open the wine, he realized that it wasn't a screw top. "I'm sorry to say that I don't have a corkscrew," I said.

"No worries." Harold reached deep into the pocket of his jumpsuit and pulled out a Swiss Army knife. He sorted through the several implements until he found the corkscrew and proceeded to open his wine.

I shook my head. "My dad would say that thing is slicker than snot on a doorknob."

Harold started laughing so hard he had to sit down. "I sure wish I could have met your dad."

"You two would have gotten along famously. He was in the Second World War. He never saw action, but he had a bunch of stories from those days."

Harold wiped his eyes, shook his head, and had one last guffaw. "No doubt."

When we were both settled in with our drinks, I told Harold about my decision to go to Billings' hearing. "Would you like to join Richard and me?"

Harold's eyes lit up. "I'd be honored. Will it be all right with your son?"

"I'm sure it will." I was becoming increasingly annoyed that people tended to think of him as my boss, but I chose to leave the topic be for now. "Come by here about one-fifteen on the 12th. We'll go together to meet Richard out front."

I wondered what a person wore to court these days. It seemed like the *Law and Order* women usually wore dark suits. I scrounged around in the back of my closet and emerged with a black pantsuit. The legs were a little wide, but heck, that style was coming back. I paired it with my white blouse. Boring and dignified, that was me. I chuckled at myself.

Harold was prompt as always and we waited outside for Richard, who picked us up in a shiny blue Tesla. Since he doesn't take me out to lunch, I hadn't seen his latest car. My son was dressed in his lawyer clothes. He was tall and slim with his dad's large ears and thick, steel-gray hair. Even if I wasn't his mother, I'd consider him a striking figure. Using the manners I'd taught him, he opened the car door for me. His eyebrows went up when Harold got into the backseat.

"I invited my friend Harold Lancaster to join us. I hope you don't mind," I said matter-of-factly as I sat down on the front seat. I introduced the two men. "Harold was instrumental in making sure the detective's plan was sound and I was safe during the purse snatching episode."

"I see."

While Richard was making his way to the courthouse, I threw the opening salvo. "Since Mr. Billings has no money, I doubt the judge will fine him, but I'm sure he'll go to jail. What do you think?"

"How do you know he doesn't have money, Mother?"

I was afraid he'd ask that question. "I did a little checking and I happen to know he's jobless and homeless."

Richard simply shook his head. He probably didn't want to know how I found this out and I hadn't planned on telling him. Since the question went unanswered, I assumed he agreed with my premise.

As we were walking into the courthouse, Richard chatted with Harold while looking him over like he was the suspicious suitor of his fifteen-year-old daughter.

We settled into our seats then I asked my son if he would arrange for me to have a moment to speak with the defendant after his sentencing. Richard nodded, got up, then confidently strode to the front of the courtroom and spoke with the young man's court appointed attorney who he seemed to know. When the judge appeared, he returned to his seat. "It's all arranged," he whispered in my ear.

Basically, the hearing went as I'd imagined. There was the "all rise" then "how do you plead." After Steve pleaded guilty to one count of purse snatching, the judge issued his orders. Since the boy had no money, he received the higher sentence of one year in a minimal security prison and no fine. Maude had contacted the detective with the description of her attacker which didn't match Steve so they could only charge him with the one theft.

Just before he was led away, Richard ushered me to where the attorney was standing with his client. I approached Steve. "Do you remember me, young man?"

"You the lady that got me arrested?" He squinted his eyes at me, as if he was afraid that I could further damage his life.

"I am and I'm glad you're off the streets and no longer stealing women's purses. I do, however, care about you and your future."

"So?" he said, sounding belligerent and suspicious.

"Would you be willing to be pen pals with me while you're in prison?"

He gave me a "Are you kidding?" look. Ignoring the expression, I pulled a piece of paper from my purse and handed it to him. "Here's my name and address. If you write to me, I'll answer. If you don't want to write, I'll understand. Even though I was instrumental in your going to prison, I hope I can help you in the future." I tried to appeal to his softer side. "Give you grandmotherly advice, send you cookies, stuff like that."

He took the paper. "Okay, lady. I'll think about it."

The officer handcuffed the boy and led him away. Even though I knew justice had been served, I felt sad for him and a tad guilty.

When we got back to the car, Richard admonished me. "Mother, what were you thinking?"

This annoying line was becoming a theme of his.

"Had I known you were going to give him your address, I would not have arranged for you two to speak." He looked behind him at Harold. "Is she always like this?"

Harold grinned. "Pretty much."

Smart man. He knew enough to keep his response short. I pulled my seatbelt across my chest. "Well, you did and I did, so it's done." I changed the subject. "Do you think he got a fair shake?"

I could see my son slip out of his father/son persona and back into his lawyer-self. "I do. Obviously, there wasn't much his attorney could say or do other than tell the judge about his current circumstances of being homeless and unemployed. Since he was arrested in the act of committing the crime, there was no other way to plead but guilty. I think a year in prison is a fair and just punishment, don't you?"

"Yes. I think it's fair. People can't go around stealing from little old ladies and get away with it. When word gets out that Steve is going to jail for a year, his compatriots will think twice before pursuing this line of theft." I looked down at my hands, trying to get in touch with what was happening in my heart. "I do, however, hope that this isn't the beginning of the end for that young man. He has a whole lifetime ahead of him, and if he doesn't change, he'll likely end up a career criminal. I don't know anything about his background—"

My son interrupted me. "You don't? How did you miss that bit of information?"

I ignored him. "As I was saying, I don't know about his history but I imagine it's pretty bleak. No one was there for him today, no one took him in when he could no longer pay rent, even his friend, the grocery bagger I talked to, had given up on him. With no support, how does a person make it in the world?"

Harold spoke up from the backseat. "I agree, Martha. His future looks bleak but if he writes to you, perhaps knowing that someone on the outside cares about him will be a turning point."

I was so happy to have Harold defend my position, I could have kissed him.

He continued. "In my experience, a letter from home often meant all the difference to a young soldier in a foxhole wondering if he was going to die tomorrow."

This comment seemed to pique Richard's interest. "You were in the military?"

"Yes, sir. I proudly served thirty years in the United States Army."

I looked over at Richard, delighted to add, "Harold's too modest to tell you, but he's a retired Lieutenant Colonel."

My son put on the turn signal and dutifully looked both ways before saying, "Well, that's impressive, Harold. Or should I call you Colonel?"

"Harold will do but thank you, Counselor."

Chapter Twenty-Two

I was walking to my apartment after my workout on a Tuesday morning when I heard loud voices coming from Agnes' office. Curious, I slowed my pace and listened. It was Madge's voice, and she sounded distressed and defensive; definitely not the usual competent and confident person I knew her to be. I could tell that Agnes was berating her for some reason.

That night at dinner, after we'd settled into our main course of meatloaf and mashed potatoes, I looked over at Madge, who was picking at her food. "How was your day?"

She didn't look up. "Awful."

"What happened?"

"Agnes harassed me about not going to meals. I told her I always go to dinner but in my quest to lose the extra pounds I've put on lately, I'm eating a simple breakfast and lunch in my apartment. She told me she considered my conduct to be outrageous and dangerous to my health."

I thought about the times I'd chosen to eat in my apartment. "What business is it of hers?"

"She said that when residents avoid meals it reflects poorly on her."

Missy jumped in. "How so?"

Madge shook her head. "She wasn't clear about that. I think she doesn't like anything to be out of line. Wasn't that obvious when she punished Martha," Madge gave me a sympathetic glance, "for providing us with a bit of diversion?"

The conversation moved on, but after dinner I caught Madge on our way to the social room and pulled her aside. We sat down near the front door where visitors usually waited. "I'm worried about you, Madge. What else is going on?"

She looked at me with an expression of wariness. "What makes you think something else is going on?"

"Just a hunch. In my various careers, I've been an advocate for women, so I recognize signs that others may miss."

Madge hung her head, reached into the pocket of her trousers, and pulled out a tissue. I waited patiently. I learned the value of silence a long time ago.

"To tell the truth," Madge gave me a once over like she was deciding whether or not to trust me, "I've been bored and a bit depressed of late. This has led me to eat things I shouldn't like the chocolate croissants that occasionally show up on the breakfast buffet and the constant cookies and ice cream on display at lunch. I can handle our plated dinners, but I don't do well with all the choices at other mealtimes."

"Does eating soothe your feeling of emptiness?"

"Yes. But then a few hours later I feel guilty about what I've eaten, and the cycle starts all over again." Madge wiped her nose. "I'm not good with people like you are, Martha. I'm only good with numbers."

She was right. Madge wasn't particularly good with people but I was wondering why she would bring it up now. "Tell me more."

She looked at me. "You're really interested?"

"Yes, I'm really interested." I looked her in the eyes and didn't flinch when she was silent for a moment.

After a few beats, her eyes lit up as if she was remembering something pleasant. "I was the first female auditor for The Royal Bank of Canada. I eventually traveled throughout Europe for my work. My only dealings with people were to talk about numbers. These were usually unpleasant conversations which didn't win me any friends, but I didn't mind because I knew I was good at my job, and that was all that mattered in those days."

Madge slouched back in her chair. "Now I sometimes regret never marrying, having children, or making life-long friends."

"Being the first female auditor was quite an accomplishment." I looked at Madge and when I saw a smile gather on her lips, I continued. "We all make sacrifices of some sort. In my case, I stayed home with kids for a number of years which made it difficult for me to reenter the business world." I carefully considered my next statement. Did I want to spend this much with Madge? Her know-it-all attitude frequently made her a pain-in-the-neck but I went ahead and asked, "What would you think of eating lunch together most days?" I quickly added, "At least for a while." A smile flickered in Madge's eyes. "I need to watch what I eat as well. We can help each other be accountable to healthy eating. What do you say?"

Her smile grew. "You'd do that for me?"

"Of course."

"All right. What time is lunch?"

Madge probably needed to add lunchtime to her spreadsheet. "Noon except on Wednesdays when I go to the library. You can ride along if you'd like to. Just seeing Winter will help you push boredom aside."

"Who's Winter?"

"The very woo-woo librarian."

When Madge pulled her eyebrows together I added, "You'll see. Want to go?"

"I'd love to!"

I got up. "Let's get over to the social room before the music ends."

The next morning, I texted Madge.

It's Wednesday. Meet me at the front door at ten-thirty so we can go to the library. Jake takes us in the minivan."

Right away, I heard my phone beep.

I'll be there with bells on.

I smiled to myself. Now, that was something I would never have expected to hear coming out of Madge's mouth or from her fingers, as the case may be.

For the next two weeks, Madge and I had lunch together. She dropped four pounds, I dropped two. Having an accountability partner seemed to be working for both of us.

As we ate, she told me of other residents who had had altercations with Agnes. A few less worldly and more sensitive women than Madge and me were upset for weeks after Agnes' dressing down. I didn't always recall the specifics of these relayed conversations, but I was making notes on the who and when of the encounters and I was beginning to think that something needed to be done about Agnes.

It had been a week since I'd last visited Maude in skilled care, so I texted her asking if today was a good day to visit. When I didn't receive a reply, I decided to go anyway. This time, I asked Missy to accompany me. She was better at directions than I was.

After arriving at the unit, we entered room 202 and found it empty. I inquired at the nurse's station. "We're looking for Maude. The last time I visited her she was in room 202. Has she been relocated?"

The young lady was all business but had a kinder demeanor than Agnes. "Are you relatives?"

"No, we're friends from when she lived in assisted living," I said.

The nurse drew us closer. "I'm not supposed to say anything to someone who isn't a relative, but Maude passed on last week."

"Passed on to where?" asked Missy naively.

The nurse gave her a sympathetic look. "You know, died. She had another bad fall. This time she hit her head, which caused a brain bleed. I'm sorry for your loss."

We heard someone desperately calling for assistance from a room down the hall.

"Excuse me, ladies. I need to find out what's going on down there."

Missy and I looked at one another. I inexplicably gave her a hug. "You just never know, do you?"

"Nope. Gotta enjoy every day." She tugged at my hand, "Come on, let's go get an ice cream."

Chapter Twenty-Three

Three weeks after Steve's hearing, I received an envelope in the mail that looked like it had been through the ringer. It was wrinkled and covered with greasy fingerprints. When I opened it, I found a letter written in difficult-to-read block letters by a person using a pencil. Even though it was the middle of the day, I turned on my reading lamp.

Mrs. Anderson. This place isn't as bad as I thought it would be. At least I have a bed and three meals a day, which is more than I had before. I'm not in a cell like you see on television. I'm in a room with a bunch of other guys. Our beds are lined up like in the old re-runs of M*A*S*H, and I'm learning how to fix cars. We work on old police cars mostly. So far, I've learned how to change the oil, but pretty soon I'm going to work on a motor. Maybe you getting me in this place wasn't so bad after all. I'm really sorry for what I done to you. Write if you have time. My address is Steve Billings, Fishkill Correctional Facility, 18 Strack Dr, Beacon, NY 12508.

I texted Harold.

Guess what?

There was a short pause, then a beep.

What? I can't wait to hear. (Smile emoji)

I just received a letter from Steve Billings. He's reasonably happy and learning a trade. He's at Fishkill (what a horrible name) Correctional Facility in Beacon, NY.

That's great news! Let's talk about it after dinner.

All right. I'll skip music. Come by early. (Smiley face)

When we entered my apartment after dinner, Harold settled down on the loveseat and I sat beside him so we could look at the letter together. He studied the words like they were written in code. "This definitely looks legit. I don't see anything nefarious here. He doesn't ask you for money, and he apologized."

I did a little humph. "I have good instincts when it comes to people, Mr. Lancaster." I poked him in the ribs. "I didn't buy into the bad egg theory the boy's friend put out. I had a feeling Steve had the potential to amount to something if given half a chance."

Harold studied the letter some more. "Hold your horses. He hasn't exactly amounted to anything yet, but if he can get decent training and become an auto mechanic, or better yet, a diesel mechanic, he might have a good future ahead of him. There's always work for those guys. At least he'll know how to take care of his own car, which is more than I can say for my son."

I got a piece of paper and a pen from the drawer and took it to the table. Harold followed me, and we sat down. "Help me write a return letter. Other than telling him I'm happy that things are better than he expected, I don't know what to say."

Harold rubbed his chin. I could see the wheels turning. "After you texted me, I looked the place up. Fishkill has a good work release program. Ask him to find out how he can qualify."

"That's a good idea." I wrote this down then looked up. "What else?"

"Ask him what he likes about working on cars and if they're teaching him how to rebuild a carburetor. They probably aren't, at least not yet, but it might keep him thinking ahead."

I added this to the letter. "I'd like to send him something. What do you suggest?"

"If you want, I'll call the place tomorrow and find out what prisoners can receive in the mail. They probably have a bunch of rules about that. Is it all right if I call?"

I smiled at Harold, thinking he was a good partner. "Of course. My son thinks my writing Steve is a bunch of tomfoolery or even risky, but I think it's worth it and having you believe in me means a lot."

Harold sat quietly while I finished writing the letter. When I glanced up at him, he seemed a bit off. "What's wrong, Harold? You look a little discombobulated."

"I'm feeling dizzy. I think I'll go sit in your recliner and put my feet up if you don't mind."

While Harold walked to my chair, I got him a glass of water. I sat the drink beside him on the table. "Are you okay?"

"I'm having some trouble breathing and I'm feeling very tired. Perhaps you should call the desk."

I pulled my emergency cord and a voice came over the intercom. "What can I do for you, Martha?"

Thank goodness it was Judy. "Harold's here and he's not feeling well. Please come right away."

"What's happening?"

"He's dizzy, suddenly very tired, and seems to be short of breath."

"I'll be right there!"

I opened my door so Judy wouldn't have to take the time to knock, then I returned to Harold, who seemed to be struggling for air. His eyes were closed. I brought a chair over, sat down, and took his hand. It felt clammy and a little shaky.

Judy burst into the room with a stethoscope around her neck, and Josh followed with a blood pressure cuff in his hand. "I'm going to listen to your heart, Harold," Judy said as she placed the stethoscope on his chest. "Are you experiencing any chest pain?"

With his eyes still closed, Harold replied in a weak voice that scared the pants off of me. "No pain. Just tired. Trouble breathing."

"You're having another Afib episode. Drink this water," Judy handed him the glass. When he'd finished the water, she said, "Good. Now, take some deep breaths."

Harold did as he was told. After several minutes, Judy put her stethoscope back on his chest. "Your heart is back in rhythm. How do you feel?"

Harold opened his eyes and gave Judy a little smile. "Better. Thanks."

"If you'd had any chest pain, I would have called 911."

"I know. I'm glad it didn't come to that," Harold said.

Judy patted his hand. "Josh and I are going to stay here for a while to make sure you're stabilized." She looked at me. "Are you okay, Martha? You look pale."

"I'm fine. Just worried about my friend here. You all stay as long as necessary. I'm going to go lie down for a bit." I gave Harold a peck on the cheek then took myself to the bedroom, where I changed into my soft clothes. I sat on the bed with my back resting against the headboard, which reminded me of my marijuana escapade with Missy.

I quickly tossed that memory aside and tried to get in touch with my current feelings, realizing that I could have lost another dear friend. This thought forced me to consider what place Harold had in my life. Not only was he my friend, but I counted on him for so many things. What I thought when we first faced Agnes together was still true; we were two peas in a pod. Perhaps not two peas but a kernel of corn and a pea.

I was suddenly exhausted and slipped down to lie flat on my bed. When I awoke in the night, my apartment was dark and I was warm but too sleepy to change into a nightgown.

The next morning, I texted Harold first thing to see how he was feeling. When there wasn't an immediate response, my heart did a flip-flop—not in a good way. I waited five minutes and texted him again, knowing that he was always up by eight o'clock. When there was still no response, I threw on my clothes, flew out the door, and headed to Harold's apartment. I knocked. When there was no answer, I tried the handle. The door was unlocked. Judy and Josh probably left it open when they took him back last night. Just as I walked through the door, Harold rushed into the living room wearing blue striped boxer shorts and a white t-shirt.

"Martha! What the hell are you doing here?"

I could tell he wasn't mad, just surprised. "I texted you and when I didn't get a response, it scared the shit out of me!" He smiled. I had a feeling he knew that very few people had heard me say that word out loud.

"When they brought me back to my apartment last night, I went straight to bed. I must have left my phone in my pocket." Harold picked his jumpsuit off the back of the chair, reached into the pocket, and pulled out his phone. "Just as I thought. It's as dead as a doornail."

"Well, I thought YOU might be dead as a doornail. I'm sure glad to see you upright!"

"Glad enough to give me a hug?"

I reached over and gave him a big hug. Tears welled up in my eyes, and I realized just how frightened I was thinking I'd lost this dear man. I pulled back from the embrace. "You look pretty cute in your undies but if you'll get dressed, I'll take you to breakfast—assuming you feel up to it."

Harold gave me a serious look. "I warned you about these episodes, Martha. Once my heart gets back into the proper rhythm, I recover but the episodes are becoming more frequent. My doctor's talking about an implant. We'll see…"

My friend trailed off. He was probably deciding whether or not an intervention like that was worth it at his age. It didn't seem like the time or place to discuss the issue so I said, "Go get dressed!" With the direct order, he marched into the bedroom.

Chapter Twenty-Four

Although my son paid my Manor bill every month, I handled my taxes, checkbook, credit card payment, and other expenses like co-pay for doctor's visits. I didn't always scrutinize my credit card statement like I should. However, three months ago, the credit card company texted me asking if I'd made a particularly large charge. When I answered no, they canceled my card and sent me a new one. Now here I was again, faced with a balance that was more than I'd expected, so I pulled the information up online.

Going through each item, I saw Amazon, Shear Play (my hairdresser), Nike.com, and RockAuto, an online auto parts store. Since I didn't wear Nike anything nor had I driven a car in more than two years, I added up their amounts, then called the 800 number on the back of my credit card. A nice lady with a heavy accent canceled my card, told me they would remove the charges, and assured me a new card would be coming in the mail.

I wondered how my card had been compromised... again. I knew that online shopping was the riskiest activity for credit card fraud but I'd had no issues until recently and I remembered paying cash at the sleazy grocery store. I decided to ask Madge about it at lunch. After all, she had been a bank auditor.

"Maybe someone took the card out of your wallet while you were away from your apartment," she offered.

"Really? That sounds far-fetched. Besides, I'm pretty careful about locking my door."

"But just think of all the people who have a master key. The maids and the medical staff, for starters."

Madge was always suspicious, which was a good counterpoint to my too-trusting nature.

Even though it was just the two of us at the table, Madge leaned across and whispered, "Maybe Agnes took your card, made a copy of the number, and slipped it back into your purse."

I frowned at this notion. She might be a disrespectful and mean-spirited nincompoop, but I couldn't imagine her stealing from the residents. If she were caught, her actions would end her career and land her in jail. I missed Madge's last comment. "I'm sorry, what were you just asking?"

"When do you expect to get your new card?"

"Later this week. They expedited it."

Madge was quiet for a moment then said, "After you receive your card, I think we should set up a spy cam in your apartment."

Her suggestion surprised me. "A spy cam! That seems a bit over-the-top."

Madge shrugged. "Perhaps, but then you'll be able to check the possibility of an intruder off your list. After all, this is the second incident in a little over two months." Madge fiddled with her phone. "You can get one on Amazon for as little as $20, a better one for $30. It seems like a good investment to me."

"I'll think about it."

When I returned to my apartment, I found my door unlocked. I could have sworn I'd locked it when I left for lunch. Maybe this was a sign that I should purchase the spy cam Madge talked about. Or maybe it was a sign I needed to, literally, get my head examined.

After lunch, I had a text from Harold.

Want to come over and watch the first episode of Fool Me Once on Netflix?

Before answering, I googled the title. In essence, the main character was trying to deal with the brutal murder of her husband when she installed a nanny cam to keep an eye on her young daughter and was shocked to see said husband in her house. Was this another sign? I texted back.

Sounds intriguing. I'm on my way.

Great. I'll microwave some popcorn.

Do you know anything about nanny cams?

(eyes up in the air emoji) *We'll talk in a few.*

I could see Harold shaking his head and thinking, "What now?"

After I entered his apartment, we settled ourselves on the couch with a big bowl of popcorn between us. Harold looked over at me. "Before I ask a more specific question, I'm curious about how you got to be so tech savvy."

I shrugged. "My mother loved having the newest household inventions. For instance, we were one of the first people in our neck-of-the-woods to have an automatic washing machine. Although I learned to sew on a treadle machine, my mother eventually had an electric. I had a microwave—this popcorn is delicious by the way—before any of my friends." I thought for a moment. "Oh, and I had one of those huge car phones." I grabbed another fist-ful of popcorn. "In today's world, being on the cusp of the newest gadgets translates to technology. I suppose it just comes naturally."

"Interesting." Harold gave me a serious look. "This leads me to the nanny cam question. Tell me more."

I explained the fraudulent charges on my credit card statements and Madge's speculation that my card might have been stolen from someone in-house. Like me, Harold was dubious.

"Like you said, it seems far-fetched, but…" Harold paused, tilting his head to one side, "Madge might have a point. For twenty bucks, you could be sure. I say why not."

"Let's see how the nanny cam works in the show we're about to watch, then decide. Deal?"

"Deal."

Harold started up the Netflix.

The nanny cam seemed pretty cool in the episode, so when I returned to my apartment, I put a Blink Mini in my Amazon shopping cart. The description said it would connect to my Alexa. As soon as my new credit card arrived, I'd place the order. I perused the other options. I imagined that Robyn on *The Equalizer* had an iSpyPen PRO.

By Thursday, my new credit card arrived and I received my Blink Mini on Saturday morning. Madge came by to help me hook it up. It was her idea, after all.

Nothing showed up over the weekend when the regular staff were off, but on Monday morning I watched on my phone as the maid came in while I was at breakfast. She vacuumed, dusted, went off camera to presumably clean the bathroom and change my sheets, and then she exited. I conveniently left my purse on the kitchenette table but she didn't touch it other than to move it from side to side when she wiped the table down.

Tuesday was so quiet I actually went to Bingo in the afternoon. The rest of the week sailed by, and I started to forget about the Blink Mini.

The following Monday, my son came for his monthly lunch. We were eating our sandwiches with less conversation than usual when, suddenly, he dropped a bombshell. "Maria's divorcing me."

It was my turn to sound outraged. "She's what?"

"She says we're incompatible. After 39 years of marriage. I just don't understand it."

I looked at my son. He didn't look as outraged as he sounded, and I wondered if there was more to this story than he was telling me. "So, what's going to happen?"

Richard fiddled with his fork. "We're putting the house on the market. When it sells, we'll split the proceeds. She'll get half of my 401K which is a hefty amount, but I'll survive. The worst part was telling the kids. Rich was mad at both of us and stormed out of the house, Susan cried, then she told us we'd ruined her life. There was a lot of drama."

"Have you told your sisters?"

"Not yet. I wanted to tell you first."

I wanted to know more, but I also wanted to respect my son's privacy so I simply said, "I'm terribly sorry about this. Life isn't easy when you're alone."

"Thanks, Mother."

My son installed me in Martyn Manor because it was close to his home. I wondered what would happen to me if he moved away. "Are you planning on buying another place here in town?" I asked.

When he looked down, I wondered if he'd thought that far ahead. "Probably. Don't worry, I won't leave you stranded here." He was quiet for a while. "By the way, your birthday's coming up. It's the big Nine-O. How do you want to celebrate?"

Redirecting. That's what lawyers did. "Frankly, I haven't thought about it. Have you spoken with your sisters about it?"

Richard folded his napkin. "I've talked with Elizabeth. She'd like to come, so would Barbara and Bobbie. Ruth will be out of the country on business. I haven't heard back from Susan or Rich yet. I think they're still punishing me for the divorce. "

I considered my growing family. I had met David, my only great-grand, at Richard's house not long after he'd been born. I hadn't seen my granddaughter Barbara and her wife Bobbie since their wedding. I was glad they were coming with Elizabeth. I wasn't surprised about Ruth being away.

"If it's all right with you, I'll make the arrangements for a family dinner once I have a final count. We still have a month or so."

"That would be lovely. Thank you."

Chapter Twenty-Five

Madge and I started going to chair yoga where we heard about another theft. A valuable watch had turned up missing. So far, the only person we'd seen on the mini cam was the maid and I was beginning to think my credit card had been compromised elsewhere.

I was eating lunch with Madge on Wednesday when I got an alert on my phone. Even though we expected to see the maid, Madge moved her chair beside mine to get a good view of the screen. We watched as a gentleman we didn't know walked through the door, pocketed a key, then went to my mini fridge. He took a soda, opened the can, then nonchalantly walked back out. As far as I could tell, he left my door unlocked. My unlocked door wasn't my imagination after all!

"Who was that?" Madge asked.

"I don't know, but he looks vaguely familiar. I'll ask Harold. He knows all of the men who live here." I thought for a moment, then remembered the false fire alarms. "I wonder if he's the guy who unlocks the fire alarm boxes and sets off the alarms?"

Madge raised her eyebrows. "Possibly. Looks like he has a skeleton key or is good with locks. If he can figure out one, he can figure out others." Madge slid her chair back to her side of the table. "Either way, he just illegally entered your apartment and stole something. It seems like that's enough to obtain a warrant to take his fingerprints which should help the Poughkeepsie Police or Fire Department make a conclusive identification if they match his prints with those on the fire alarm."

"Two birds with one stone. We're regular sleuths, Madge," I said.

A rare smile crossed her face. "Indeed."

Later that afternoon I showed the video to Harold who identified the intruder as Joey Russo.

"Do you think he's the guy who sets off the fire alarm?" I asked.

"All I know is that he's from Brooklyn and he comes to the woodworking shop. Next time he's there, I'll ask him if he can help me with a lock problem and see what he says. In the meantime, what are you going to do with this video?" Harold handed back my phone.

"I think I'll hang on to it until after you have a talk with Mr. Russo. Depending on how that goes, we might have enough evidence to convince the police or fire department to fingerprint your friend."

Harold bristled. "He's not my friend. He's an acquaintance. In fact, I think he's a bit of a Space Cadet."

When I frowned, Harold explained. "He acts weird, even by Manor standards. I admire your patience. You're wise to accumulate as much information as you can. You'll have less chance of it being dismissed."

"I agree. I'm finding that as an old lady, I'm taken less seriously than I was when I was younger."

Two days later, in the middle of the afternoon, Harold texted me.

Spoke with Russo. He bragged about his "incredible" knowledge of locks including those on safes. Bingo, I think we have our guy.

(thumbs-up emoji)

Since I didn't want Agnes to know about the mini cam, I decided to wait a while longer before informing the authorities. I appreciated Harold's acknowledgement of my patience but in reality, I wasn't a patient person so holding on to this evidence and waiting for someone else to show up in my apartment was out of character for me. I set a deadline of two weeks before I made a move.

A week and a half later, there was a ping on my phone. Once again, Madge and I were in the dining room eating lunch. This seemed to be the ideal time of day for illegal entry into my apartment.

"It's Agnes!" I shout-whispered. Madge hustled over to my side of the table. We watched as Agnes entered the living room then put a key in her pocket. She called out my name (there was even sound on the device) then went directly to my purse. She took out my wallet, removed my new card, pulled a notepad from her pocket, jotted down the pertinent information, then returned the card to the wallet and the wallet to my purse before exiting.

"I was right!" Madge said with such exuberance others in the dining room turned to look.

I put my finger to my lips. "Shhhh. You want the whole place to know what's going on?"

Madge moved her chair back. "I can't believe she'd take such a big risk. She obviously found out that you canceled your card when she tried to use it again and had to come back for the new numbers."

"She certainly would have skedaddled had she known we were watching her. Now what do we do?"

Madge set her napkin on the table. "Let's get out of here. We don't want her to get wind of the fact that we know anything. This place has a bunch of big ears," Madge looked at the residents eating at the nearby tables, "if you know what I mean."

Madge and I walked to the chairs by the piano, where no one sat this time of day.

"I say we let her make more charges then we'll have both the video and the evidence from your new credit card bill. We can either contact the credit card company or the police," said Madge.

"Since I have history with Detective Warren, I think he's our best bet. Plus, he's acquainted with Agnes."

Madge turned to face me. "When we talk with him, I think we should also tell him how Agnes treats some residents as well as the disappearance of the watch. Perhaps that robbery was reported, perhaps not, but it could be connected. It might be a good time to show him the video of Russo also."

On the way back to my apartment, I stopped by Harold's to fill him in on what was happening. He was more incredulous than I was but there was no denying the video.

Later in the week when I looked at my credit card account online, I noticed irregularities such as a charge to Express Scripts, an online pharmacy, and Instacart at a local grocery store. I thought Agnes made decent money, so I was curious why she'd need my card to pay for essentials like these charges suggested.

I once again canceled my card and was relieved of the fraudulent charges. At lunch, I told Madge about the new illegal purchases. "I'm going to make an appointment with Detective Warren. I think talking with him is our best course, don't you?"

Madge set her fork down. "I agree. See if you can get in to see him tomorrow."

I returned to my apartment, made the appointment for the next morning, and arranged for an Uber.

After arriving at the precinct, Madge and I were ushered into the familiar interrogation room and sat at the same battered table. Whoever preceded us needed to use Degree or Secret. The place smelled like a cheap gym.

Warren looked at me with impatience written all over his face. You'd think he would show more respect considering I'd solved two cases for him. "What can I do for you ladies?"

I didn't say a word as I handed over my phone, which was queued up to the video of Agnes taking my credit card from my wallet.

"My gawd! Is that Miss Duly?" Warren asked.

"It is," I replied, holding my tongue with some difficulty.

"Has she used it to buy things?"

I looked at him like he was an ignorant schoolboy. "Of course she has. Since my card was compromised twice before this episode, my friend Madge here," I looked over at her, "had the idea of installing a spy cam. I thought it was a long shot, but I was wrong."

Madge spoke up. "In addition to this unlawful behavior on the part of Agnes, you should know that she's regularly demeaning and generally unkind to residents. We've also heard about a valuable watch going missing. Has a theft at the Manor been reported recently?"

"Not that I know of," Warren said.

I jumped in. "We believe it seems strange that, in some cases, Agnes's credit card charges are for essentials like car parts, groceries, and drugstore items. I believe there's more to this story than meets the eye, don't you, Detective Warren?"

Without answering my question, the detective hollered out the door for a tech guy. Almost immediately, a young man in a police uniform, to whom we were not introduced, took my phone and made a copy of the video. He also took a photo of the two credit card statements which I'd printed out. When he was finished, Warren ushered us out the door. "I'll handle everything from here, Mrs. Anderson." He gave me a stern look. "It's important at this stage of the investigation that you keep your findings completely confidential." When I nodded, he asked, "Does anyone else know about this?"

"I've shared everything with Harold Lancaster."

To his credit, the detective looked slightly embarrassed. "Oh yes, Mr. Lancaster. I trust he will keep a lid on this?"

"I'm certain he will." I shouldered my handbag. "And I trust you'll keep us informed of your progress?" I pointedly asked.

He nodded unconvincingly. He was no Marcus Dante, the New York detective from *The Equalizer*, that was for sure.

Our encounter left Madge and me feeling unsatisfied. We considered eating fried food to drown our frustration but since we were committed to losing weight and healthy eating, we directed Ted to take us back to our boring lives and non-greasy institutional food.

That evening after dinner, I stopped by Harold's apartment to give him the rundown of our meeting.

"You need to stay on top of this, Martha. I think good old Detective Warren," Harold said his name with disdain, "is prone to lollygagging."

"Fortunately," I held my phone up, "I have his cell number right here."

"You do?"

"Yes. He gave it to me before the purse snatching scheme."

"He'll regret that." Harold smiled mischievously.

"Not if he does his job."

I didn't hear from the detective for two days, but I did see his assistant, Detective Niles, in clothes even plainer than her dark suit, talking with residents after Agnes had gone home for the day. I presumed she was gathering information about the other robbery and, possibly, about the mistreatment.

Chapter Twenty-Six

Because of the less-than-satisfactory meeting with the detective, I decided to share the video of Russo directly with the fire department, hoping they'd be more receptive. I started with a phone call.

"If this is an emergency, hang up and call 911."

"This isn't an emergency."

"Then how may I help you?"

"This is Martha Anderson. I live at Martyn Manor where there's been a rash of false fire alarms in the last six months," I paused to make sure the woman understood.

"I'm aware of the false alarms. A very disturbing circumstance for our firemen as well as for Martyn Manor residents."

"Very. I think I have a clue as to the person who is setting them off."

"Really?"

I ignored the question. It sounded like a what-does-this-old-lady-know kind of statement.

"If someone will come to my apartment, I'll show them a video that may lead to the perpetrator or at least to obtaining a warrant for taking fingerprints."

"A video?"

"Yes," I said with authority. "A video."

"All right. I suppose we could check it out. I'll send over an investigator right away."

"I'd rather you send someone after six o'clock this evening," I countered.

"Is there any particular reason?"

"It would be more convenient." I rushed on so there was no time to pursue the timing. I wanted them to come after Agnes had left for the day. "My apartment number is 206. Please ask whoever is coming to be discreet; no uniforms. I'd rather no one knows about the video just yet. I'll tell the front desk I'm expecting a visitor."

"I understand. Lieutenant Smith will be coming."

"I'll be waiting. Thank you."

After I hung up, I texted Harold.

Lieutenant Smith from the fire department is coming to my apartment about six this evening to look at the video of Russo. Come over after dinner so you can fill her in on your findings.

I'll be there. (thumbs-up emoji)

I informed the front desk of my expected visitor then returned to my apartment to dress for dinner.

Lieutenant Smith was a middle-aged, attractive woman dressed in jeans and a plain black sweater, so no one would suspect she was a fire inspector. She had a nondescript back-pack resting on her shoulder. I invited her into my apartment and introduced her to Harold.

"I understand you have a video of the person who may be setting off the recent false alarms," she said.

Without preamble, I cued up the video and handed her my phone.

"Looks to me like he's stealing a can of soda. I'm afraid you need to take this up with the police," she said after viewing the video.

I took back my phone and looked at Harold. "Mr. Lancaster will be able to shed additional light on this perpetrator that may convince you otherwise. Harold…"

Harold cleared his throat and told the lieutenant what he knew of Russo. "In my opinion, he's the only person in this facility capable of unlocking the fire alarm cases," he concluded.

Smith studied Harold. "I see," she said. "So this video, combined with Russo's knowledge of locks and keys, led you to believe that he's the person setting off the false alarms."

"Yes." I didn't add the don't-you-think-so-too part.

"You do have a point. I can see why you came to us first. Setting off a string of false alarms is certainly more concerning than stealing a can of soda."

Harold shifted in his chair. "We thought so, too."

"Who do I need to speak to about dusting the alarms for prints?" Smith asked.

I jumped in. "Judy." I reached for my cord. "I'll call her right now."

Judy promptly responded. "How can I help you, Martha?"

"Can you come to my apartment? It's not an emergency. Someone's here I want you to meet."

"I'll be right there."

After Lieutenant Smith showed Judy her identification and told her the story of Mr. Russo, Judy escorted her down the hall to the fire alarm. Harold and I stayed behind. We didn't want our neighbors to associate us with this investigation. Presumably, the lieutenant also dusted the alarm on the first floor before returning to my apartment.

"Before we request prints from Mr. Russo, I want to run what I just took through our database." Smith stood. "I'll be in touch, Mrs. Anderson."

Three days went by without word from the police or the fire department. The following Monday morning, however, I saw no sign of Agnes and wondered if at least one case might have progressed. I was encouraged when I saw a notice that a resident meeting had been called for three o'clock that afternoon.

The CEO of the entire continuing care organization, Cynthia Robertson, was standing at the front of the room when Madge and I entered. We sat in the front row with great anticipation. Harold joined us.

"Thank you all for coming. I want to personally inform you that Agnes Duly, the Assisted Living Supervisor, no longer works at Martyn Manor. Her temporary replacement is your night supervisor, Judy Johnson. The management team thought the transition would be smoother if a familiar face served in the interim while we look for a permanent replacement for Ms. Duly. Are there any questions?"

I let out a sigh. Finally! For the magnitude of what happened, the message was certainly short and sweet.

Harold raised his hand.

"Yes?"

"What happened to Agnes?"

"As you'll read in tomorrow's newspaper, she was arrested at her home yesterday morning on charges of credit card and jewelry theft. Miss Duly's arrest is a regrettable circumstance for Martyn Manor, as we pride ourselves on hiring the best staff possible. Of course, she was thoroughly vetted, but apparently, her behavior deviated from when she joined us two years ago, and we had no other choice but to take swift and decisive action." Robertson surveyed the audience. "Are there any other questions?"

When there were none, she adjourned the meeting emphasizing that nothing like this had happened since their opening and reassuring us that nothing like this will happen again.

My face was practically hurting from holding in an ear-to-ear smile. I looked over at Madge, who literally had her hand over her mouth.

"Let's go to my place," said Harold.

Madge and I followed him into the elevator then down the hall. After we all trooped in and he closed the door, Madge and I let out cheers.

"We did it!" Madge said with an exuberance I'd never seen from her.

"Congratulations you two," said Harold. "Good detective work." He went to his kitchenette and pulled a split of Prosecco from his mini fridge. "This calls for a toast."

Harold poured a small amount of bubbly into three plastic cups. We held them up and Harold made a toast. "To justice and the two smart women who made it happen!"

"To justice," Madge and I said in unison before clicking our glasses.

Chapter Twenty-Seven

U nfortunately, my monthly lunch with Richard was later the same week as the announcement about Agnes was made public. When I approached the table, I could see a newspaper sitting next to his napkin. After I sat down, he held up the paper with the article about Agnes front and center. The headline read, "Martyn Manor Staff Member Arrested."

"Do you know anything about this, Mother?"

I gave him my innocent look. "Maybe."

"Maybe you were present for the announcement, read it in the paper, or…" he paused, "maybe you had something to do with the supervisor's arrest?"

"Maybe all of the above." Poor Richard. As we used to say regarding problem teenagers, I'm sure he saw me as a handful.

He shook his head. "When will you stop playing amateur sleuth?"

I thought for a moment. "Perhaps when there are no more crimes happening under my nose."

"Can't you leave all this to the authorities?"

"Apparently not." I didn't say anything about the spy cam or the fact that I was a victim. This information would upset Richard further and might cause him to move me to another facility. I was tempted, however, as it would justify my actions.

I changed the subject to the birthday celebration and he took the bait. I also knew how to play attorney games and redirect conversations.

"Your birthday dinner will be Sunday, October 6th, at Maloney's Irish Pub and Steakhouse. They have karaoke most nights but not on Sundays so it will be quiet. I think you'll like the atmosphere, it's very Irish."

A big smile tried to bubble up but I tamped it down. "Sounds lovely."

"Rich and Samatha will be there with little David so we'll eat early—about five-thirty. Barbara and Bobbie are flying in with Elizabeth. As I said before, Ruth is out of the country."

"What about Susan?"

Richard's face clouded over. "My daughter is still upset about the divorce."

"I see," I said, but actually I didn't see. This was my party and it had nothing to do with Susan's parents, yet she couldn't come for me? She grew up as a self-centered girl who was spoiled by her father. I tried to tell Richard at the time but he wouldn't listen. Now he was reaping the results of his actions as a parent.

Just so I was clear about the participants, I summarized.

"Yes. Plus, you and me, of course—unless you'd like to invite Harold."

I considered his offer. "Let's keep it to the family."

Richard nodded.

"Barbara and Bobbie can stay here. I'll arrange for the visitor's apartment," I said.

Richard looked relieved at my suggestion. "That would be ideal. Rich said his Aunt Elizabeth could stay at his place. There's no room in my temporary apartment."

I looked up. "You have an apartment?"

"It was too stressful for Maria and me to live in the same house while it's on the market so I moved out."

"I see." I seemed to be saying that a lot lately but the messy details of Richard's life were none of my business.

After lunch, I arranged for the apartment, then put the party out of my mind. It was three weeks away and I planned to wear the fancy blouse and slacks I wore to the city and the French restaurant since none of my family had seen the outfit.

Ping. The text was from Harold.

I talked to Russo at the shop today. I have news. Come by after lunch.

(thumbs-up emoji) *Finally! I'll be there.*

I settled into Harold's navy blue couch with thick cushions and wide arms. I could see how Marcella slept comfortably there. "What's the news?" I asked.

Harold took his time sitting down. He liked to create drama. "Well…"

"Good grief, Harold. Spit it out!"

"Patience, Martha. I'm getting there. I was in the woodworking shop when Russo walked in. Seeing that he was down at the mouth, I asked him what was wrong. He told me the fire inspector, accompanied by the police, came to his apartment and confiscated his tools and keys."

"Really?"

"Yes, really. Want to hear the rest?"

"Sorry."

Harold made his usual throat-clear noise. "Russo was quite incensed. He told me they accused him of setting off the fire alarms and unlawfully entering a resident's apartment. When I asked him if he did it, guess what he said?"

Harold was milking this for all it was worth. "What?"

"He admitted doing the deeds! Just like that, he proudly said that he'd figured out how to unlock the alarm cases and entered a few apartments with a skeleton key just for the heck of it. But the weird part is he doesn't seem to understand why everyone is so upset since he didn't take anything of value or hurt anyone."

"Did he say anything else?"

"He told me he was fined a thousand dollars for setting off the alarms and booked but put on in-house probation for the other. I'm not sure what that means but it seems to me that he got off easy. Probably because he's old. I guess there are a few perks."

"Well, if we ever decide to be the bad guys instead of the good guys, perhaps our advanced age will be a benefit."

Harold frowned. "Seriously?"

"Of course not! I don't have a thieving bone in my body. Besides, I like being the sleuth who solves crimes. It's so much more fun than being the perpetrator."

Harold frowned again.

"Not that I'd know about that of course."

With my "cases" closed, I was feeling blah. Had I become addicted to the adrenalin rush of masquerading as a private eye? I hoped not. I needed to learn to live within the confines of the normal life of an old lady.

At least my birthday party was coming up. Drama always played a part at family gatherings. Not that I wanted that kind of excitement. In fact, I hoped the staff at Murphy's wouldn't recognize me. If they did, I wondered what questions might arise. After all, I was last there on a date with a lovely lady with whom I sat on the same side of a booth and teared up when she sang *Moon River* to me. It was a scenario that would take a lot of explaining.

Chapter Twenty-Eight

Barbara and Bobbie knocked, rushed through my door, and nearly toppled me with their hugs. "We're so glad to see you, Gran," my granddaughter said after settling onto my love seat and taking her wife's hand.

Barbara still had the look of a college coed even though she was approaching thirty. She was tall and willowy with straight brown hair that touched her shoulders and inquisitive brown eyes. By her appearance, no one would guess she was my granddaughter, or her mother's daughter for that matter. In her short, sleeveless, fitted dress, she could have passed for a model, except that she wore no makeup, not even lipstick. Her only jewelry was a simple gold wedding band and small diamond studs in her ears.

Bobbie, on the other hand, had short hair similar to mine but blonde and curly, reminding me of Missy's flyaway curls. She had big blue eyes shadowed by long lashes swiped with mascara and expressive, carefully filled-in eyebrows. She was a good three inches shorter than Barbara and had an athletic build. She had attended college on a soccer scholarship. She had on black…what did Winter call them? Oh yes, flares. Her tucked-in blouse was lemon yellow and open wide at the collar. She wore a gold band that matched Barbara's, a small monogram necklace, and gold hoop earrings.

"We've missed you. What have you been up to?" Barbara asked.

Nestled together, they were as cute as two kittens in a basket. I'd never imagined my granddaughter having a wife but since she did, I was glad she'd married Bobbie. "What has your mother and Uncle Richard told you?" The question seemed like a good place to start. I didn't mind them knowing about my personal life, but I didn't want to repeat what they already knew.

"They said you made the front page of the local newspaper when you were involved in a police sting," Bobbie said.

Barbara added, "And Uncle Richard told us that the guy was arrested and sent to prison. Is that true?"

"That's all true. However, the young man, Steve Billings is his name, isn't as bad as he sounds. He did a very bad thing and deserves to be in jail, but we've become pen pals, and I think he will return to the outside world as a contributing citizen."

The two young ladies looked at me with the same expression my son had.

"Really?" Barbara finally said.

"Yes, really. He's taking classes to be an auto mechanic. He has apologized for his earlier actions and regrets what he did. People can change you know." I hoped I hadn't said that unkindly. I was aware of how defensive I tended to be about my involvement with Steve. Thankfully, they moved on.

"Uncle Richard also told Mom that you might have been involved in an investigation that got the supervisor fired. She wasn't sure about your part in this, and Uncle Richard couldn't confirm either way. What's the story there?"

I briefly relayed the preliminary information, then added, "I used a mini cam to not only discover credit card thefts by the supervisor but also to nail down the person who was setting off fire alarms here at the Manor. His mistake was to enter my apartment and steal a can of soda. Because of the mini cam, I realized he had the tools and know-how to breach locks."

Seeing that the girls were wide-eyed, I added a cautionary note, "Please don't pass my involvement in these operations on to your mother or Uncle Richard. It will only upset them and your uncle might consider moving me to another location. I have made good friends here, and I certainly don't want to start over someplace else."

"Our lips are sealed." Both girls ran their fingers across their lips. "Wow, Gran. That's pretty cool," Barbara added.

I smiled, "My life here isn't as dull as you might imagine."

Barbara twisted in her seat. "Speaking of friends, is there a special friend?"

"Special as in romantic or otherwise?" I asked.

She clarified. "Romantic, of course."

My granddaughter always was a sucker for romance. "Possibly."

"Come on, Gran! Give us the scoop. We won't tell. Promise."

"There is a certain gentleman, his name is Harold. Your uncle has met him. He's a retired Army Colonel. He's very kind. For instance, he made sure I was safe during the purse snatching sting. We became close when my friend and I rescued him after his son abducted him."

"Rescued?" Bobbie asked with raised eyebrows.

"That's a story for another day. Let's stick with the relationship side of things for now." I wondered if I should say anything about Missy. These two would certainly understand.

"And…" Barbara prompted.

"I also have a lady friend. Missy has a lovely singing voice and she's fun to be with."

Barbara leaned so far forward, she practically fell off the couch. "You?"

"Yes, me. You keep asking that rhetorical question." I pushed the handle on my recliner and my legs jutted out. Barbara settled back onto the couch cushion. "Old age is an interesting time of life, perhaps akin to the college years when the world's your oyster. There are opportunities to explore without as much consequence as when you're in the more responsible years of your life." I gave the couple a serious look. "Like where you are now."

Barbara leaned forward again. "Have you ever been interested in a woman before Missy?" Without giving me a chance to answer, she went on. "You were married to Grandpa for a long time and had two husbands before that. Right?"

Bobbie looked at her wife. "I didn't know that."

Barbara turned to her partner. "There's probably a lot about my gran you don't know. Obviously, there's a lot about my gran that I don't know either."

I put my legs down, got up, and walked to my kitchenette. "Anyone want a soda?"

"No thanks," Barbara said. "Stop stalling."

I got myself a glass of water and sat back down.

"Well?" My granddaughter got her impatience from her mom, who got it from me.

"I knew an artist in Paris who was quite fascinating."

"How fascinating?" Bobbie asked.

"An infatuation from afar. Nothing came of it. It was a tiny blip on my romantic radar screen."

"What about when you were younger?" Barbara asked. She could have followed in her uncle's footsteps and become a lawyer.

"The whole notion of same sex couples wasn't even talked about or thought about in those days—except, of course, by those who were biologically predisposed. And as far as I know, most of them didn't act on their feelings. They buried who they were, got married to someone of the opposite sex, and had children like the rest of us. It makes me sad to think about it. Even in the mid-80's when Rock Hudson came out as gay, people were in disbelief."

Both girls looked at me.

"You haven't heard of Rock Hudson?"

They shook their heads from side to side.

"Never mind." I sipped my water. "I didn't personally know an openly gay person until I participated in a therapy group when I was in my fifties. Remember, I've lived most of my life in a small town in Iowa. Not that there aren't gay people in Iowa but even in recent years, I suspect they're careful about sharing information regarding their lifestyle. One couple I knew had to pretend they were roommates or they would have lost their jobs. I'm glad to see you two living your lives openly. It's a terrible thing to have to hide who you are."

Bobbie looked at me with those intense blue eyes. "It's not always easy. Even for us. Living in a big city like Chicago helps, but when we hold hands in public we still get looks that are meant to shame us."

"We've learned to shake it off, like a wet dog shaking off after a bath," Barbara interjected.

I had to laugh. "Sorry. I'm not laughing at what you must endure, I'm laughing at the wet dog bit. You sound just like my dad. Witticisms must be in your genes."

Barbara smiled. "I realize that's a compliment Gran, because I know how much you loved my great-grandpa."

I glanced out the window. It was a sunny morning and a beam of sunshine lit up Bobbie's golden hair. I felt the presence of multiple generations merging together. When I forced myself back to the present, I changed the subject. "Let's move on from my boring life and talk about you two. Are you planning on having children? What's new in your world?"

Barbara looked disappointed. "If you want to save the rest of this conversation for later, we'll move on." She reached over and gave my outstretched leg a gentle poke. "However, we shall return. You're not getting off the hook that easily."

My frankness with the girls opened them up to speaking frankly about their life. They explained how they planned to start intra-vaginal insemination, or IVI, as soon as they returned to Chicago. They had already consulted with professionals. The next step was to purchase sperm from a sperm bank.

"Barbara will insert the sperm into her vagina with a needle-less syringe," Bobbie explained. "I'll be the pregnant partner for baby number two."

All this was a bit TMI for me but I really appreciated their willingness to share the intimate part of their life. "I imagine it could take a while to get pregnant," I offered.

Barbara agreed. "You're right but it's the least expensive option. If IVI doesn't work, we'll eventually go to Plan B."

Bobbie gave me a serious look. "Please keep our plans confidential. We haven't told anyone else."

I looked from one girl to the other. "I'm very good at keeping secrets. Good luck to you and please keep me posted. I'd love to have another great-grand before I die."

After the extended sitting, I slowly got up from my chair. "Now that we've all shared our secrets, I think we should go to lunch."

Chapter Twenty-Nine

The fancy clothes I was planning on wearing to my birthday party were a bit loose, thanks to the heathy eating I was doing with Madge, but it was too late to order anything else so they would have to do. Grandson Rich was bringing my daughter, Elizabeth, to the party. Richard was coming on his own still hoping his daughter would change her mind and want a ride from the train station. I ordered an Uber for the girls and me. They liked being on their own in the Manor's guest apartment and they hadn't felt the need to rent a car for their brief visit.

"Good to see you, Mrs. A," Ted said when he picked us up at the curb.

"You know the driver?" Bobbie whispered.

"Ted, meet my granddaughter, Barbara and her wife, Bobbie. They're here from out of town to attend my birthday party."

Ted turned in his seat. "Nice to meet you and happy birthday, Mrs. A."

"Thank you."

He turned back. "Where you headed tonight?"

"Murphy's."

"I hope you know there's no karaoke on Sunday."

"I do. My son planned this event. He's not big on karaoke."

"Ahh, so that's why your lady friend isn't with you."

"Yes."

I was astonished that everyone but me seemed to have such excellent memories. It was just before five-thirty and clouds were gathering in the October sky when we walked into Murphy's. Richard waved at us from a large table in the corner.

"Are you with that group?" asked the hostess looking in his direction.

"Yes." I said.

"You do know we don't have karaoke tonight."

"I'm aware."

The hostess continued. "I'm sorry your girlfriend won't be gracing us with her beautiful voice tonight."

I took a few steps forward so there would be no further conversation. "No need to show us to our table," I said before I looked at the girls and did a lip-zipping motion. They smiled conspiratorially.

Richard was sitting next to Elizabeth. Rich and Samantha, were sitting across from them. My great-grand, David, was in a baby carrier set in a special chair near his mother. Barbara skirted around me and sat next to her mom with Bobbie to her left. After I greeted everyone, I sat beside Samantha. David was sound asleep with his little mouth puckered up and his hand next to his rosy cheek. I hoped he'd wake up before the party was over.

Elizabeth turned to her daughter. "Did you have fun with Gran today?"

"Of course. She told us all about her Canasta club, Bingo on Wednesdays, and the stringy beef." She winked at me.

Elizabeth looked at me from across the table and then spoke loud enough for me to hear. Unfortunately, the rest of the restaurant guests could also hear her. "I hope you haven't been up to any more purse snatching operations, Mother. Richard sent me the link to the news article. Good heavens! What were you thinking?"

How had I managed to raise such unadventurous children? Ruth must have gotten all of the adventure genes, and I was paying the price by her not being at my party. I ignored the question. "It's been quiet at the Manor lately. Not much going on."

The waitress came to take our drink orders. When she got to me she smiled. "A Corona Lite, if I remember correctly."

"Yes, thank you."

Richard came to attention. "You didn't tell me that you'd been here before. During the week this is a college hangout with karaoke. I can't imagine…" He trailed off.

I ignored him and addressed the waitress. "And three baskets of onion rings, please," I added.

"Our bar isn't as busy tonight as it was when you were last here, so I'll bring them with the drinks."

"That will be lovely."

Everyone looked at me. I fiddled with my pocketbook. When my son continued to stare at me, waiting for an answer, I pointed to the stage. "The karaoke is over there."

He responded with, "We'll talk later, Mother."

Just as the drinks and onion rings arrived, my son waved at someone near the entrance. When I turned, I saw Susan walking toward us.

"Happy Birthday, Gran," she said, leaning down to kiss me on the cheek.

"I'm glad you decided to come. Pull up a chair and sit next to me," I said.

Susan dutifully pulled a chair from an adjoining table and squeezed it next to mine. The waitress came forward and asked for her drink order. "I'll have a vodka martini, please. Extra olives."

"Susan…" Richard started to speak but stopped when I held up my hand.

"That's my friend's favorite drink," I told Susan. She smiled at me. "What have you been up to lately?" I asked.

"Mostly, I've been trying to figure out how to live in a world without a family," she said with an edge to her voice.

I gestured around the table with my hand. "I see your family all around. Right here, right now. The living arrangements might have changed but you still have a family."

"Mom's not here," she said pointedly.

"Neither is your Aunt Ruth but I'm still enjoying myself."

"But it's just not fair!" Susan's cheeks reddened and I was afraid she was about to cry.

When Susan's martini and the onion rings arrived, I insisted she take one. "You're right. Life's unfair and it's just as well you learn that lesson sooner rather than later."

Her full, red lips gathered into a pout but quickly reversed course when she took a bite of an onion ring. Susan thought she had a miserable life but, truth be told, she was blessed in many ways. She was beautiful, with long, shiny black hair, dark brown eyes, and smooth olive skin which she inherited from her mother. Susan's grandfather on that side of the family immigrated from Spain when he was in his late teens. She was willowy like her cousin, Barbara, but in a sexy way with breasts that were noticeable in her sleeveless, rust-colored dress. Her makeup was perfect and her long nails matched her lipstick. Smart like her father, she had an Ivy League education and, at twenty-three, she was already working at a top investment firm in New York City making more money than I'd ever earned in my life. But she was used to getting her way and her parents' divorce definitely wasn't her idea.

Susan took a sip of her martini. "I was supposed to go on a cruise this fall with my parents but of course, that plan has changed."

She sounded like a two-year-old but it wasn't my place to address her attitude. "I would think you'd rather take a vacation with your friends," I suggested.

She dabbed grease from her lips. "I have a few business acquaintances but not many friends." Her lovely face fell. "It's not easy making friends in the city, Gran."

"I suppose not."

I heard a mewing sound coming from the baby carrier. The waitress had just taken our orders and her shuffling about had probably awakened David. His mother reached in and released him from the restraints.

"Would you like to hold him while I get his food ready?" Samantha asked me with the baby wiggling on her lap.

"I'd be delighted." I reached out and she placed my great-grandson in my waiting arms. I wanted to snuggle him close but he had other ideas. He strained to face the table. When I turned him around, someone took a photo. He started fussing and I bounced him on my knee. He was heavier than he looked and my arms quickly tired. When the bouncing didn't settle him down, I returned him to his mother.

It was difficult to have a conversation across the table. My hearing wasn't terrible but it wasn't that not great, either. I was content, however, to pick up my conversation with Susan since I rarely had an opportunity to be with her. She was eating a Caesar salad with grilled chicken. I was relishing a well-cooked, not stringy, steak and baked potato with sour cream and chives.

"Gran?" Susan looked at me with an expression that reminded me of when she was a little girl about to ask her father to buy her something.

"Yes."

"Would you consider going on a trans-Atlantic cruise with me? My treat of course."

When I didn't respond, she rushed on. "We'd embark from the Manhattan Port so you'd only need to take the train and a taxi. I'd meet you there. Or I could pick you up at the Manor." She took a quick breath. "It's eight-nights on the *Queen Mary Two*. We can attend stage shows every evening and eat fabulous food any time, day and night." She looked over at me. "I know how much you love live entertainment and good food."

"My goodness, that's quite an invitation! Is this the trip you were planning on taking with your parents?"

Before she could answer, Richard stood up and clinked his glass with a spoon. "May I have everyone's attention please."

All heads turned in his direction.

"I'd like to offer a toast to our mom, gran, and great gran," he said holding up his half-filled water glass.

Everyone responded by holding up their glasses.

"To an ageless woman who is full of life and love."

It was such a lovely toast. Suddenly, tears filled my eyes as I looked at all the beautiful faces saying, "To Gran, Mom, Martha." Right on cue, the waitress brought in a chocolate cake topped with flaming candles. Certainly not ninety, but enough to make me wonder if I could blow them all out. I closed my eyes and made a wish for one more healthy year and an abundance of health, wealth, and love for my family and friends. When I was only able to blow out half the candles, Susan blew out the rest. David squealed with delight and Richard sat down with a satisfied look on his face.

I had requested no gifts, so the party was over when the cake was eaten and the dishes removed. I was unable to resume my conversation with Susan before her father whisked her back to the train station. She promised to call me. Elizabeth asked if the girls and I could meet her for lunch the next day.

"I think you should go on the cruise with Susan, Gran," Barbara commented on the ride back to the Manor. "It would be fun and maybe you'll meet a sexy Frenchman," she paused, "or woman." She cocked her head and grinned.

"It's amazing how everyone but me seems to have such good hearing," I said.

Barbara looked sheepish. "I didn't mean to eavesdrop, but Susan's voice carries."

"That's all right, I'm glad to have your advice. It's a generous offer. Memory seems to be my biggest handicap and on board a ship, I guess I couldn't go far if I got lost. Worst case scenario, I'd be sauntering down the halls until someone found me. Other than that, I guess I'm healthy enough to make the trip. I know there are doctors on board but there are no specialists or operating rooms between New York and Southampton."

Bobbie, a physician's assistant, spoke up. "You seem very fit. I say go for it. Especially if your doctor gives you the green light."

"If you decide to go, be sure to take the opportunity to walk the outside decks and enjoy the fresh air," suggested Barbara, a physical therapist. "Just be careful. Falling is one of the main hazards aboard a ship. Wet surfaces, high door sills—you get the picture."

"If I decide to go, I'll be careful. Thanks for your concern," I replied, and said I'd see them tomorrow.

Chapter Thirty

When the girls and I arrived at the restaurant the next day at noon, Elizabeth was already sitting at a table for four. After a few minutes of chit-chat, the topic of Richard and Maria's divorce came up. Elizabeth's father, my first husband, and I divorced when she was a young adult, so she had empathy for Susan but now that she'd been divorced for five years, she could see the situation from both points of view.

Elizabeth was my youngest child and the only athlete in the family. At fifty-three, she was short like me but muscular. She worked full-time as head of the HR department in a large hospital, played pickleball regularly, and was somewhat of a gym rat. She had short dark hair, brown eyes, a pale complexion, and a million-dollar smile. From the beginning, she had embraced Barbara's lifestyle but her husband had not. It was a bone of contention between them that eventually led to their divorce.

After we ordered our lunches, Bobbie, perhaps not wanting to hear more about failed marriages, abruptly changed the subject and asked me about my childhood. The girls were past the self-absorption of teenagers and young adults and in the narrow window just before the overwhelm of child-rearing so I obliged knowing this was a rare opportunity that would quickly pass.

"Start with the basics," Bobbie said. "The others know about your beginnings but I don't."

The restaurant was chilly, so I pulled my shawl closer. The room was quiet, making it easy for me to hear the conversation around the table, and the atmosphere was quaint with chintz curtains and an antique sideboard along one wall which served as a beverage station.

After the waitress delivered our iced teas, I began. "I was the youngest of three girls, my mother was a housewife, and my father owned a grocery store. We lived in a two-bedroom, one bathroom bungalow just off the town square in Ames, Iowa. My dad walked home for lunch if he had a clerk to back him up that day."

"How did you manage with five people in such a small house?" Bobbie asked.

"All the girls slept in one room. We had a bunk bed and a twin. The oldest got the twin. Being the youngest, I had the lower bunk."

"I can't imagine three girls plus a mom using one bathroom. Did your dad ever get in? We're only two people, and we have two and a half baths," Barbara said.

"We took turns. No extended primping. None of my friends had more than one bathroom back then either, so we never thought about it."

"Were you poor?" Bobbie asked.

"Other than plenty of food on the table, we probably didn't have much but at the time, I was unaware of what we didn't have. What I remember most was having loving parents and sisters who were also my friends. I miss them all. It's difficult being the last one."

"I can imagine it is," Bobbie said sympathetically. "What did you do for fun?"

That girl liked to stay positive. "We did simple things for fun, like ice skating and sledding in the winter, but I also had responsibilities at home like dusting and drying the dishes when I was young and helping my dad in the store when I got older."

"Were there hills in your town?" Barbara wondered out loud.

Picturing the cornfields of Iowa, I replied, "Not many, but my dad tied our sleds together with a rope and pulled us down deserted country roads behind his car. It was a daring thing for him to do and he was the only parent who did it. Perhaps I got my 'bend the rules' spirit from him. Although until recent years, I was very rule-abiding."

"Bending the rules? Are there stories you haven't told us?" my daughter asked.

The girls cleared their throats.

"Maybe, but let's stick with the past for now," I said.

"Okay," Elizabeth reluctantly replied when the girls gave her a 'let Gran talk' look.

"I went swimming nearly every day after work in the summer, rode my bike, and roller skated. My girlfriends and I played with dolls when we were young. We pretended our husbands were at war since many dads were away. My dad served for four years in the Army. He enlisted right after Pearl Harbor. My mom, my sisters, and I ran the store while he was gone. It was fortunate that he returned. More than 400,000 U.S. soldiers died in World War II."

There were sad faces all around so before Bobbie could ask, I returned to talking about fun things. "We played jacks and jumped rope—complicated rope tricks, sometimes with two ropes like you see on *America's Got Talent*."

"Were you allowed to date?" Of course it was Barbara who asked this question.

I recalled Dave Kelly, my first love. "Yes, I had boyfriends, but we were innocent by today's standards. Kissing and hand holding was the extent of what I did. I was a virgin when I married Elizabeth's father. I thought my friends were too but, years later, I found out I was alone in that category."

The girls snickered.

Elizabeth asked, "Do you have any regrets, Mom?"

"That's a big question." I paused to think. "I regret not learning earlier in my life the value of confronting people when it's necessary. I was afraid of confrontation because I thought it would cause me to lose the person I was confronting. I learned the hard way that the opposite is true. When I didn't confront, I built up resentment towards that person, which ultimately damaged the relationship."

The waitress brought our lunches. The turkey wraps, salads, and cups of soup all looked delicious. I was about to take a bite of my wrap when Elizabeth asked, "Anything else?"

I knew she wanted me to say something about my divorce from her dad. She, like Susan, took it hard even though she always had a good relationship with both of us. I laid my wrap aside. "I'm sad I got divorced but I can't say I regret it. The loss of our family unit was every bit as catastrophic to me as when Marvin died so suddenly. However, as a result of my divorcing your father, I think we were both happier and you and your siblings eventually adjusted."

Elizabeth's forehead was creased in a frown. She probably didn't agree with my assessment but she was quiet, apparently deciding to keep her opinion to herself for now. I hurried on. "I've had momentary regrets when I've been judgmental or spoken harshly to someone, but those weren't long-lasting. I can't recall any specific instances."

The faces watching me were still engaged, but I didn't want to bore them. "Enough about me. What's new in your life?" I asked my daughter before taking a large bite of my wrap.

She brought me up to date on her life as a single person. I encouraged her to get out more and travel—even if it was by herself.

When lunch was over, my three girls called a cab to take them to the airport. They'd brought their carry-ons with them to lunch. Since the Manor was in the opposite direction from the airport, I called Ted. I was sad to see the girls leave, but I was also looking forward to returning to my routine.

As promised, late that afternoon, Susan texted.
Is this a good time to talk, Gran?
It's fine. Call me.

My phone buzzed and Susan came on the line. "Well, have you had time to consider going on the cruise with me?"

Just like her dad, this girl got right to the point. "I've given it careful consideration and I've decided to take you up on your kind offer. A transcontinental cruise will be great fun. When do we go?"

"Gran! I'm so happy you said yes!"

I heard muffled talking in the background. "Sorry. I'm at work and someone has a question." Susan paused, said something I couldn't quite hear, then resumed our conversation.

"The ship departs on October 25th, arrives in Southampton, England on November 1st, then we fly home. I know it's not much time to prepare, but do those dates work for you?"

"Well, I'd have to give away my Taylor Swift concert tickets."

"Really?" Susan responded in a loud voice.

"No, just kidding. Those dates are just fine."

"You crack me up, Gran."

"I'll try not to bore you on the cruise."

"I'm not worried about that." There was a pause and I heard keys clicking. "I'll book the cruise and the flight."

"Thank you."

Susan continued. "I'm so happy to have something to look forward to, and it'll be good to spend time together. When I was a kid, I didn't appreciate your visits but believe it or not, I've matured."

"I'm sure you have." More talking in the background. "Let me know what I need to pack. Will there be a formal night?" I asked.

"I think those have gone by the wayside, but I'll check."

I heard someone call Susan's name.

"Gotta go. I'll be in touch. Love you!"

"Love you, too."

Chapter Thirty-One

My friends had a gift sitting on the table at my place at dinner that night. "What's this?" I asked.

Madge explained. "Just a little something for your special birthday. We know you don't want more stuff but we did it anyway. Open it."

I untied the blue satin ribbon and tore away the white tissue from a box about the size of a saucer. I opened it and pulled out a square China dish inscribed with *Never Forget The Difference You Have Made.* Tears filled my eyes. Since I'd never been a crier in the past, I wondered if tears were something that increased with old age.

"I can't imagine a greater gift than knowing you've made a difference." I looked at Missy, Madge, and Molly—and was very much aware of Margaret's and Anna's absence. "What a lovely gift. Thank you."

Missy gave me her special smile. "I'm sure you've made a difference in many lives over the years but most recently, you've made a difference in ours."

The other two nodded.

Molly added, "You've helped us keep the spark of life lit and we appreciate your kindness and caring. Happy birthday."

Moving things along, Madge asked, "What looks good for dinner? I'm starving."

After dinner, the pianist for the evening stuck up a rendition of "Happy Birthday" and everyone sang. To put an exclamation point on my unending birthday celebration, Harold was leaning against the wall when I returned to my apartment. "Happy birthday, Martha."

"Thanks. Want to come in?"

He was holding his usual brown paper bag but tonight, it wasn't bottle-shaped. When I didn't offer him anything, he took a seat on the loveseat. I sat next to him. "Here's a little something for your birthday. I hope you like it." He pulled a ring box out of the paper bag.

My heart leaped, but not in a good way. I was worried about what might be in the box and what I'd say. I cautiously opened it. Nestled on the black velvet was a black and white, antique cameo pin about the size of a dime. I took it out of the box and held it up. "This is lovely! Thank you."

"It belonged to my mother," Harold offered in a serious voice.

I pinned the cameo on my sweater. "Many years ago, all my jewelry was stolen from my house. Much of it had once belonged to my mother, grandmother, and mother-in-law. I had a cameo very similar to this that was my grandmother's." I looked down at the pin. "What was your mother's name?"

"Ruby. You would have liked her."

"I'm sure I would. She raised a thoughtful son."

Harold got up from the couch. "It's late. I know you want to change into your comfy clothes." Harold leaned over and kissed me. "Good night and sweet dreams. Welcome to the Nine-O Club. We're as scarce as hen's teeth."

I smiled at Harold. "Men like you are as scarce as hen's teeth. Thanks again."

Our new Assisted Living Director, Joe Henderson, arrived soon after my birthday. He was in his mid-fifties, had movie star good looks, and southern charm. He was all "yes, ma'am" and "if you please." Best of all, he was kind to the staff and residents. He made Judy his deputy and hired a replacement for night duty. By the second week, he addressed everyone by name.

A week before the cruise I made appointments to have my hair, nails, and toes done. I wanted to look spiffy. Earlier, Susan had texted me saying there was a Captain's Night where everyone dressed up. Not in formal gowns and tuxedos, she assured me, but dressy.

Maria, my son's soon-to-be-ex-wife, texted me just as I was wondering what dressy meant. She'd obviously heard about my upcoming trip with her daughter and offered to take me shopping. Maybe she didn't want a dowdy old lady accompanying her beautiful daughter on a cruise. "That's snarky, Martha," I said to myself.

We scheduled our shopping trip for the following day right after lunch. The cruise date was getting close and I needed to pack.

"It's so good to see you," Maria said after she'd picked me up in front of the Manor. "How have you been?"

"Good. You?" I responded after I'd settled into the front seat of her baby blue Lexus SUV.

Maria looked beautiful as always—her glossy black hair was cut into a bob that fell just below her ears and her dark complexion was radiant.

"Other than the fact that my daughter will barely speak to me, I'm good, I guess. The divorce has been very stressful but life's too short to be unhappy."

"I hadn't realized you and Richard were unhappy," I said.

"Well, we were."

Maria fiddled with her phone. I hoped she wasn't going to text and drive. I tended to be a nervous passenger even when the driver paid attention to the road.

Abruptly changing the subject, Maria asked, "What kind of clothes do you need for the cruise? We could go to EB. They'll have dresses and accessories."

"EB?"

"Elsa's Boutique. You haven't been there? Everyone goes to EB."

"I shop online."

Maria was certainly the right person to take me shopping. She had impeccable taste. At EB, she helped me choose a lovely purple lace dress that fell just below my knees, a matching jacket, and low-heeled black suede pumps.

"Have a good cruise," Maria offered when she dropped me off. "Susan is very excited about you going with her. I'm sure you won't disappoint her."

I felt incensed about the "disappoint" remark, but I let it go. "Thank you for taking me shopping," I said as I pulled my two large bags out of the back seat. "Keep in touch."

Maria said, "I will. We're still family, after all."

"Yes, and I believe it's important for Susan to understand that." I wondered if she got the hint about communicating with her daughter.

Later that week, I made an effort to pack light but, knowing the weather would be chilly, at the last minute I added the black, all-weather coat I wore on a visit to Iceland years ago.

The night before I left, Harold walked me back to my apartment from the after-dinner music. "I'm going to miss you," he said with sad puppy dog eyes.

"I'll only be gone eight days."

"Nine if you count coming and going."

I gave him a punch on the shoulder. "Whatever."

He pulled me in for a kiss. I held up my hand. "Let's go inside."

I barely had the door closed when he pulled me into his arms. "Be careful, Martha. I've heard that falling is the biggest risk on a ship."

"So I've been told."

"And don't let any French dandy sweet talk you into anything." He possessively put his arm around my shoulders.

"Why Harold, I think you're jealous."

He winked. "Who me?"

"I hope you have a wonderful time," he said sincerely.

"Thanks." I looked into his eyes. "I'll be back before you know it with good stories to tell."

His look grew serious. "Don't get into trouble, Martha. Keep your head down and mind your own business."

I gave him a salute. "Aye, aye, Colonel."

Chapter Thirty-Two

Susan took the train and then a taxi to pick me up at my apartment. Apparently, she wanted me to arrive at the port safely and on time. I appreciated not having to wrangle my suitcase and carry-on. It was enough for me to carry my purse.

I'd read that the *Queen Mary* 2 was the only transcontinental ocean liner in service in the world. It held over 2,600 passengers and was christened twenty years ago. I had looked at photos online but when we finally embarked the ship and I walked into the grand entry, it took my breath away. Two wide spiral staircases, crystal chandeliers, dark wood trim, and rich blue rugs gave the vast space a sense of old English charm.

Susan and I had adjoining rooms, each with a small balcony. The first two days were lovely with smooth seas, fabulous food, and a stage show reminiscent of Broadway. Day three brought wind, rain, and rough seas. I wasn't seasick, but I was ultra cautious when I walked the inside, carpeted hallways, and I didn't dare venture onto the wet, slippery deck. That afternoon, I watched a movie in my room and Susan and I ate our dinners in her cabin. She didn't want me to take the chance of falling by walking through a rocking ship.

Day four was back to calm seas, and I took the opportunity to lounge in a deck chair after eating a late lunch. Susan wanted to work out before changing and meeting me for dinner, so I was sitting alone. The sea breeze was cold and the tepid sun provided little warmth, but I was comfortably snuggled in a blanket. By late afternoon, everyone had left the area to return to their cabins and change for dinner.

I was already in my dinner clothes and planned to meet Susan in the dining room, so I had no need to return to my cabin. I had a good book, a fabulous view, and I welcomed the alone time. The blue water, accented with glittering crystals, danced alongside the ship. White, billowy clouds floated across the sky. No land was visible, but I'd gotten used to that by now.

I was drifting off, lulled by the gentle pulsing of the ship, when loud voices brought me to attention. I looked up to see two men standing dangerously close to the railing. They were pushing and shoving and calling out obscenities to one another. Suddenly, the older man hollered, "She's mine!" and pushed the younger man over the rail. I froze, not believing what I'd just witnessed. When I saw the assailant running down the deck toward the front of the ship, I threw my blanket aside, got up and yelled, "Man overboard!"

When I realized no one was around to hear my cry, I grabbed my book and ran to the door. In my haste to get back inside the ship, I tripped over the tall sill but I was able to regain my balance and walked as quickly as I could until I found a steward exiting a cabin. "A man just went overboard! Call for help!" I said breathlessly.

To his credit, he didn't question me but grabbed his walkie-talkie and pushed a button. "I have a guest who just reported a man overboard." There was a pause, then the man said, "Yes sir," and returned the device to his cart. "If you don't mind, madam, they asked that you stay here with me. They're sending someone to speak with you."

"Of course."

I texted Susan telling her I'd be late for dinner because I'd witnessed a man going overboard and was being detained.

OMG!!! Where are you, Gran?

I looked at the room number.

I'm standing in front of room 1303.

Deck 13?

I asked the steward and when he confirmed our location, I texted back.

Yes, deck 13, room 1303. A cabin steward is with me.

I'll be right there!

I could tell the boat had slowed. There was less sway and sudden quiet. Before Susan arrived, two men in plain clothes approached. "Please come with us, madam," said one of the guards who introduced himself as the Master at Arms. His tag read William Johnson, Bermuda. He reminded me of Detective Warren. The man with him had a smaller build. His tag said Ben Wilson, Canada.

"I have to wait for my granddaughter. She's on her way."

Johnson looked at his watch. "This is an emergency, madam. I'm terribly sorry, but if she's not here in five minutes, we must leave without her."

There was no chit-chatting. They were all business. This was as it should be, of course. Good grief, a man had probably just lost his life—and it was murder. When I registered this thought, my heart sped up, and I felt weak in the knees. "Could someone get me a chair?"

The steward, an older gentleman with a kind face and gray hair, opened the door to a nearby cabin, went inside, and returned with a desk chair. Relieved to be sitting, I had time to consider the what ifs. Just as I was wondering whether or not the killer had seen me, Susan rushed up. "Are you all right, Gran?"

"Not really."

Johnson spoke to Susan. "We're taking your grandmother to be questioned. Apparently, she witnessed someone going overboard."

"Not just going overboard," I said. "The individual was pushed."

"Pushed?" Johnson asked. "Why didn't you tell us this earlier?"

"You didn't ask and I'm telling you now," I said emphatically.

Wilson intervened. "Let's go." He helped me up from the chair.

Johnson led the way, with Susan and me walking behind him. Wilson brought up the rear. I felt like we were being taken to the gallows aboard a pirate ship. We passed only a few passengers as most were at dinner. The staff, however, was out in force. We saw maids, stewards, and runners from the galley delivering meals to cabins. It was the time of day that staff did their work while the cabins were empty. I walked as fast as I could, but it didn't suit the guard in front, who kept looking back and motioning us forward.

"My grandmother is ninety years old, sir." Susan said sternly. "Have a little patience."

After being chastened, Johnson slowed his pace. Still, it seemed like an eternity before we entered a door marked "Staff Only" and were led down a dark, narrow hallway to another door standing half open. When we entered, a man dressed in a white uniform with shiny brass buttons stood up and held out his hand. "I'm Chief Mate Davies," he said in a heavy English accent. "And you are?"

Susan stepped up. "I'm Susan Petty and this is my grandmother, Martha Anderson."

Davies, a handsome middle-aged man with a ruddy complexion and blue eyes, shook our hands. "Please be seated."

It felt like I was back at the Poughkeepsie Police Station. The overly warm room, smelling faintly of fuel, held a narrow table surrounded by six straight-backed chairs leaving barely enough space to open and close the door. After taking a seat at the head of the table, Davies said, "Tell me what you saw, Mrs. Anderson."

"Yes, of course. Less than thirty minutes ago, I was dozing in a lounge chair on an upper deck when I heard loud voices. I opened my eyes and saw two men, one young, the other older, scuffling near the railing. Suddenly, the older man yelled, 'She's mine,' and pushed the younger man over the rail. The older man was taller and bigger than the younger. Then the man ran toward the front of the ship and through the first door he came to. I yelled 'man overboard' but there was no one around, so I got up, found a steward, reported what happened, and here I am."

Davies narrowed his eyes. "Did you tell the steward that the man had been pushed?"

"Not at first. My main concern was for him to be rescued. When the guard," I pointed toward Johnson, "questioned me, I told him that the man had been pushed."

The officer steepled his fingers. "I see."

"May I have a glass of water?" I asked.

"Wilson, get Mrs. Anderson a bottle of water," Davies ordered then continued. "Did you recognize either of these men?"

"No. I had never seen either one of them before."

"So, you don't know them."

"If I've never seen them, I certainly don't know them." I was getting hungry, which is never good. 'Hangry' is when a sweet lady turns into a crab because she needs to eat. I was on the cusp.

Davies turned to Susan. "Can you confirm that your grandmother has made no male friends on this cruise?"

"Yes. Definitely." She gave him a hard look. "You should be out there looking for the murderer, not harassing an elderly lady."

Susan was her father's daughter through and through, and she was probably also hangry. It ran in our family.

The Chief Mate was not pleased that a young lady, lovely or not, had just told him off. His response was gruff. "I can assure you that we are investigating any suspicious persons and assessing the overboard report." He turned back to me. "Can you describe the two men?"

"As I said, one was older and bigger, and other was younger and smaller. Both were white, both wore long pants and sweatshirts, both had short hair. The older man wore glasses."

"What were their approximate ages?"

"It's hard to say."

"Guess."

Wilson returned with my water, unscrewed the cap, and handed it to me. Davies drummed his fingers on the table while I took a long drink. "The older man was probably in his late sixties. The younger one more like late forties or early fifties. He had dark hair, the other man's was gray."

"Any other distinguishing characteristics?"

"The older man was built like a football player but with a paunch. The younger man was medium height and slim like a runner or tennis player, not heavily muscled like the murderer."

Davies gave me a stern look. "Let's not jump to conclusions, Mrs. Anderson. It's too early to assume there was a murder. If word got around that there's a killer at large on this ship there would be panic among the passengers. You don't want that, do you?"

"I saw what I saw, sir. One man pushed another man over the side of this ship. I suppose if the man is pulled out of the ocean alive, it's attempted murder. If not, well, that's murder in my book."

We were interrupted by a knock on the door. "Come," said Davies.

A man in plain clothes entered the room and spoke to Davies. "Sir, the man in question has been pulled from the water."

"And—" growled Davies.

"He's dead, sir. Drowned. No discernible injuries."

"Were they able to identify the body?"

"Yes, sir. He had his cruise card in his pocket." The guard looked at a small notebook. "The deceased is Harry North, cabin 405. According to our records, he was traveling alone."

With that settled, Susan appealed to our investigator. "May we go now? My grandmother's blood sugar level is falling and she needs to eat. You don't want a killer AND an unconscious woman on your hands, do you?" She gave him a steely look. "Besides, it's not like we're going anywhere."

Davies sighed. "I'll have Wilson escort you to one of the smaller dining rooms. After you've eaten, go directly to your cabins. Lock your doors and do not, I repeat, do not let anyone in. If your steward knocks, have them identify themselves by name. We'll be in touch in the morning. Until then, stay put."

I rose from my chair. "Old ladies are quite invisible." I looked at Davies to gauge whether or not he understood me. "I doubt if the killer saw me but I appreciate your caution. We'll stay in our cabins after dinner."

Without commenting on my observation, Davies spoke to Wilson then motioned for us to leave. We followed the guard up from the lower decks to higher decks and, eventually, to the door of a small Italian restaurant. "The ship will pick up your tab," he said before turning us over to the maitre'd.

The restaurant looked like it had been transported from Tuscany. Rough stone walls the color of brick, classic red and white checkered tablecloths, battery-operated candles in bottles on each table, and soft music with lyrics in Italian. The maitre'd, young, handsome, and with a strong Italian accent, winked at Susan. We'd definitely been transported to Italy!

"Isn't this a nice side benefit to witnessing a murder?" I whispered to Susan after we'd been escorted to a table for two. "A dinner at a specialty restaurant that's not included in our fare."

"Well, that's looking at this from the bright side," Susan growled, putting her elbows on the table. "What an ordeal!"

Ignoring Susan's negative attitude, I replied, "I prefer to think of it as an adventure." I picked up the menu. "I'm starving, and there's nothing like pasta to fill one up."

The waiter arrived to take our drink orders. Susan asked for a martini with extra olives and I ordered a glass of chianti—when in Italy, etc. The waiter promptly brought our drinks along with a basket of warm Italian bread and a saucer of olive oil with a colorful swirl of balsamic vinegar in the middle. Susan drank a third of her martini in one gulp.

"You better have some bread," I said, handing her the basket.

"I can't believe this is happening." She took another sip. "You were very cool and calm during the questioning. It was like you'd experienced this type of thing before." She looked at me closely. "Have you recently been questioned by the police?"

"Maybe."

"Drink your wine and tell me about it. What happens on a cruise stays on a cruise," Susan proclaimed and smiled for the first time in over two hours.

Over appetizers, I told Susan about my interrogation around Harold's disappearance, leaving out the three-way accusation and the part about the erotic library book.

"How did they think you abducted him? Did they think you threw him over your shoulder and walked out of the building?"

"My sentiments exactly."

"You and your friend found him even after the police had investigated?"

"We did."

"This on top of being the hero in a purse snatching scheme. Anything else?" Susan looked genuinely interested.

Our main courses arrived. They smelled like heaven. I helped myself to another piece of bread and dipped it in the oil. "Let me eat first, then I'll tell you more. It's been an interesting two years at Martyn Manor." After my second glass of wine and several forks of pasta, I told Susan about the mini cam, Agnes, and the fire alarm guy.

"Good thing my dad doesn't know all this. He'd have a heart attack."

"My sentiments exactly," I repeated.

After a monumentally delicious, four-course Italian feast ending with tiramisu and decaf cappuccinos, Susan and I returned to her cabin. "What do you think will happen next?" I asked after settling into a desk chair.

Sitting on the edge of her bed, she pulled her phone from a small handbag. "Let's Google and find out." Her fingers flew over the keyboard. "It seems that murder at sea is complicated. One source says that the FBI has authority through the Special Maritime and Territorial Jurisdiction

Code if the victim is a U.S. citizen. But…" She swiped up, "another source says that the law of the country the ship is registered in prevails. The flag state of this vessel is Bermuda." She looked up at me. "Maybe you'll get an additional vacation in Bermuda out of all this."

I didn't smile. "I don't want an additional vacation. I want to return home immediately after we dock."

"I'm sorry. This isn't anything to joke about." She kicked off her impossibly high wedges and pulled her knees up to her chin. "Do you think I should call Dad?"

"I certainly do not." I softened my stance. "Not yet, anyway. Let's see what tomorrow brings."

When there was a knock at the door, butterflies fluttered in my stomach. "Who is it?" Susan called out.

"It's Priscilla. I'm here to straighten your cabin and turn down your bed."

Susan jumped up and looked at a card on the desk. Priscilla's name was on it. "Come in."

I got up from my chair. "Seems like this is a good time for me to go to my cabin. I'll see you in the morning. Knock on my door when you're up and dressed. Just to be extra cautious, use your full name to identify yourself."

Susan gave me a hug. "Are you sure you'll be all right alone?"

"Yes, I'm sure. Thanks for being there for me."

"I love you, Gran. Good night."

Chapter Thirty-Three

The knock came early. I was still in bed but not asleep. I sat up. "Who is it?" I called.

"Susan Lucia Petty, at your service."

I was happy to hear a smile in her voice. She was giving up part of her holiday because of me after all. I swung my legs to the floor, reached for my kimono, padded to the door on bare feet, and opened it a crack. Susan was standing there holding a covered cup in one hand and a basket of French pastries in the other. Wearing a gold cashmere sweater over ripped skinny jeans, she looked like a ray of sunshine.

"Good morning, Gran. I thought you'd like a little something to get you started this morning."

"My goodness, you must have gotten up early." I opened the door wide and she handed me the basket.

After she checked that the door was tightly closed and locked, she followed me inside and sat at my desk. I settled into an easy chair, she handed me the tea, then I took a still-warm, almond encrusted pastry from the basket.

"Any news?" she asked.

"Not yet."

She looked over at my house phone. When I followed her gaze, I saw a red light blinking.

"You have a message. Have you listened to it yet?" she asked.

"No. I wasn't aware I had a message. I didn't even hear the phone ring. Who on earth could it be?"

"It's probably Davies or Johnson. I'll cue it up then put the call on speaker." Susan pushed some buttons and a woman's voice came on the line.

"Please excuse this intrusion, Mrs. Anderson, but I need to speak with you as soon as possible. I learned last night that my friend, Harry North, drowned after falling overboard. I obtained your name and suite number because I believe you may be in danger. Please return my call. I'm in cabin 505. Do not speak to anyone but me. My name is Tess. I'll stay by the phone all morning. Please call me back. It's urgent."

When the phone went dead, neither of us spoke. Then Susan finally said, "What the fuck was that?" She quickly covered her mouth. "I'm sorry. I didn't mean to say the F-word but that was intense!"

I took a sip of tea. It was Earl Gray, the only tea flavor I didn't like. Perhaps it was a sign of the morning to come.

"Gran! How can you be so calm?"

"I'm thinking." I sat my tea on the end table. "Do you suppose she knows who the killer is and wants to warn us? I wonder if she's spoken with the police or guards or whatever they're called and how did she find out my name and cabin number?"

"Strange too that she's exactly one deck above the cabin of the man who died," Susan added.

"I didn't pick up on that. Do you think it means something?"

Susan picked at her croissant. "I have no idea."

"First things first," I said taking a big bite of my flaky pastry. "I'm getting dressed." I heard the phone ring while I was in the bathroom and opened the door a crack.

"Yes, this is Mrs. Anderson's cabin. I'm her granddaughter. What do you want?" I heard Susan say.

"Why would you ask a question like that?" Susan asked after a long pause.

"She burnt the pot, okay? She's had a few memory issues and my father, her son, is very protective so, yes, he relocated her to an assisted living facility two years ago. I don't see what bearing that has on this case," I heard Susan say with venom in her voice.

Proud of her for standing up for me, I quickly finished dressing. When I returned to the lounge, I asked Susan about the call.

"It was Johnson. He was asking questions about you. He'd done his research—I'll give him that. He knew where you lived and asked about your competency. I think they're trying to wiggle out of this being a murder. Maybe they'll say that you aren't capable of remembering what happened. I have a feeling that's what his conversation with me was all about." Susan's face was red, her lips in a grim line. "We can't let them do that! Of course, you're a reliable witness. All they have to do is talk with you to know that you're totally with it!"

I appreciated her intense loyalty and high opinion of my ability to remember. "Do they want to interrogate me again?"

"He didn't say. He just reaffirmed that we are to stay in our cabins."

I sat back in the chair and swigged down the now cold, awful-tasting tea. "Do you think we should set up a meeting with Tess, our mystery woman?"

Susan narrowed her eyes like her father when he's in deep thought. "But what about Johnson and his insinuations?" She also had his tenaciousness.

"We can't do anything about that right now. All we can do is wait and address the issue when we speak with him in person." When Susan didn't respond, I repeated my question. "Should we call the woman?"

Susan paced the short distance from the desk to the door and back. "Yes, I think we should call her back and have her come here. Tell her to come empty-handed. No bag or purse. Then we can be sure she's unarmed."

"Unarmed?" I repeated with some alarm.

"Well, we need to be cautious."

"You're right," I said. "Make the call." Before I came on this cruise, I wanted something exciting to show up so I could step back into my amateur sleuth persona. I guess I should have been careful what I wished for.

Susan punched in the number. "This is Mrs. Anderson's granddaughter returning your call."

"Come to our cabin if you wish to speak to us," Susan said after a long pause. "Knock, then identify yourself. In addition to your name, use the code word JASPER and don't bring anything with you. Come empty-handed. Do you understand?"

"Good," Susan said after a shorter pause. "We'll see you in a few minutes."

I put a pillow behind my back. The chair was too big for me and I was uncomfortable. I missed my recliner. I looked at Susan. "Well, this should be interesting."

Ten minutes later, there was a knock on the door. Susan called out, "Who is it?"

"Tess. Code word JASPER."

Susan went to the door and peered out. "Show me your hands." Apparently, the woman was empty-handed because Susan escorted her into the cabin and offered her the desk chair. Susan sat on my bed. "I'm Susan Petty, and this is Mrs. Anderson, my grandmother," she said.

"Nice to meet you both. I'm terribly sorry for interrupting your holiday. Thank you for allowing me to speak with you."

Probably in her mid-fifties, the woman was what my dad would describe as 'drop dead gorgeous.' She had auburn hair pulled back into a ponytail, blue eye shadow, long false eyelashes, and legs that went on forever covered in expensive, trendy jeans, the kind with extra holes. She wore a tight, low-neck red sweater and long, dangly earrings. She looked like a combination of a Radio City Rockette and a high-class hooker.

"Nice to meet you, Tess," I said. "Do you have a last name?"

"Boudin. Tess Boudin."

"I'm Martha. Now," I leaned forward, "let's get down to business. Why do you want to speak with me?"

Sitting up straight, head held high, the woman had a confident air but her midnight blue eyes betrayed her. She looked frightened and something else. Guilty? Ashamed?

"I believe my husband pushed Harry—ahh, Mr. North—over the railing."

She looked down at her red lacquered, elegant fingers nervously moving in her lap.

"And what brought you to that conclusion?" Susan asked impatiently.

Susan had yet to learn the value of silence.

"Late yesterday afternoon, my husband confronted me about my relationship with Harry, then stormed out of our cabin in a fit of rage," Tess said in a quiet voice.

"So, you think your husband located Mr. North, accused him of having an affair with you, then pushed him overboard?" I asked.

"Yes. He probably didn't intend to push Harry overboard, but he's a much bigger man and…" Tess trailed off.

Susan said. "Describe your husband."

"Six-foot-four inches tall, sixty-two years old, short gray hair, glasses. He played football in college but has since gone to seed."

"Seed?" Susan asked innocently.

Tess responded. "You know—macho guy gone soft. Muscles that have turned to fat. The sad thing is, he still thinks of himself as the star quarterback."

I understood the "going to seed" bit. When I was younger, men frequently complained about their wives going seed. I pulled my attention back to the issue at hand. "How did you meet Harry?"

"My husband, Ezra, retires early, so because I don't want to miss the nightlife on the ship, I go out by myself. I have a drink, listen to music, that sort of thing."

When she paused, Susan prompted, "Go on."

"The first night of the cruise, Harry was also sitting alone at the bar and we struck up a conversation. After we'd both had a few drinks, he asked me to dance. Although it was all very innocent at first, I knew right away that we were attracted to one another. He is, was, handsome, smart, and funny. He said he was divorced and had no one to travel with, so he took the cruise alone. It was some kind of sales reward. He sold pharmaceuticals."

I nodded my understanding. "And then you met him the next night and the next."

Tears gathered in the woman's lovely eyes. "Yes, and now I'm the reason he's dead. Just as sure as if I'd pushed him myself."

Always the practical one, Susan ignored the drama and asked, "Where is your husband now?"

"He's probably at a bar somewhere contemplating what to do next."

"Did he return to your cabin last night?" I asked.

"No. When I heard that a man had gone overboard, I thought right away that something happened between Ezra and Harry. I texted them both and when neither answered, I started asking around."

Susan glared at Tess. "Have you gone to the Chief Mate or the Captain with this information?"

Tess's tears overflowed. "Not yet. I hate the thought of turning my husband into the authorities, you know?"

"No, I don't know," Susan replied.

"Why did you call me?" I asked.

"Because I didn't want something to happen to another

innocent person. I have enough of a guilty conscience already."

"How did you find out that I'm involved in all this?"

"It wasn't difficult to convince someone to tell me what happened," Tess said, crossing her legs.

"You mean because you're beautiful, men give you what you want," Susan spat out.

"You should know," replied Tess with a smirk.

"Now ladies, let's stick to the topic and let the authorities decide how and where Tess got her information." I gave the woman a sympathetic look. "I appreciate your concern about my well-being, but you must speak to Chief Mate Davies about this. He's the lead investigator."

My house phone rang. Tess handed me the receiver.

"Yes, this is Mrs. Anderson."

"Have him identify himself and use the code word JASPER."

"Yes, really! We're taking your advice. Also, there will be another person of interest coming with us. She's here in my cabin."

"Yes, I'm quite sure. Goodbye." I handed the receiver back to Tess.

Two pairs of eyes looked at me intensely. "That was Johnson. He's sending someone to escort us back to the interrogation room."

Susan looked at Tess. "That was good timing. Now you can join us and straighten this whole thing out."

Tess nodded, took a tissue from the box on the desk, blew her nose, and dabbed at her eyes.

As I settled back into my chair, I couldn't help but think, *Harold's never going to believe this!*

Chapter Thirty-Four

BANG, BANG, BANG! Susan yelled, "A knock will do." She walked to the door but didn't open it. "Identify yourself?"

"Johnson sent me. Code word is JASPER."

Tess and I joined Susan. When she opened the door, the man showed us his shield. "Follow me, please."

Once again, we trooped single file down halls, through doors, down more halls, down on the elevator, and through the Staff Only entrance located in the bowels of the ship. Chief Mate Davies was waiting for us. No longer crisp and ramrod straight, he looked rumpled and tired, like he'd been up all night. Pointing at Tess, he tensely asked, "By whose authority is she here?"

"Good morning, Chief Davies," I said in a friendly voice. "This woman called me, came to my cabin by my invitation, and told me a very interesting story I think you'll want to hear."

"Sit down. All of you," he ordered. He looked at Tess. "Well?"

I gave Tess a reassuring look. "Tell the chief your story."

Tess told Davies her name and spilled out the story nearly word for word as she'd told us. I thought she was brave for being willing to expose her tawdry behavior in the interest of solving the case.

"Have you spoken to your husband since your encounter with him yesterday afternoon?"

Tess shook her head. "He hasn't come back to the cabin. I called him last night and this morning, but he didn't answer. By now, I assume his phone's dead."

"Do you have a photo of your husband?"

Tess pulled a phone from her pocket and scrolled through her photos until she found one. She held it up to the chief. He took her phone and showed the photo to Johnson, who was standing near the door. Johnson took a screenshot with his phone.

"Find that man!" Davies commanded. "Bring on as many men as you need. Haul them out of their berths if you have to but locate Ezra Boudin ASAP."

"Yes, sir," said Johnson, backing out.

Davies turned back to Tess. "How the hell did you find out about Mrs. Anderson's involvement?"

"I…"

Susan stood up and interrupted. "How she found out about my grandmother's part in this case has no bearing on us. May we go?"

"No, you may not! Please sit down!"

Tess told him how she talked to maids who talked to other maids and stewards, who led her to others who had the information. "There are few secrets on this ship, sir. I can't implicate those I spoke with because I don't know their names. Besides, it's my husband you need to find before he hurts someone else—or himself. I'll take whatever punishment you wish to dole out later."

Davies glared at Tess then, with some effort, softened his tone. "Please show the photo of your husband to Mrs. Anderson."

Tess handed me her phone.

"Is that the man you saw at the railing?" Davies asked me.

"Yes. That's the man that pushed Harry North over the railing late yesterday afternoon." Davies raised his eyebrows.

"Perhaps I left a pot boiling on the stove, Chief Mate Davies, but I'm perfectly clear about what happened yesterday aboard this ship."

He ignored my statement. "Would you be willing to testify in a court of law about what you saw?"

"If I can do it via Zoom. Once this trip is over, I don't plan on taking another long- distance excursion. And," I gave him a challenging look, "I doubt if a judge will demand that a ninety-year-old woman journey to Bermuda, or even Washington D.C. for that matter, to testify. I'll sign a written statement before I disembark this ship."

Twenty minutes passed with Davies shuffling papers, Tess nervously swinging her crossed leg, and Susan checking her email. I was content to sit still and be quiet.

I jumped when the door slammed open. Johnson and a man in handcuffs entered. "Mr. Ezra Boudin," Johnson announced.

"Sit down, Boudin," Davies demanded. "I'm Chief Mate Davies and we're here to get to the bottom of what happened yesterday afternoon between you and a Mr. Harry North. This is a chance to tell your side of the story."

Johnson pushed Boudin into a chair. Ezra looked across the table and said, "Tess! What the hell are you doing here?"

Davies said, "Never mind, Boudin. Tell us about your encounter with Mr. North." Davies pushed a button on a machine in the middle of the table. "You're being recorded."

Boudin narrowed his eyes. "How do you know I had an encounter with North?"

Davies put his hands flat on the table and glared at his suspect. "We have a witness."

Boudin looked at Susan and me, then back at his wife. "Other than my wife, I've never seen anyone in this room before."

I spoke up. "See? What did I tell you? Invisible."

Davies frowned at me. "Please don't interrupt." He turned his attention back to Boudin and asked, "Where were you yesterday afternoon about five o'clock?"

"I was in my cabin."

"Don't lie, Mr. Boudin." Davies shot him a look. "Now, let's try this again. Where were you late yesterday afternoon?"

Boudin shouted across the table at his wife. "What did you fucking tell them? Isn't it bad enough that you hooked up with a perfect stranger?" His face turned red and a vein pulsed in his neck. "What have you done, Bitch?"

Davies pushed the button on the recorder. "Johnson, please escort the ladies from the room."

By the time we were escorted back into the interrogation room, it was close to noon. Susan and I were 'hangry' and Tess was beside herself with guilt and remorse. Boudin's cuffed hands covered his face.

"Please take your seats ladies," said Johnson.

After we sat down, Davies made an announcement. "Ezra Boudin has signed a confession saying he accidentally pushed Harry North over the ship's rail and to his death. He will be placed in the ship's brig until we reach South Hampton, then he will be turned over to the United States authorities, presumably the FBI." Davies looked at Johnson, "Get him out of here!"

After Johnson escorted Boudin from the room with Tess tearfully trailing behind, Davies passed me a legal pad. "Please write down exactly what you witnessed on the Lido Deck yesterday afternoon. Once you sign the statement, you're free to go."

I took the pad and started writing. I was brief but careful to include the details. I passed the page to Susan to read. After she nodded her approval, I signed the statement and handed the pad back to Davies.

He read the statement then said, "You and your granddaughter are free to go, Mrs. Anderson. Thank you for your cooperation."

I couldn't help myself—I had to have the final word. "I hope you learned something about dealing with senior citizens, Chief Mate Davies." I didn't wait for his reaction. I grabbed Susan's arm and we walked out of the room with our heads held high. We stopped at the nearest restaurant and went through the lunch line. I ordered a cheeseburger and fries, Susan, ever disciplined, picked up a Cobb salad.

"Can I text my friend Harold at the Manor?" I asked my granddaughter after we sat down with our meals.

"Of course. Your rate will be skyhigh so I'd suggest you keep it short."

I pulled out my phone.

Had a BIG adventure. Don't worry, everything is under control now. Don't reply. It's too expensive. See you soon. Miss you (I have yet to meet a sexy Frenchman). (Heart emoji)

Before I put my phone back in my pocket, Susan asked. "Would you mind giving me Harold's number? Just in case?"

"Of course." I handed her my phone and she synced his number to her contacts. "Harold gave me his son's phone number and address just before he was abducted. That's how Missy and I were able to locate him."

"I certainly hope you won't be abducted, Gran. But, given your track record of late, one never knows."

After lunch, I returned to my cabin for a nap and Susan went to work out. The Captain's dinner was tonight and I wanted to be at my best. After sleeping for about an hour, I laid out my purple lace outfit and pumps. Just as I sat down to read the ship's daily newsletter, there was a knock at the door. I called out and when no one answered, I walked to the door and peered out. There was a large envelope in the message cubby. I pulled it out, went back inside, and sat down with the missive in one hand and a bottle of water in the other.

The envelope had my name written in fancy calligraphy across the front. I took a drink of water then I opened the flap and pulled out an ivory card with an embossed seal across the top.

Captain's Reception — Britannia Restaurant

You are cordially invited to join
Captain Dumas at his table

Cocktails and reception - 5:00 p.m.

Dinner - 6:00 p.m.

Thank you for your recent cooperation
with the ship's personnel.

Just as I laid the invitation on the desk, there was another knock on my door. "Coming," I called out.

Susan, still dressed in her workout clothes, stood there with an envelope in her hand. "I've been invited to sit at the captain's table tonight. Did you receive your invitation? I'm sure you're the reason for this gesture."

I was happy to see my granddaughter excited about something. I secretly hoped she'd meet a ship's officer at the reception. Without waiting for me to answer, she swept through the door. "Isn't this exciting?"

"Quite exciting. I'm glad your mother took me shopping."

"Shopping?"

"Yes, your mother took me shopping for the cruise. I bought a fancy dress and shoes for tonight. As you well know, Maria has wonderful fashion sense."

Susan plopped down on my unmade bed. "I'm surprised she called you."

"I don't know why you're surprised. We're still family. She even took me to EB, her favorite store."

Susan got up and walked to the side of the bed where I'd laid out my clothes. "This is lovely, Gran. You'll be the belle of the ball."

"Thanks. Now, don't you think you'd better hop in the shower? We don't want to keep the captain waiting."

Jumping off the bed like a frog, Susan gave me a hug. "Another advantage stemming from our adventure. Right?"

"Right. Now scram."

An hour later Susan showed up in a short, emerald green, off-the-shoulder satin dress. Her dark hair was gathered up on top of her head and her makeup was perfect. She wore long emerald earrings, which were a college graduation gift from her mother, and a matching choker. She was stunning.

I wore my usual makeup with a little extra mascara. My purple ensemble was a bit tight after the burgers and pasta but I still felt good in it. I added my cameo pin from Harold to the collar of my jacket.

"You look wonderful," Susan said.

"Thanks. So do you," I replied.

She hooked her arm with mine. "Come on, Gran, let's go get the party rolling!"

Chapter Thirty-Five

All the stops had been pulled out for the Captain's Dinner. White damask tablecloths, yellow roses in low vases, a string quartet, and servers circling the room with flutes of champagne and hors d'oeuvres on silver trays. The sun had just set, giving the room a rosy glow. I took a dainty puff pastry from the tray. After taking a bite, I discovered it was filled with delectable crab meat. Susan and I toasted each other with our champagne glasses held high. "To us!" we said in unison.

Our one-time nemesis, Chief Mate Davies, was at the front of the receiving line introducing the captain to those in attendance. Davies held out his arm. "Ahh, Mrs. Anderson, so glad you and Miss Petty could join us this evening." He looked to his left. "May I present Captain Andre Dumas."

The tall, straight-backed captain looked debonaire in a formal black jacket with brass buttons and four gold stripes up the sleeve. "The famous pair from New York, I believe. I am quite pleased to meet you," he said in a heavy French accent.

"Bonsoir capitaine ravi de vous rencontrer," I replied.

"Not only are you a hero, but you speak beautiful French as well. Please sit next to me at dinner. I have a feeling we have much in common."

I executed a little bow. "Avec plaisir."

I floated down the reception line as others introduced themselves. French men have always had that effect on me. Perhaps they have a certain effect on most women. I looked over at Susan to gauge my premise. Even though the captain was nearly three times her age, she too had a swoony look about her. Out of the corner of my eye, I saw Dumas motion to a server and whisper something in his ear. He immediately approached Susan and me.

"Madame Anderson, please follow me." He took my elbow and ushered me forward. Susan followed. The captain's table seated ten and was positioned in the center of the room. The server pulled out my chair, waited for me to be seated, pushed the chair in, and did the same for Susan. He unfolded the napkin and placed it in my lap. "May I bring you an aperitif?" When I didn't respond right away, he suggested, "A pastis perhaps?"

"A pastis is perfect. Please bring one for my granddaughter as well."

He bowed. "At your service, madame."

The server glided away, and Susan looked at me with raised eyebrows. "What was all that?"

"All what?"

She cocked her head to the side. "You know. Speaking French to the captain, the aperitif. What is a pastis anyway?"

"A pastis is an aniseed-flavored aperitif. An aperitif is a liquor taken before dinner to stimulate the appetite."

"And you know this how?"

"I lived in Paris for a year when I was younger—much younger—then I returned fifteen years ago. As a result, I love all things French."

"Including French men. That's a statement, not a question," she said with a grin.

"Was I that obvious?"

Susan rolled her eyes. "You practically swooned. You absolutely charmed him with your French and cute little bow."

"You looked a bit swoony yourself, my dear," I replied.

Our drinks arrived on a silver tray placed on a rolling cart. A small glass pitcher containing a yellow liquid, a pitcher of water, and a crystal bowl of ice sat on the tray. Indicating I was to tell him when to stop, the server slowly poured the pastis into a heavy-bottomed, flared glass. When I held up my index finger, he added two ice cubes then topped off the glass with water. He repeated the process for Susan and rolled the cart away.

Susan took a sip.

"What do you think?" I asked.

"Tastes a bit like a black jellybean," she whispered. "But the presentation was lovely."

"I guess it pays to sit at the captain's table," I replied.

Just as I said this, the captain took his seat beside me. He smelled of musk and something woodsy. He pointed to my drink. "A woman of good taste, I see." Our server was instantly at his elbow. After he ordered his own aperitif, he picked up the menu card. I noticed he wasn't wearing a wedding ring.

I perused the options on my own card, then asked, "What do you suggest?" Without hesitation, he began. "I'd suggest soufflé au comté for your starter, the une entrée." When I nodded, he continued. "For un plat de résistance, or main course, you must have pot-au-feu, which as you probably know, is literally 'pot on the fire' in English. It's a French beef stew which is typically served in winter. It's the most celebrated dish in France."

I looked out the window. After the lovely sunset, I was surprised to see rain pelting the panes. Waves were crashing and the boat was swaying more than usual. I hoped the Capitan had a competent person at the helm. "Pot-au-feu sounds perfect for this weather." I indicated the window, but he only smiled. Men tend to enjoy being in control. It's taken me years to learn when, where, and with whom to be accommodating. This was definitely the right time and place to give the reins to a man who knew what he was doing.

"Now for the un plateau de formage or cheese course. Our table will be offered a platter featuring at least three kinds of cheese, each representing a different type of milk—cow, goat, and sheep. Most likely there will be a soft cheese such as Brie, a Roquefort, and a heat-pressed cheese like Beaufort. They will be placed around the platter from mildest to strongest. That way, there's something for everyone. The cheese course will come with a simple salad. Does this please you?"

"Immensely. I do recall having salad near the end of the meal when I was in France. So different than the order in which we Americans eat our greens."

The waiter appeared and Captain Dumas placed the order for our starters and main courses. He also ordered wine. When the waiter moved on to the next guest, Dumas turned his attention back to me. "And now un dessert. What is your pleasure, Mrs. Anderson?"

"Please call me Martha."

"Ah, Martha. The name fits you like a glove." He looked back at the menu. Up close, I could see that Dumas was older than I had first thought. He was probably in his mid to late sixties and close to retirement. I was shocked when I realized that he was close to my son's age. Dumas had a fair complexion, steel-gray eyes that matched his thick hair, and full lips. Deep creases were carved into the corners near each eye, which suggested that he'd laughed more than he'd scowled. The captain's deep voice pulled me back from my thoughts. "I'm sorry. Please repeat the choices," I said.

"Will you have tarte tatin, crème brûlée, tarte au citron, or mousse au cholocat?

"The mousse. One can't go wrong with chocolate. Do you agree, Captain?"

"Please call me Andre."

When the wine arrived, the sommelier poured a small amount into a goblet for the captain to appraise. He swirled, sniffed, and took a sip. When he nodded his approval, my glass was filled, then Susan's, then the captain's.

"I would agree with you about the cholocat or chocolate as you would say in English. We will order this when we order un café and un digestif. Yes?"

I smiled. I'd heard enough about food. I knew how much the French loved talking about all things gastric, but

I was interested in knowing about the man. "Tell me how you decided to take on a life at sea, Andre," I asked as I sipped the heavenly French red wine.

Dumas unspooled his story starting from his boyhood love of sailing miniature boats in the local pond growing up in Grasse, France, a town located in the Provence-Alpes-Côte d'Azur region between the Mediterranean Sea and the French Alps. He spoke of Grasse being the perfume capital of the world for the last three centuries. He was a second-generation seaman who had followed in his father's footsteps.

Andre's face grew somber when he told me why he'd never married. "Watching my mother pine away for her husband was influential in my decision to not marry," he explained. "I didn't think it fair to be away from a family for weeks, if not months at a time so I chose not to have one. Now that I'm about to retire, I'm reconsidering the wisdom of my decision."

I looked at Andre sympathetically. "It's not easy living alone, but there are some advantages."

"So, you're a widow?"

"Yes. I've been divorced once and widowed twice. Quite French of me to have had three husbands, don't you think?" I regretted saying this as soon as it was out of my mouth. I blamed my faux pas on the alcohol. When a grin spread across Andre's face, I backtracked. "I didn't mean to be disrespectful of the French. I only meant that I'm experienced in relationships. Actually, I love all things French."

"And just what are these 'all things French' you love? Perhaps there's a Frenchman at your assisted living facility?"

I frowned. "How do you know where I live?"

"As the captain of this ship, it's my job to know about my passengers—especially those who witness murders."

That statement sobered me up. I wondered what else he knew about me.

As we chatted, I became concerned about Susan until I saw her enthusiastically speaking with her tablemate—a handsome officer close to her age.

By the time a rancio sec, the French equivalent to sherry, arrived, I was exhausted, my dress was bursting at the seams, and my head was filled to the brim with beautiful memories. I realized Andre was speaking to me about the final aperitif. Of course, the conversation had returned to food.

"Rancio sec is brewed in Roussillon, a stone's throw from Aix-en-Provence, in the South of France near my childhood home. It's a one-of-a- kind French wine you've probably never heard of."

I smiled at the handsome, charming Frenchman I had somehow attracted into my life for a few hours. "A one-of-a-kind wine to top off a one-of-a-kind evening with a one-of-a-kind gentleman. Merci capitaine."

"Tout le plaisir est pour moi, Mme. Anderson."

Chapter Thirty-Six

At breakfast the next morning, I asked Susan about the gentleman sitting next to her at the Captain's Dinner.

"He's one of the ship's doctors, based out of New York, with a house on Long Island. He's single."

"And…." I prompted. Susan was usually so thorough in her explanations.

"And, what?"

I gave her a look. "You seemed to be hitting it off. Will you see him when he returns to New York? Were there sparks? Remember—what's said on the cruise, stays on the cruise."

"Oh, Gran, now I know where Dad gets his interrogation skills." Susan fiddled with her spoon, finally taking a bite of yogurt. "He said he'll call me but I'm not holding my breath—shipboard romances and all that. I'd love to see him again, and yes, there were sparks."

"All righty then. Promise you'll keep me posted."

Susan nodded. I could tell she was trying not to get her hopes up, but I felt optimistic. Why wouldn't he call my beautiful, smart, moderately spoiled granddaughter?

The restaurant was busy with people stuffing themselves one last time before tomorrow's departure. I had a food and alcohol hangover so I only ate a piece of toast and a dish of mixed fruit. On our way back to our cabins, Susan asked about the captain.

"He's your father's age," was my only reply. I was a little disappointed when she didn't ask for details. Perhaps her head was too far in the clouds.

For our final dinner, Susan and I returned to the Italian restaurant. She'd been a strong supporter through my ordeal, and I wanted to treat her to another special dinner. "I'm sorry your vacation was disrupted because of me," I said to Susan as I dipped my warm bread into the fragrant olive oil.

She smiled. "And you were worried that I'd find traveling with you boring. I have a feeling that being around you is never boring. Besides, we had a great adventure."

"I see you've learned how to reframe a negative experience. I wonder if you can do the same regarding your family?"

Susan tilted her head to one side as if she was cataloging my comment for later consideration, then forked a big piece of lasagna into her mouth. After our meal, I took Susan's arm and led her in the opposite direction of our cabins. "I have a surprise for you. When it's not being used as a music venue, the 3D cinema, Illuminations, is a planetarium, and I have tickets for tonight's show."

When we arrived, we found comfortable seats in the large theater. Soon, the planetarium dome was sending us on an epic voyage across the solar system. The "Tour of the Night Sky" program showed scenes of stars, planets, and other celestial objects, making them appear and move realistically to simulate motion. We learned that the ship had a partnership with the Royal Astronomical Society.

After the show, we returned to our cabins, completed our last minute packing then parked our suitcases in the hall outside our doors to be picked up during the night in preparation for our morning departure. I'd had an amazing trip, but I was ready to return to my apartment, my friends, and my simple routine.

The next morning, we claimed our luggage then hailed a porter who loaded it onto a cart and proceeded us down the gangplank. There were people with cameras waiting at the bottom, and I assumed there was a famous person on board they wanted to interview and photograph. I was taken aback when a woman with a microphone and a cameraman trailing behind her approached me.

"Mrs. Anderson?"

"Yes."

"We understand you witnessed a man being thrown overboard to his death. Is that true?" asked the woman as she pointed the microphone at my mouth.

Susan intervened. "Mrs. Anderson can't comment on an open investigation."

"And you are…?"

"I'm Mrs. Anderson's granddaughter. Please allow us to pass. We have a plane to catch."

The reporter withdrew but the cameraman followed us as we proceeded toward the taxi stand.

The flight home was uneventful. I read, ate the dinner they provided, and slept. Susan pounded away on her laptop's keyboard. She was preparing to reenter the worka-day world. Poor thing.

Once we were through immigration, we entered a large room filled with people waiting for the arrivals. Some held flowers, others held signs saying welcome home or a person's name.

I heard someone yell, "That's them!" and a group of people pushed their way through the crowd toward us.

"Mrs. Anderson, may I…."

"Mrs. Anderson, I'm from the…."

"Mrs. Anderson, I'll just be a moment…"

I let Susan handle them. I'd heard celebrities talk about the annoying, if not dangerous, crush of paparazzi clam-oring around them, but I had no idea what it was really like—until now. It certainly wasn't pleasant.

"Please, just one question," pleaded a young woman with untidy hair wearing a wrinkled jean jacket with a hole in the elbow. I couldn't help but take pity on her. She was probably a fledgling reporter who had been given an assign-ment that could make or break her career. She looked des-perate, so I stopped in front of her. "Just one question."

Susan glared at both of us.

The reporter stepped closer, her phone ready to record. "What was it like to witness a murder knowing you were marooned on a ship with the murderer?"

With a "killer" question like that, the young lady might have a future after all. I chuckled to myself at my clever thought. "It was frightening, of course. However, the ship's authorities were very professional and handled the situa-tion with expediency. Captain Andre Dumas keeps a tight ship." I could see the reporter winding up for a follow-up question. "Now, if you'll excuse me, I'd like to return to my residence and have a rest. It's been an eventful journey."

Susan grabbed the handle of my suitcase and whisked me away. Perhaps whisked is an exaggeration but I managed to totter along behind her, keeping the pace for fear I'd get lost in the crowd. Even Harold would have difficulty finding me in a place like that.

We'd been in flight for over eight hours and in transit for more than fourteen. When Susan suggested I stay at her apartment overnight, I nearly took her up on the offer but decided to push toward home. She and I took a taxi to the train station. From there, I assured her that I could continue on my own. "I'll arrange for Ted to pick me up at the station and Harold to meet me in front of the Manor. They'll handle my luggage."

When Susan agreed, we said our goodbyes.

"Thank you for taking me on this grand adventure, Susan. I wouldn't have missed it for the world."

"Thanks for coming with me, Gran. You rest up. I'll come to see you soon."

We hugged, and I was on my way.

I texted Ted from the train and he texted back.

Have the porter put your luggage on the platform. I'll be waiting and take it to my car. You can count on me, Mrs. A.

Next, I texted Harold but he didn't respond. After a few minutes I called, but all I got was voicemail.

As arranged, Ted, Uber Driver Extraordinaire, was waiting for me on the platform when I stepped off the train. "You look done in, Mrs. A. I'll get you home as soon as possible," he said, pulling my luggage topped with my carry-on with one hand and guiding me to his car with the other. When he heard me leaving another message for Harold to meet me at the entrance, Ted intervened. "Don't worry. I'll take your luggage to your apartment if you can't reach your friend."

"Thank you. I'd appreciate that very much."

It was nearly four o'clock in the afternoon when I finally closed the door to my apartment. I went straight to my bedroom, took off my clothes, put on my nightie, and fell into an exhausted sleep. I awoke at eight to go to the bathroom, and then I went back to sleep. Unfortunately, at four in the morning my eyes popped open, and I was famished. I couldn't remember when I'd last eaten. I got up and rummaged around in my cupboards. All I found was a half jar of peanuts, four mini sodas, and a Kind Breakfast Bar. I ate the peanuts and the bar, then chased them down with a Dr. Pepper. I showered, dressed, and emptied my suitcase. By then, it was time to go to breakfast. Before heading to the dining room, I texted Harold again, but there was still no answer. By now, I was getting worried. He was always up by eight o'clock so when I left my apartment, I went straight to his.

I knocked and when there was no answer, I tried the doorknob and found it locked. With growing alarm, I walked to Judy's office. Early as always, only now at the opposite end of the day, Judy was sitting at her desk working at her computer. She was young to have such a responsible position and I was proud of her. She looked up when I knocked on her door.

"Come in!" She got up from her desk, came around, and gave me a hug. "Welcome home. How was your trip?"

"Very eventful."

"Tell me."

"Later. I'm here on a mission. Have you seen Harold? He's not answering his phone or his door."

Judy ushered me to the chair that faced her desk. When I sat down, she said, "He's in the hospital recuperating."

I gasped. "Recuperating? From what?"

"He had a very serious heart episode just after you left. The next day, his cardiologist examined him and told him he wouldn't survive the next one without a pacemaker. He finally relented and had the surgery two days ago. The doctor kept him in the hospital an extra day due to his age. He's scheduled to return either to his apartment or skilled care later today. The hospital is supposed to call me this morning."

I was flabbergasted. Harold had talked about the possibility of a pacemaker, but he'd also spoken about his unwillingness to go through the procedure at his age. Apparently, he'd decided there was still a reason to live. "Is he going to be all right?"

Judy gave me a kind smile. I was glad to be talking with her instead of Duly. "I believe so. The fact he may be returning to his apartment is a good sign."

"I wonder why he hasn't returned my texts or calls?"

"He's probably busy with rehab or perhaps he forgot his charger. Either way, you should be able to see him soon."

I got up to leave. My stomach was rumbling. "Thanks, Judy. If it's not against the rules, will you text me when he returns from the hospital?"

"Of course. By the way, I miss our evening get-togethers. I'll try to stop by after my shift so you can talk about your trip."

Chapter Thirty-Seven

While I was eating my Grape-Nuts, Madge stopped by my table with the *New York Times* under her arm. She was wearing gray sweats and didn't look like herself at all. Even her usual neat bun was in disarray. "Welcome back. We missed you," Madge said as she sat down opposite me at the table. She opened the paper, turned to the *Lifestyle* section, thumbed through a few pages, folded the paper, then set it down in front of me. "You made the papers again."

"I what?"

She thumped her knuckles on the article. "Read."

My picture was there and I looked old. The young reporter I spoke to in the immigration hall had quoted me correctly. She filled in the rest of the story from what, I assumed, was reported by the cruise line.

"Trouble follows you wherever you go—even to the middle of an ocean," Madge observed.

I handed the paper back to her and took a sip of my tepid tea. "I was napping on the deck when two guys starting fighting."

Madge stood, picked up her paper, and turned to leave. "You can tell us the whole story at dinner. Get some rest,

Martha. You look like hell." With that encouraging remark, she was gone.

I returned to my apartment and looked in the mirror. There were dark circles under my eyes and my face was puffy. Assuming I was dehydrated, I went to the sink, filled a glass with water, sat down in my recliner, and closed my eyes thinking that it was a good thing I'd declared the cruise to be my last trip. I must have dozed off because I was momentarily confused about where I was when my phone buzzed. I finally answered it. "Hello."

"This is Judy. Your phone nearly went to voicemail. Are you okay?"

"I'm fine. Just taking a nap in my chair. Have you heard from the hospital?"

"I have, and it's good news. Harold's granddaughter is picking him up from the hospital this afternoon. She'll bring him to his apartment and get him settled in. The doctor wanted him to go to skilled care but he insisted on the apartment. His granddaughter told me that she assured the doctor that he'd be well cared for here."

I was relieved. Perhaps I was more worried about Harold than I'd acknowledged. "That's great news and a credit to you, Judy."

"Thanks, Martha. I have a feeling your presence here might also be a motivating factor. I know you don't like walking to skilled care on your own."

"You're right, I don't," I said. "I got lost once and Harold had to come find me." I wasn't afraid to admit this to Judy because I knew she wouldn't use it against me.

"I understand. When Harold's back, I'll text you a thumbs-up. See you later." She hung up and I set my phone back on the end table. I guzzled down my water then I went to the sink and refilled my glass. The inside of an airplane was like a desert, and my body was suffering the consequences.

After my rehydration, I felt better so I texted Missy.

I'm back. Want to go to yoga? I need to stretch and it will be good to see you.

Two minutes passed.

Absolutely! I'll come by after lunch. Missed you. (Heart emoji)

On our way to the exercise studio, I gave Missy a brief account of my trip—lovely time with my granddaughter, witnessed a murder, sat next to the captain at dinner.

"Madge showed me the *NY Times* at breakfast. Unfortunately, I made the *Lifestyle* section," I said.

"Oh dear! Will your son be furious again?" Missy rarely forgets anything. However, she didn't look well. She had lost weight and was walking even slower than I was. I wondered what was happening with her health, but I decided to ask her later.

After our chair yoga class, in which Missy barely participated, I had a thumbs-up text from Judy. I said goodbye to Missy then I went to my apartment to change out of my workout clothes and into my skinny jeans and an aqua sweater. When I checked my face in the mirror, I still looked haggard, but my cheeks had pinked up and my energy had returned thanks to exercise and hydration.

Without texting first, I walked to Harold's apartment and knocked quietly on the door. A woman opened it. "You must be Martha," she said when she saw me. When

I nodded, she continued, "I'm Harold's granddaughter, Sarah. I've heard so much about you. Please come in."

Harold was in his recliner, looking pale and older than I'd remembered. "Hello, Martha."

"Please have a seat," Sarah said. "Can I get you something to drink?"

"Water, please," I said.

When Sarah disappeared into the mini kitchen, I walked over and gave Harold a kiss before sitting on his comfy couch. "How are you doing?" I asked him.

"I survived. I'm feeling better now that you're here," he gave me a weak smile.

Sarah put my water on a nearby table then turned to Harold. "Is there anything else you need before I leave, Grandpa?"

"I'm all settled. Thanks for everything, Sweetie."

She gave her granddad a kiss on the cheek, then picked up her coat and purse. "So nice to meet you, Martha. I'm sure you two have a lot to catch up on." She turned back to Harold. "I'll come by tomorrow and check on you. Text me if you need anything before then."

"I will," Harold said, holding up his phone.

Sarah closed the door. Harold and I were silent for a beat as each of us waited for the other one to speak. I finally jumped in. "So, you did it. You got a pacemaker. I'm glad you chose life, Harold." I wasn't going to beat around the bush.

"Yep."

"That's it? Just yep. No long story about your medical adventure?"

"Nope."

I wondered if he was tired, in pain, or simply feeling non-communicative. I was brought back when I heard him speak again. "What was that?" I asked.

"How was your trip? Your text came through just before my procedure. I was worried, given your penchant for getting into trouble. Also, I think I saw a video of you on the BBC while I was channel surfing in the hospital. Was it you?"

Poor Harold. If it weren't for me, maybe he could have waited another year before he had to get a pacemaker. "The trip was good, I had a lovely time with Susan, the food was fabulous, and, yes, that might have been me on the BBC if I was chasing after my granddaughter pulling our suitcases." Still feeling like a camel, I drank half of my water.

"Good grief, Martha."

Harold sounded exasperated, so I made an effort to explain. "I was minding my own business and keeping my head down just like you asked me to do." I paused long enough to be sure he'd gotten this.

"Go on," he said.

"In fact, I was napping in a lounge chair on the Lido Deck when two men started arguing. Then, right in front of my eyes, one threw the other over the rail and into the ocean. I reported the incident and I found out later that the man thrown overboard had drowned."

I looked over at Harold who was leaning forward. When he didn't say anything, I continued. "The interrogation reminded me of our time with Detective Warren. Anyway, the next day they found the perpetrator and put him in the brig. After I wrote out my witness statement, Susan and I resumed our holiday. There are a few more details but that's the gist of what happened."

Harold was shaking his head. "Details or not, that's quite a story! You're like a magnet for trouble."

"Well, I'm demagnetizing and laying low. I've had enough excitement to last me the rest of my life."

"Really?" Harold looked doubtful.

"Really. Now tell me how you're feeling. You look done in."

"That bad, huh?"

"You're still a handsome devil but a tired one." I gave him a big smile and he finally smiled back.

"And you're still as cute as a button, but I'm betting you could use some rest, too."

I finished my water and took my glass to the alcove. When I returned, I kissed Harold goodbye. "You're right. Now, you get a nap and I'll come by after dinner to say good night."

Chapter Thirty-Eight

At dinner, the girls filled me in on all the gossip. Distracted by everyone's appearance, I barely heard the verbal barrage. Madge didn't look much better than she had at breakfast, although she had changed into her baggy slacks and oversized sweater. Her eyes were bloodshot and her complexion was pasty.

Molly seemed distracted, constantly looking at someone sitting across the room. At least she'd gotten fitted for hearing aids and was able to keep up with the conversation. She looked even more charming than usual, with her hair in a new updo.

Missy was quiet, picked at her food, and had no color in her cheeks. Her sparkle was missing, her eyes were dull, and I wondered how my friend could have changed so much in a little more than a week.

As soon as our table was cleared, Molly traipsed across the room in her dangerously high-heeled shoes. She obviously wasn't joining us for music. "What's up with Molly?" I asked Missy.

She took my arm as we slowly walked to the social room. "While you were gone, she reeled in a man. He's a new resident who's young-ish, attractive, and sexy. I don't know about the sexy part, but that's how Molly described him."

"And Madge? She doesn't look herself," I said.

Missy shook her head and pulled me over to the side. "I think she's drinking. A lot. Once or twice, I could swear she was drunk at dinner. I'm worried about her," Missy whispered.

"Has anyone asked her about it?"

Missy started walking again. "No. You know how she is—doesn't want anyone in her business."

Madge had already found a seat by herself, so Missy and I sat at the opposite end of the room. "And what about you? How's your health?"

Missy's intense blue eyes looked into mine. "I'm not well. I hate to admit it, but I can't lie. You know me too well. My diabetes has brought on cardiovascular disease, and the doctor wants me to move to skilled care so I can receive daily oxygen and they can keep a closer eye on my insulin levels. So far I've resisted, but I'm afraid it won't be long before I'm ineligible to live in assisted. When I can't check off enough boxes on the daily living chart, they'll insist I move."

I was completely taken aback. First Harold and his pacemaker, Missy probably moving to skilled care, and Madge drinking too much. At least Molly was on the upswing.

I took Missy's hand. "I'm so sorry to hear about your health. It seems like one day we're acting like college girls," I whispered in her ear, "smoking marijuana," I smiled, "and the next you're fearing a move."

She squeezed my hand. "In the blink of an eye."

Her statement gave me pause and by the time music ended, I was completely wrung out. I knew my exhaustion was a repercussion from my trip and all the bad news, however, I'd promised Harold I'd stop by and I wasn't going to let him down. On my way to his apartment, I made a wrong turn and had to backtrack.

When I walked in, Harold said, "I thought you weren't coming."

"Well, I'm here. Perhaps a little down at the heels but I promised to check on you," I said as I eased myself onto his couch.

"What kept you?"

"I missed a turn and had to backtrack so it took me a while to get here. That and I had some bad news from Missy," I confessed with a sigh.

"What?" His concerned expression probably matched my own, although his was possibly more about my getting turned around than it was about my friends.

I reiterated what Missy and I had discussed. "I can't believe so much happened in just a week."

"In the blink of an eye," said Harold. He had his maroon jumpsuit on and his hair was neatly combed. He smelled like Old Spice.

"That's exactly what Missy said." I put my head back and briefly closed my eyes. "We're getting up there," I added.

Harold drank some water. Perhaps wine was off his menu for now. "I hate to break it to you, but we're already there."

I ignored his comment and got up from the couch. "Well, I for one am planning on sticking around a bit longer, so I better get my beauty sleep." I walked over and gave Harold a quick kiss. "You too, Colonel. Go get some rest."

Just as I got to the door, Harold asked, "Was there a Frenchman?"

"I'll tell you all about it tomorrow. Good night and sweet dreams."

The next day, I knocked on Madge's apartment door. I didn't text first because I wanted my visit to be a surprise. As soon as she appeared, I could tell she was inebriated. "Martha," she said with a little slur, "what brings you here? No bad news, I hope."

"May I come in?"

"Of course. Have a seat," she removed newspapers from the couch, then walked unsteadily to the mini kitchen to stuff them in the trash receptacle.

I was completely taken aback by the clutter. Besides the just-removed newspapers, there were used glasses on the table tops and a few articles of clothing tossed over a chair. "No bad news," I said taking a seat. "I just want to get caught up on how you're doing. I'm sensing that something's off."

Madge slumped into a chair. "It's not good, and since you're my one true friend, I'll tell you."

She paused so long I finally asked, "Tell me what?"

"I'm afraid I've exchanged my addiction to sweets for an addiction to alcohol. Does that shock you?"

She looked so distraught and vulnerable that I was at a loss for words. I finally asked, "Have you been down this road before?"

"Yes. Drinking too much was one reason I left the bank. I could no longer keep up with my duties. Thankfully, my drinking coincided with my retirement plan, so I left with my dignity intact. I thought coming here would give me a new outlook and solve my problem. It did for a while. Of course, I was using sugar as a crutch, but then I started drinking again a few weeks before you left. My usual nightly vodka multiplied and now I'm back in the ditch."

I appreciated Madge's honesty. It seemed rare for someone to admit they had a problem of this magnitude. "Is there anything I can do to help you?"

Madge shook her head. "I've been speaking with my younger brother in Canada. He wants to bring me back there so I can get treatment under his supervision. He's a doctor."

I leaned back into the couch cushions which weren't nearly as comfortable as Harold's. In fact, this couch was downright lumpy. The whole room was depressing with the curtains drawn and no color to speak of. There were beige walls, brown furniture, and just one picture—some kind of colorless abstract. "How do you feel about returning to Canada?"

"I think he's right. I came here on a whim. My brother advised against it, but I was stubborn and determined to start over. I don't regret coming but it's time I return to my homeland and what's left of my family." Madge took a drink of whatever was in her glass. She was back in her sweats, her hair uncombed.

"I'll certainly miss you," was all I could think of to say.

"We had some good times, didn't we, Martha?"

"We did."

Two nights later after enjoying evening music, I started walking back to my apartment and got turned around—again. It seemed to happen mostly in the evenings when I was tired. Perhaps I was going to be the next one to go down the road of poor health and to a life of dependency. I went to bed with a heavy heart for myself and my friends.

Chapter Thirty-Nine

A week later, I was on my way to work out when I got a text from Susan.

Do you have a minute to talk?

Of course. Just let me get to where I'm going so I can sit down.

Ok, call me when you're there. (Smile emoji)

I hurried along the hall then took the elevator down to the workout room on the first floor. Thankfully, no one was there and I made no wrong turns. I sat on the stationary bike seat and called Susan.

"Guess what, Gran?" she said with so much excitement in her voice I wasn't sure it was my granddaughter.

"What? I hope it's good news. I could use some."

"It is good news! Michael actually called me, and we're going out this weekend."

"Remind me who Michael is." She acted like I should know this guy, but I had no idea who he was.

"The ship's doctor. Remember?"

"I remember what you'd said about the ship's doctor but I'd forgotten his name."

"Well, I never in a million years thought he'd actually call, but he did. His ship docked in New York last night and he called me right away. We're going to dinner on Saturday. Isn't that wonderful?"

I shifted on the bike seat. It wasn't the most comfortable place to sit for an extended conversation but I was delighted with Susan's good news. "Yes, that's fantastic. Have you told your parents about him?"

"Not yet. I want to see how the date goes before I tell them anything. But I'd promised you I would follow up so here I am, following up."

She sounded like a teenager. "Thank you for not forgetting your promise. Will you let me know how the date goes?"

"Of course, but let's pretend we're still on the cruise and keep our motto of what's said on the ship stays on the ship. Okay?"

"You got it. I'll look forward to your call on Sunday."

"Bye, Gran. Wish me luck."

"You don't need luck, Susan. You just need to be yourself. Bye now."

The conversation with my granddaughter perked me up enough to do three miles on the bike and three weight machines. And best of all, I found my way back to my apartment without a hitch.

As promised, Susan called me on Sunday evening just as I was getting into my soft clothes. "I think I'm in love, Gran. Is that even possible after just one real date?"

I had to smile at the exuberance of youth. "Anything's possible, but don't get ahead of yourself." When she didn't respond right away, I added, "So, I'm guessing the date went well?"

"It was perfect. He's perfect. Just think, if you hadn't agreed to go with me on that cruise, none of this would have happened. I have you to thank."

I thought it best to ask a practical question. "How long will he be stateside?"

"One more week, then he leaves for two. Actually, because I'm so busy at work, his schedule works out for me."

"Where did you go for dinner?"

"A French restaurant. I think the captain's French-ness has worn off on him. The food wasn't as sublime as it was that night on the ship, but the evening was wonderful. He's such a gentleman and so interesting. He's been all over the world. Also, he makes me laugh. You always said that's a good thing. Right, Gran?"

"Yes, it's a good thing. Do you have interests in common?"

"All kinds of things—music, movies, healthy living, the desire for a family in the future."

"My goodness, he does sound ideal."

Susan's voice became serious. "But I'm taking your advice and going slow. I'm not sleeping with him until at least the third date."

That comment was beyond my purview so I let it go. "Sounds like you have a plan. Keep me posted and don't forget that you promised to visit me."

"I'll text you a date next week."

"Great."

"Bye. Love you."

"Love you too."

I sat on my recliner, book in hand, trying to sort it all out. Susan is in love with the ship's doctor and she's waiting until the third date before sleeping with him. I hoped she wasn't going to get her heart broken.

If one bit of good news on top of multiple bad news wasn't enough, I had a call from Barbara the following week. She started out with the same question as Susan.

"Guess what, Gran?"

"What? Are you and Bobbie all right?"

"Yes! We couldn't be better." She paused and I heard Bobbie come to the phone. They must have been on speaker. "We're expecting!" they said in chorus then Barbara came back on. "We wanted you to be one of the first to know."

"That's wonderful news! Congratulations. Do you know if it's a boy or a girl?"

"Not yet. We find out in about six more weeks. I got pregnant on the first try—right after we came to see you."

I heard Bobbie calling in the background.

"I gotta go," Barbara said. "We're off to do some shopping for the nursery. I just wanted to give you the good news."

"Thanks for thinking of me."

"We love you."

"Love you both, too."

I felt like I was on a tilt-a-whirl where one side goes up and the other side goes down—over and over.

Before I knew it, Christmas was just around the corner and I had a flurry of texts from various family members assuring me they were coming for a visit. On top of that, I received a Christmas letter from Steve.

After wishing me Merry Christmas, he wrote that he was getting out of prison early, but he wasn't sure of the exact date yet. He wrote that he'd be reporting to a parole officer for a year, he'd lined up a job as a mechanic, and a reentry program had put him on a list for an apartment.

Earlier, Harold found out that the best thing we could do for Steve was to fund his spending account at the prison, so that's what we'd been doing. He thanked us for the money that allowed him to buy magazines, snacks, stamps, etc. Harold and I were both proud of the progress he'd made. I wondered if we'd see him when he got out.

Chapter Forty

My errant daughter, Ruth, visited the week before Christmas and stayed in one of the Manor's apartments for two nights. Although she's the middle child, Ruth doesn't live up to her birth order hype. Instead of being the family mediator, she's positioned herself as the "distant one." Fifty-nine and single, she's spent her life traveling for her work as an international business consultant. Since I rarely saw her, it was a treat to have her visit.

Neither tall like her brother nor short like her sister, Ruth was average height and weight. However, that was the only average thing about her. She was a Rhodes Scholar and a medal-winning gymnast in college. During most of her adult life, she'd worked in exotic places like Thailand, China, and Myanmar. Her home base was Chicago so she had a good relationship with her niece, Barbara, spending time with her and Bobbie when she was home. Her condo on the Magnificent Mile allowed her the opportunity to enjoy all the city had to offer.

Ruth arrived late in the evening, so my first opportunity to see her was early the next morning. When she walked in at nine o'clock, I was overcome with emotion at seeing her after more than a year.

She drew me into a hug. "Oh Mom, it's so good to see you!"

Teary, I simply nodded against her shoulder. Although still looking "put together," I was surprised by how much she'd aged. Her brown hair was threaded with gray, she had crow's feet at the corners of her eyes, and a furrowed brow. Her smile, however, was warm and her embrace was firm.

She stepped back, still holding both of my hands. "You look wonderful! You haven't aged a bit. How are you?"

"Fit as a fiddle as your grandpa would say," I replied. "My memory isn't as good as it once was but then, it was never very good. My new hip is working like it should and I'm still enjoying life."

"So I hear." Ruth gave me a look that told me she'd been talking with her sibs and, possibly, her niece.

"Let's go to breakfast," I said, whisking her out the door.

We were both dressed in jeans—her's "flared," mine were still skinny. She wore a plain black sweater accented with a lovely silk scarf, on which I remarked. She touched her scarf as if to remind herself what she was wearing. "It's from India. I brought one for you along with a few other things."

We loaded our breakfast trays and looked around for a private table. After we were seated, I asked, "Tell me what's new in your life. It's been so long since we've had a chat." Just as Ruth was about to speak, Harold stopped by to say good morning. "This is my daughter, Ruth," I said by way of introduction. I looked at Ruth wondering how to introduce Harold. "And this is my dear friend, Harold."

Ruth raised her eyebrows and then smiled. "Nice to meet you. Would you like to join us?"

"Oh no. I wouldn't want to interrupt. I know what a rare opportunity it is for the two of you to be together," Harold said then stepped away. "See you ladies later."

Ruth turned back to me. "So, just how dear?"

"You're as bad as Barbara, always thinking everything is about romance," I said in response to her question.

"Well, is it a romance?"

I took a sip of my tea. "Yes, I suppose you could call it that. We look out for each other, smooch occasionally, and enjoy each other's company. Would you call that a romance?"

"Yes, definitely." She gave me a warm smile. "I envy you, Mom. I'd like to get off this roller coaster I'm on and find someone to share my life with. I plan to retire in another five years but then what? I have no idea how to do life without work since it consumes about ninety percent of my time."

Although Ruth was smart and successful and lived the life many dreamed of, I felt sad for her. After all, what was life without relationships? Romantic or not, male or female, I couldn't imagine a life without good friends. "Will you stay in Chicago after you retire?" I asked.

"I plan to. My few friends live there and I enjoy spending time with Barbara and Bobbie. Aren't they just adorable?"

I smiled at her description and bit my tongue so I wouldn't reveal their secret about being pregnant. "They are. I enjoyed their visit when they were here for my birthday."

"Besides Harold, have you made other friends here?" She looked around the dining room. "From what I've heard, most people don't like living in a continuing care facility but you, on the other hand, seem content." Ruth looked at me intently to gauge if this was true or not. Perhaps she felt guilty about leaving my living arrangements up to her brother.

Molly was the only friend I saw at the moment and she was whispering something into her boyfriend's ear. "I started out with five good friends; that number has dwindled to three and I'm about to lose those. Molly," I pointed in her direction, "has a lover or boyfriend or whatever and is constantly occupied nowadays. Two friends died, one will be going over to skilled care right after Christmas, and my friend Madge is returning to her homeland of Canada. The six of us were quite the troop but things change quickly here. We're all living on borrowed time."

Ruth looked genuinely sad. "I'm sorry, Mom." She took a bite of her avocado toast. "With your girlfriends gone, will you and Harold move in together?"

I looked at her aghast. "Heaven's no! We're both way too set in our ways for that. Besides, what we have now is working for us. I've lost three husbands, I certainly don't want to lose a fourth."

Ruth took a sip of her coffee and changed the subject. "Tell me about your cruise. I heard that it was quite an adventure."

I gave her a little smile. "Well, there was a Frenchman involved. Let's go to your apartment and I'll tell you all about it after I see what you brought me. I love surprises."

Chapter Forty-One

The new year brought the changes I'd predicted. Molly was spending all of her time with Harry, her friend-with-benefits. Madge's brother arrived, packed up her belongings, and flew her back to Canada. Missy was unceremoniously moved to skilled care on January second.

Missy's move was a real heartbreaker for me. In recent weeks, I'd watched the life force drain out of her while I helped her sort through her belongings and put what she wanted to take with her into boxes and a suitcase. All her spunk and desire to come up to, and occasionally cross, the line had disappeared.

"I feel like a sittin' duck just waiting to die," she told me just before her move.

I promised to visit her regularly but in my heart, I knew my trips "across town," as I thought of it, would dwindle. I was losing confidence in my ability to navigate the halls of my own space, much less the hallways to and from skilled care.

Before my friends left, I told Harold about their imminent departure, and he suggested that we eat dinner together.

So, just after New Year's, Harold approached my table while I was waiting for dinner to be served.

"Is this seat taken?" he asked. He'd set aside his jumpsuit for the evening and was dressed in his out-to-eat clothes.

"Yes, it's taken," I said in response.

Harold looked so shocked that I hurried on. "It's reserved for a friend who wears jumpsuits to dinner. Have you seen him?" Falling into his chair, Harold said, "Don't kid me like that, Martha. I've got a bad heart."

I reached over and patted his hand.

Adjusting to my friends' departure was more difficult for me than moving to the Manor had been. After my sisters died, friends had taken a similar role in my life. Even with Harold's caring companionship, I felt sad and alone. I allowed myself to wallow throughout January, then on February first, I gave myself a pep talk about making an effort to meet new people and establish friendships. I decided that the first step was volunteering to be an ambassador for the Manor so on my way to breakfast the first Monday of February, I stopped in to see Judy. At least she was still around.

"Good morning, Martha. What brings you in so early?"

"How do I become an ambassador?" I asked, sitting in the chair across from her desk.

"You talk with Sophia, our volunteer coordinator." Judy pecked away on her computer. "I told her you'd stop by after breakfast. She'll be expecting you."

"Wow, you're efficient. Thanks."

Judy looked closely at me. "You look down. What's going on?"

I gave her a weak smile, happy to have someone really notice me. "Basically, I've lost all my friends except Harold. I allowed myself to mourn my losses, but now it's time for me to get on with my life. Hence, the volunteering. I'm hoping to meet and befriend some new arrivals."

I looked down at my hands. I didn't want to sound pathetic but I was willing to be vulnerable in front of Judy. "I've always needed friends in my life. You know my range of friendships," I paused, and when Judy nodded her understanding, I continued, "all the way from Madge to Missy. You can't get much more diverse than that. So, I figure I should be able to make new friends."

"Of course you can, Martha. You're a friend magnet. You just need to get back in the game."

I rose from the chair. "My sentiments exactly. I'm looking forward to talking with…"

"Sophia. Room 203," Judy filled in.

"Could you write that down for me?"

Judy wrote down the information then handed me the slip of paper. "Here you go. Good to see you. Drop in anytime."

After speaking with Sophia and going through an hour training session, I was made an official ambassador and I had the name tag to prove it. Marjorie Lawson was the first person I was asked to contact. She'd been living at the Manor for four days and the staff was concerned that they had only seen her outside of her apartment twice, each time to go to dinner. I called Marjorie and invited her to join me for lunch. Without much enthusiasm, she agreed to meet me just outside the dining room. I told her I'd be wearing a brightly colored silk scarf around my neck.

We met as planned. Marjorie was short and thin. Not curvy-model-thin but never-ate-a-bite-of-crusty-Italian-bread-dipped-in-olive-oil thin. Crepey skin hung on her arms, I could count the tendons in her neck, and her hair was gray and waspish with no particular style. She had small blue eyes and a mouth that turned down at the corners. All in all, she didn't present a pleasant appearance. She wore a patterned blouse that hung on her shoulders and black wool pants that were popular in the eighties.

We greeted one another then proceeded to the lunch line. After filling our trays, we found a table for two near the windows. Although the days had been cloudy and cold all week, today the sun was shining and I could imagine spring coming soon.

Marjorie set her plate, fork, napkin, and drink glass down, then placed her empty tray on a nearby table. She sat down and immediately launched into a monologue of complaints. "My children forced me to leave my beautiful home and moved me here. I hate communal living. I've never even lived in an apartment or a condo. I like my privacy." She paused for a moment to look down at her salad. "I hate the food and my apartment. I appreciate you inviting me to lunch, but so far, I've not met anyone interesting. And what is there to do here anyway?"

I opened my mouth to answer but she prattled on. "Boring Bingo, amateurish evening music, and ridiculous chair yoga is all I've found to do. I don't even see an interesting lecture in the lineup for this month. Once you get in here, is there any way out?"

Assuming it was another rhetorical question, I continued to eat my tuna melt.

"Well? Is there?"

I looked up. Perhaps she was asking a genuine question after all. "Is there what?"

She gave me a sharp look. "Are you even listening? Is there a way out of here once you're in?"

Sick of her bellyaching, as my dad would say, I let her have it. "There are several opportunities to leave here. Two of my good friends left by way of dying, one returned to Canada to enter rehab, and a fourth was recently moved to skilled care even though she dearly wanted to stay in her apartment." I gave her an uncompromising look. "See? You have a number of opportunities. Which one suits you?" Her eyes widened. She finally managed to respond with an indignant, "Well!"

I returned to my tuna and allowed the silence to hang in the air between us.

Marjorie pushed her half-eaten salad aside. "Is there anything in this place that you find pleasing?"

Raising my sweaty glass of iced tea to my lips, I took a long drink. I slowly returned the glass to the table. "As a matter of fact, I find many things and people at the Manor to be pleasing, starting with Judy, our assistant director. She's a peach. Two women in my original group of five were the best friends I've ever had. I find the food to be acceptable and I'm comfortable in my small but cozy apartment."

"But what do you DO?"

"I used to play Canasta but my partner is no longer here. I workout downstairs several times a week, go to Bingo occasionally, take the minivan to the library, listen to books while embroidering, and particularly enjoy the amateurish music you mentioned. I've even been known to sneak out with my friends and go to karaoke. I watch television in the evenings. I'm especially partial to *The Equalizer* and football."

Marjorie had a sour look on her face. My lineup apparently didn't interest her.

"What did you do before you came here?" I asked.

"I had my book club and card club…"

I interrupted her. "We have those. The book club meets monthly and there's Canasta, bridge, and mahjong."

She looked at me as if I was making this up.

I ignored the look and asked, "What reason did your children give for moving you here? I know it's a personal question so feel free not to answer."

"Well…" she whisked the napkin off her lap and set it on the table. "They were concerned that I'd had some rather nasty falls of late and I got lost driving home from church so they didn't want me living alone any longer. I've been divorced for more than twenty years. My son and daughter both live in Brooklyn but they couldn't locate a suitable residence near them so they put me here in Poughkeepsie. What kind of a name is that anyway? I'm from Rochester. Everyone's heard of Rochester!"

I was growing weary of this woman. It was time to end this unpleasant and disappointing lunch in which I had such high hopes. She was even an M! Looking directly at her, I said, "Poughkeepsie has a rather interesting meaning. You should look it up." When Marjorie didn't respond, I concluded our lunch meeting. "Nice meeting you, Marjorie. I hope you adjust to living at the Manor. It's the best alternative as far as I can see." I scooted my chair away from the table and got up. "Perhaps I'll see you around."

I returned to my apartment with even more determination to find new friends. I also made a vow to myself to never be like Marjorie. I did, however, find a bit of empathy in my heart for her as I wondered what in her life had caused her to become so negative.

Even though it was only one o'clock, I texted Harold. *Any good movies on Netflix?*

Long pause.

I'm sure we can find something. Perhaps tonight? I'm finishing up a woodworking project right now. See you later.

I was definitely going to have to find a girlfriend. In the meantime, I decided to "befriend" a character in my new book, *Hester.* Witches had always fascinated me.

Chapter Forty-Two

The following week I had a new ambassador assignment, a gentleman named Bob. I wasn't crazy about escorting a man around. In my experience, a purely platonic relationship with a man was rare. I'd had them in my life. Well, I'd had one. After my years of being a full-time, stay-at-home mom, I'd done script writing for Steve, a professional photographer and video producer. He became like a brother to me. The catch? He was happily married and I knew his wife. As far as I knew, Bob was single.

As with Marjorie, I invited Bob to lunch so we could get to know one another. I told him I'd be wearing a blue sweater and I'd meet him outside the dining room.

Bob was much younger than I'd imagined him to be from his husky voice—probably mid to late seventies. At first glance, I wondered what had brought him to the Manor. I knew that most men don't do well on their own, but perhaps he also had a medical condition that triggered the move. As I approached him, I could see that my assumption was correct. Bob walked with some difficulty and his left arm hung limply by his side. I guessed that he'd had a stroke.

He looked put together in pressed jeans, not dad jeans but jeans that fit, and a long-sleeved golf shirt with a little alligator on front. He was bald and probably shaved whatever hair was left but it didn't take away from the fact that he was handsome with high cheekbones, smiley blue eyes, and a kind demeanor. We shook hands and went into the dining room.

Unlike Marjorie, Bob began by asking me a question. "What brought you here, Martha?"

"I burnt the pot." I briefly told him my story and shared how my memory was declining but otherwise, I was doing pretty good for ninety. He raised his eyebrows when I said my age which was a mood lifter.

When it was his turn to share his story, he confirmed my suspicions that he was a widower and had suffered a serious stroke more than a year ago. He'd been rehabbing in Manor's skilled care and was happy to have gotten strong enough to move over to assisted living. "I'm lucky to be alive," he said with a broad smile. "The paramedics got me to the hospital in the nick of time and I was able to have emergency surgery to relieve the pressure on my brain caused by an aneurysm."

Now that he mentioned it, I noticed an indentation and a scar on the left side of his head.

"In the beginning, I couldn't speak or walk. I was in bad shape, and I knew right away that I'd never be able to return to living alone. It took me a long time and a lot of hard work to get back and, as you can see, I'm still left with an arm that doesn't work, a limp, and a mind that can no longer work with complex mathematics. I was an investment banker and numbers were my bread and butter."

I followed Bob's story with empathy but he clearly wasn't looking for sympathy. He was simply stating the facts. He had lived on Long Island most of his life and commuted to the city for work. In addition, he owned a second home in the Poconos which he was trying to sell.

After we shared our stories, I got to the point of our meeting. "My job as an ambassador is to help new residents adjust to life at the Manor. What can I help you with, Bob? Have you found any activities you enjoy or other ways to meet people?"

Bob laid his half-eaten burger down. "Men seem to be a rare breed around here so I'm concerned about making male friends. I'm not into crafts or cards and I'm puzzled about how guys spend their time."

I understood his predicament and I had a possible solution. "I think you'd like my friend Harold. He's a retired Army man, enjoys woodworking, and knows most of the men who live here. He can introduce you around and give you ideas on what to do. Would you like to join us for dinner tonight? I'm sure he won't mind."

"I'd love to."

"We'll save you a place. Meet us here around 5:30." After finishing my lunch and saying goodbye to Bob, I left the dining room and headed to my apartment. When I turned the corner of the hallway, I realized I was on the wrong floor. The numbers were reading in the three hundreds and my apartment was on the second floor. It took me five minutes to locate the elevator and take it down to my floor.

When I finally entered my apartment, I was wrung out. The anxiety of knowing I was mentally declining was exhausting. They always say, "Knowing you have dementia is worse than the dementia itself." I needed to do what I could to mitigate my condition so I finally called Judy and asked her to make an appointment for me with the gerontologist the next time he came to see patients at the Manor. It was something I should have done months ago. Then, I ordered colored Post-it notes from Amazon.

Later that afternoon, I texted Harold.

We're going to have a third at dinner tonight. I hope you don't mind.

Pause

All right. What's her name?

She's a he, and I can't remember his name but he's a nice guy. You'll like him.

A longer pause.

If you say so.

Harold didn't seem to be as amenable to my idea of a dinner guest as I thought he'd be. When he arrived at our usual table, I was disappointed to see him wearing a jumpsuit. I'd hoped he'd dress up to meet our guest. I wanted him to make a good impression. "Hold out your hand and introduce yourself as soon as he gets here," I told Harold when he sat down.

"How come?"

I gave him my "Really?" look. "That way I won't have to introduce you. I'm embarrassed that I've already forgotten his name. But I've come up with a solution for my name-forgetting issue."

Harold looked up absentmindedly. He wasn't his jovial self tonight. "Solution for what?"

"A solution for how to manage forgetting names. You'll see." I looked toward the door, saw our guest, and waved.

Harold dutifully stood up and stuck out his hand. "I'm Harold Lancaster. Have a seat."

"Nice to meet you, Harold. I'm Bob Bell." He looked over at me and smiled. "Nice to see you again, Martha."

Halfway through dinner, Harold must have realized that Bob wasn't a threat because he warmed up and returned to his charming self. The men chatted, as men do, about concrete things like woodworking projects, what cars they used to drive, and the most recent disturbing weather story on television.

I sat back and enjoyed the back and forth. I was certain Bob would quickly attract a female companion and then Harold and I would have a couple to socialize with. Though I felt good about this new acquaintance, next time I hoped I'd meet a woman I could befriend.

Next time came sooner than expected. The following day I had a call from Sophia. "I have a new move-in for you to meet, Martha," she said when I answered my cell.

"Man or woman?" I asked.

Sophia chuckled. "Woman. Her name is Laura Jones, she's ninety-two, and she's from Chicago. I thought you'd have location in common since your granddaughter lives there."

"You met my granddaughter?" I asked.

Sophia chuckled again. She was a jovial person. "Yes. I had the pleasure of meeting Barbara and her wife, Bobbie, when they were here last year for your birthday."

"Well, what do you know," I paused, "did you happen to meet my daughter, Ruth? She's also from Chicago although she's rarely in town."

"I don't believe so. Maybe I'll meet her the next time she visits. Gotta run. Have a nice meeting with Mrs. Jones. I'll text you her name and number. Bye."

As soon as the text came through, I called my new assignment before it slipped my mind.

"Yes, this is Laura Jones. How may I help you?" she said after answering her phone.

Her voice was weak and scratchy. I wondered how I sounded on the phone. After all, she was only two years older than me. "This is Martha Anderson and I'm a Resident Ambassador for the Manor. I was wondering if you'd like to join me for lunch tomorrow so I can answer any questions you might have and we can get to know one another."

There was a long pause and, for a second, I thought she'd hung up, thinking I was a crank caller.

"That would be lovely, dear. What was your name again?"

"Martha."

"Oh yes, Martha. My grandmother was a Martha. It's a charming, old-fashioned name. What time do you go to lunch?"

We arranged the particulars and I told her what I'd be wearing. She wasn't an "M" but she sounded friendly.

Laura had the stereotypical grandmother look—thin white hair that gently framed a face full of wrinkles, a widow's hump that caused her to lean over and walk with a cane, and wire-rimmed glasses. However, all of her old-lady-ness flew out the window when she gave me a bedazzling smile and gently took my hand. "So nice to meet you, Martha. Shall we go in?"

The waitress helped Laura with her tray and we settled at a nearby table. Laura looked and sounded frail but her facial expressions and words showed me that she was still very much with it. "What a lovely scarf. It must be Indian," was her opening salvo when we started eating.

"Why yes, it is. My daughter travels to India and brought me the scarf. How did you know?"

Laura's eyes danced with merriment. "I wasn't always this frail, little old lady. My husband was a medical doctor and we were missionaries in China and India for many years. I was an author. I still write occasionally."

"You must have had a very interesting life. Are your books still available? I'd love to read one."

She took a hanky from her pocket. I was impressed. Ladies rarely had hankies or pockets these days. She wiped her wet eyes. "Why do they call it dry eye when I have tears perpetually flowing?" she asked. When I raised my shoulders, she continued. "My books are still out there somewhere but I'd be glad to loan you mine. You can pick one up at my apartment after lunch."

Laura and I had a lovely conversation. It was such a contrast to what's-her-name.

After lunch we walked together to her apartment. She lived on my floor, which was helpful for future visits. I could tell that walking was painful for her but she persevered.

When I entered Laura's apartment, I thought I'd been transported back in time. A brown and gold flowered love seat sat against one wall, two solid brown recliners sat against the other. An old-fashioned credenza held a small television. The table was a drop-leaf antique with a bowl of fake fruit sitting in the middle on top of a crocheted doily. "Please have a seat, Martha. I'll just pop into my bedroom and locate that book."

Laura returned with a dog-eared, hard cover book in her hand. "This book has seen better days. I believe it was published in 1961 so it's probably not available online." She passed the book to me and I studied the cover while she continued talking. "I wrote *Silk Slippers* while we were living in China. I hope you'll enjoy the story. If not, I won't be offended. It's written in an old-school style which is no longer popular."

"I'm sure I'll find it fascinating especially since I know the author. Thank you. I'll take good care of your book."

When I turned to leave, Laura stepped forward. "May I give you a hug?"

"Of course," I said as I gently placed my arms around a potential new friend.

I returned home and found an Amazon package someone had kindly set in front of my door. I hung my key on the hook then ripped it open. My multi-colored Post-it-notes fell out. After locating a pen, I sat down at the table and considered my strategy. Blue for family, pink for friends, yellow for acquaintances, and green for miscellaneous. This was going to be my new memory system for names.

Family names still came easily to me and I wrote them on blue pages according to family units. Friends were also easy since, nowadays, I had so few. I took a chance and put Laura's name down, Judy, Molly (even though I rarely spoke with her), Missy (I'd only seen her once since her move, but we regularly talked on the phone), and Harold.

Acquaintances were more challenging. I'd forgotten the name of my Uber driver so I just put U-driver. I remembered Jake, the minivan driver, Bob the new guy, Kathleen my hair person, Winter and Mrs. Fayerweather from the library, and Ada my cleaning lady. I didn't bother writing down the night staff since they stopped visiting after Judy moved to days. I'd forgotten the new director's name so I just put director on the miscellaneous green note along with Susan's doctor-boyfriend with a question mark. I hoped this was still a thing and I made a mental note to call her.

I stuck my Post-its on the wall near the door so I could glance at them on my way out in case I was meeting someone.

That evening Harold escorted me home from dinner. "Want to come in for a bit?" I asked.

"Sure. I promise I won't stay long," he answered as I unlocked my door.

He didn't notice the notes and I didn't mention them. "You go change into your soft clothes while I make myself comfortable."

When I came out of the bedroom, Harold was sitting in the recliner facing the door. He pointed to the wall across the room. "What's that all about?"

I got a glass of water then settled myself on the couch. "That's my system for remembering names. I can't do much about finding my way through the halls—unless I leave breadcrumbs—but I can use notes to help me remember the names of people in my life. You're on a pink one under the friend's category," I looked over at him. "Just in case you're wondering."

When Harold looked at me, I saw understanding in his eyes. "That bad, huh?"

"My memory is noticeably declining. Judy made an appointment for me to see Dr. Kinney when he comes next week. I'm trying to be proactive and do as much as I can to keep my life rolling along."

Harold nodded. "Good girl. I'm proud of you for taking charge. Know that I'm always here for you."

His comment humbled me. "Thanks, Harold. Perhaps you can escort me back from dinner more often. I seem to get worse when I'm tired."

"Anytime."

We settled into a conversation about Bob. Harold had been enjoying his company in the woodworking shop, and we'd both seen him escorting a woman to music after dinner. "Next time you talk to Bob, why don't you invite him and his new lady friend to have dinner with us," I suggested.

"Good idea. You don't know her?"

"Nope. I think she's new, but Sophia hasn't asked me to meet with her yet." Surprised that I'd remembered the volunteer director's name, I immediately got up and added her name to the miscellaneous list on my wall along with Dr. Kinney.

The following evening at dinner, there were four of us at the table. Bob introduced his lady friend, Audrey Metcalf. I guessed that she was in her early seventies, very young by Manor standards, and wore a black low-cut tight-fitting sweater, a shiny black skirt, and red sling-back kitten-heeled shoes. She didn't look like Bob's type but then again, I barely knew the guy. Audrey said she'd been an actress in New York and had come to the Manor after a serious bout of Covid left her with breathing difficulties, occasional dizziness, loss of taste, and a fuzzy memory. She was renting, which was not an uncommon practice for someone who wants to try the place out before committing.

"I've been told my symptoms are likely temporary," she said in a southern accent, which made me wonder about her New York acting story. Maybe the whole Southern Belle thing was a role. Besides the sexy clothes and heavy accent, she had poufy blonde hair, shrewd blue eyes, and ample red lips. Actress or not, she certainly looked the part. Bob seemed enchanted. Even Harold was starry-eyed.

As we chatted through dinner, my intuition told me that something about Audrey was off. Since the attention was completely focused on her, I also considered the possibility that I was feeling jealous.

Since I'd already met Audrey and she was adjusting just fine, I had no need to do my ambassador thing, but I was curious about her past. I considered inviting her to lunch but that seemed weird since we barely spoke two words at dinner. I decided to ask Sophia about her instead. Maybe another ambassador had been assigned and given Sophia feedback. I called and asked if I could drop by.

"Of course. What's on your mind?" she asked.

"I'll come by after lunch and we can chat."

"All right. I'll be waiting."

I had to figure out a natural way to bring up Audrey. I couldn't just blurt out, "I think this lady has something shady going on, what do you think?" I figured I'd start by reporting my official lunch with Bob and then ease into the fact that he and Audrey were an item.

Sophia was talking on the phone when I arrived so I sat down and waited. When she hung up, she said, "Good to see you, Martha. What's up?"

"I had a good visit with Bob Bell the other day. In fact, last night Harold and I had dinner with him and Audrey Metcalf. Do you happen to know her?"

Sophia thought for a moment. "Yes, I've met Audrey. I'm glad to hear that two of our newer residents have become friends."

I crossed and uncrossed my legs remembering crossed legs weren't a good idea after hip surgery. "Did another ambassador meet with Audrey?"

"No. I didn't assign anyone as she seemed to be adjusting very well. Also, she might be leaving soon."

I crossed my arms over my chest. For some reason I felt uncomfortable. "I heard she's renting. Is she from around here?"

Sophia frowned as if trying to remember. "I believe her last known address was another senior living organization. Why?"

"Just wondering. She seems awfully young and healthy to be living here, that's all."

"Do you have a particular concern about Audrey?" Sophia asked, leaning forward. I could tell she was getting impatient with my probing questions.

"Not really." I got up from my chair. "Thanks for seeing me. Oh, I found Laura Jones to be very interesting. Did you know she's written several books?"

"I didn't know that. I'm glad to see you're embracing your volunteer job, Martha. Bye now."

I turned to leave. "Bye."

Feeling dissatisfied with our visit, I returned to my apartment and fired up the MacBook Air my kids gave me for Christmas. First, I googled Bob Bell, investment banker, New York. He popped right up, photo and all. He wasn't just any investment banker; he owned a firm along with a partner. After visiting their website, I concluded that Bob was, most likely, a wealthy man.

Next, I googled my new friend Laura Jones, the author. She, too, was way more than a hobby writer. She was a legit author and had several books published by Simon & Schuster. Although that was decades ago, she certainly was who she said she was and more.

Audrey Metcalf, actress, New York was another situation entirely. The Audrey Metcalf with the most information was born in 1911, acted in the movie *The Blob,* and died in 2003. The other Audrey Metcalfs were either too young or too dead to be who I was looking for. I decided to talk to Harold. Maybe he'd learned something from Bob.

After music that night, Harold offered to walk me to my apartment. "Come in for a few minutes. I have something to ask you without the big ears listening in," I said as we walked along.

Harold settled himself on the couch and I joined him. "Has Bob said anything about Audrey?"

"What do you mean?" Harold frowned.

"I think there's something fishy about her."

Harold threw up his hands. "You're not going back to your PI routine again, are you? I thought the murder on the cruise was the final case."

I gave him a sheepish grin. "It's hard for me to ignore my instincts."

"And," Harold prompted.

"In the case of Audrey Metcalf, my instincts are telling me that she's a con artist who goes from location to location and dupes men out of their money or has them buy her expensive gifts, then moves on."

"And you think this because?"

"Well for one thing, I googled her, and absolutely nothing came up, which seems odd if she was an actress at some point in her life. Also, she's renting short-term and doesn't seem to have the Covid symptoms that supposedly brought her here."

When I paused, Harold prompted, "Go on."

"For instance, considering she says she's lost her taste, she sure can put away the food and I haven't heard her wheezing or coughing or showing any indications of being short of breath. She lived at another senior facility before coming here. Don't you think that's odd?"

Harold let out a long sigh. "I don't know and I don't care. It's none of my damn business."

"But aren't you concerned about Bob's welfare?"

"Bob's a big boy who can take care of himself, and I think you need to mind your own business too." Harold got up to leave.

"Is that an order, Colonel?" I was pissed.

"Just a suggestion. Good night, Martha. See you tomorrow."

Chapter Forty-Three

The next morning I was still angry with Harold, but I also had to agree with him that what happened between Bob and Audrey was none of my business. It was hard, however, to let go of trying to figure out her angle because she was the type of woman who gave the rest of us a bad name.

I left my apartment for breakfast and immediately saw Audrey walking with my one-time nemesis, Ethyl Haggerty. They were chatting amicably. I hadn't forgiven Ethyl for snitching on my friends and me the night we snuck out on our first excursion. Since then, she'd added fuel to that fire by being as ugly as possible whenever our paths crossed.

For instance, if I entered the game room, she made sure to let me know there wasn't space at her table. If I saw her in the workout room, she reminded me to wipe down my equipment or rudely turned off the television even though she knew I liked to watch HGTV while I was on the bike.

And now, there she was, all chummy with Audrey and probably giving her an earful about what a terrible person I was. While they were waiting for the elevator, I caught up to them. "Don't believe everything she tells you, Audrey," I said.

They both looked at me with daggers in their eyes. "I can see that it's already too late." The elevator arrived and they walked in, leaving the door half-closed behind them. I made no effort to save it. I didn't want to be in the same elevator with them anyway.

Life continued as usual at the Manor. Winter droned on, and I spent more time in my apartment than usual. I read and embroidered when I wasn't working out or in the dining room. Facebook had turned into an old people's domain and I enjoyed the various groups of old ladies who hung out there.

In March, I had a call from Barbara telling me that their expected baby was a girl and they were busy considering names. Then a week later, she called back.

"Hi Gran, it's Barbara and Bobbie on speaker phone. How are you?"

"Fine. What's up?" They rarely called just to chat.

"We'd like to name our peanut after you but call her Marti. Would using the nickname upset you?"

"Oh my!" This announcement definitely took me by surprise.

"Well?" the girls prompted.

"I'd be honored and I think the nickname is perfect. Certainly more current than Martha. What do your parents have to say about the name?"

"This is Barbara. We're not telling anyone else until after she's born. We don't want discussion or opinions about the name. We figure it's our choice and ours alone. We just wanted to tell you since we're using, then altering, your name."

"That's very considerate of you. I won't tell a soul. Is everyone healthy?"

The girls chimed in together. "Yes!"

"Barbara is already showing, and besides throwing up some mornings, she's doing well. She's due August 10th. The baby's fine. We're thrilled knowing we're having a girl, although a boy would have been fine, too. We're still in shock that it happened so fast."

"I'm sure you are. Keep me posted and thanks for letting me know about the name. I'm delighted!"

"Bye, Gran," the girls said together.

Having a great-grand named for me was certainly motivation to live a while longer. After talking with the girls, I ordered two receiving blankets, one white and one pink, along with extra embroidery floss. When my package arrived the next day, I started embroidering flowers in the four corners. I finally had a project I could get excited about. I listened to my audible books while I sewed. It was a relaxing way to spend the dreary afternoons of late winter and early spring.

In the middle of April, I had a call from Susan. She'd been periodically updating me about her romance with Michael and things seemed to be progressing.

"What would you think about having a couple of visitors for the first weekend in May?" That was my granddaughter. She was never one to chit-chat but always got right to the point. "You and who else?" I asked.

"Duh, of course me. And," she paused and cleared her throat, "Michael and I would like to come for a visit. Will you reserve the Manor's guest apartment for us? I know it's a couple of weeks away, but with his travel schedule, we have to plan ahead."

"Of course. I'd be delighted."

"You don't have Taylor Swift concert tickets for that weekend?" She snickered.

I laughed, remembering the joke I'd played on her last year. "There are no concerts in my future or much of anything else. That weekend will be great. I'll set it up."

"I'll text you once we're off the train. We'll Uber over, probably arriving sometime in the afternoon."

"I'll be ready. Remind me of Michael's last name."

"Michael Moore. He's looking forward to seeing you again. Oh, and will you make dinner reservations at that French restaurant you told me about? If you loved it, I'm sure he will too. Also, feel free to invite Harold. Gotta run. Thanks, Gran. We're looking forward to our visit."

Whew, her calls were always such a whirlwind, probably like her life in the city. Before I forgot again, I got up and wrote Michael Moore on a Post-it and added it to my miscellaneous row. I didn't know where else to put him. Then, I texted Harold.

Two questions.

Long pause.

Sorry, I was unlocking my door. Ask away.

First, would you like to go to dinner with my granddaughter, Susan, and her boyfriend in a couple of weeks? Second, what's the name of the French restaurant you took me to the night of our first kiss?

(Haha emoji) *Funny you should reference the kiss. Yes, to the first question and Brasserie 292 to the second. Want me to make a reservation? They're usually booked at least a week out. I'm assuming that's where we're going.*

I'll make the reservation. The boyfriend—Susan's, not mine—(smile emoji) loves French food and Susan wants to treat all of us. I'm wondering if there's an announcement or something. I guess we'll have to wait and see. Talk at dinner.

(Thumbs-up emoji)

During dinner, Harold had news of his own. "Bob and Audrey are going to Bob's house in the Poconos next week. When the house didn't sell, he took it off the market. At least for a while."

Although I was alarmed, I kept my voice calm. "How are they getting there?"

"Apparently Bob had a car in storage. Audrey wanted to see his place and offered to drive the two-plus hours to Lake Wallenpaupack, near Hawley."

"Lake whatta?"

Harold chuckled. I wondered how he was finding humor in all this.

"Lake Wallenpaupack," he repeated. "It's near the small town of Hawley in the Poconos. Bob said the location is beautiful."

"I'm sure it is."

Harold frowned. "That's all you got? No theory about the," he leaned in and whispered, "dangers of Audrey?"

I gave Harold my pissed-off look. "And you don't have concerns?"

"Maybe, but as I said before, it's none of my business."

I narrowed my eyes at him. "When all of this comes crashing down, I promise that I'll try not to say I told you so."

Harold just shook his head. "Eat your dessert. I have a good movie cued up on Netflix."

The following week I received a call from someone at skilled care stating that Missy was asking for me. I wondered why she hadn't called me herself. Since the call came at the end of the day, I told the person that I'd be over to visit the first thing in the morning.

"Would you mind walking me back from visiting Missy tomorrow morning?" I asked Harold at dinner.

"Of course not. Want me to walk you over too?"

"I'll be all right. I plan to go over early while my head is still on straight."

"What's happening with Missy? I thought you two usually spoke on the phone." Harold's expression reflected the concern I was feeling.

"Someone from the unit called me just as I was getting ready for dinner. They said Missy had asked them to call and that she wanted to see me. I also wondered why she didn't make the call herself. It doesn't sound good."

Harold patted my hand. "It sure is rough outliving our friends." He leaned back. "I'll keep an eye on my phone all morning and watch for your text. If you get turned around going over, just let me know."

I nodded and then started eating my stringy Swiss steak. I felt warm inside just knowing Harold always had my back.

Right after breakfast the following morning, I set off for skilled care. My mind felt sharp and my body needed the walk. By the time I got to Missy's room, I was still feeling chipper until I saw her lying in the bed with multiple tubes attached to machines. She was as white as the sheet she had pulled up to her neck, her eyes were closed, and her curly hair had thinned and needed a wash. I pulled a chair up to the bed and took her hand.

"Martha, you came," she said in a voice I could barely hear.

"Of course, I came. What's going on that you couldn't call?"

Tears trickled out of the corners of Missy's eyes. "Bring the head of my bed up, would you?"

I found the button and pushed it until she said stop then I handed her a tissue. "I wanted to see you one last time but I couldn't navigate the phone." Missy took a raspy breath. "You know I love you, right?"

I nodded, too choked up to speak.

"More than a friend," she added, squeezing my hand. "My best recent memories are of times we spent together. I think you could have been the love of my life. Even though you aren't predisposed to being gay, I'm glad you were open to new experiences." She closed her eyes for a moment, then continued. "I didn't want to leave this life without telling you how much I love you."

This was a lot to take in. Now I was crying. I took a tissue, blew my nose, and wiped my eyes. When I finally got myself under control, I said, "I hope I didn't lead you on. What you just said is partially true, but you are more than just a friend. I love you too, just not in quite the same way. Or," I paused for a moment, "maybe I'm not aware of how I love you." I shook my head. "Love continues to be a mystery to me. But one thing I know for sure, we've always had a special connection."

Missy pointed to the drawer beside her bed. "Will you hand me the zippered bag that's in there?"

I opened the drawer, pulled out a small jewelry bag someone would use for traveling, and handed it to her. She rummaged around, took something out, then zipped the bag close. "My mother gave me this ring when I started menstruating. It was her way of welcoming me into the world of women. Little did she know the role women would play in my life." Missy closed her eyes for a moment then resumed. "I want you to have this ring and think of me when you wear it. Will you do that?" Missy handed me a gold pinky ring with a tiny diamond.

I admired the child-size ring then slid it onto my little finger. I held out my hand so we could both see it. "Thank you. Yes, I'll always wear this and think of you. The ring will remind me of the fun we had and the sweet feelings we have for one another." I had more tears. I wasn't used to the waterworks; they had arrived with old age.

When Missy's breathing became labored, one of the machines started beeping and a nurse rushed into the room. "You need to go now," the nurse said to me. "Miss Wellesley needs to rest." She turned to Missy. "Say goodbye to your friend. I'm going to give you a sedative," she added before leaving the room.

Missy opened her eyes, motioned for me to come close, gently pulled my head down, and softly kissed me on the lips. "I love you," she whispered.

I stood up. "I love you too." I brushed the curls off of her forehead and she closed her eyes. The nurse returned with a syringe and a serious look on her face. I obediently took my leave. Just outside Missy's door, I texted Harold. He texted back saying he was on his way.

Missy's sweet kiss lingered on my lips as I waited for Harold. I was aware of the irony but I dismissed it for later consideration. As I waited, my mind returned to the kiss. I'd never been kissed on the lips by a woman, not even my mother. Come to think of it, we didn't show much affection in my family although I always knew my parents loved me.

I had a lot to process and I was anxious for the quiet of my apartment. When I saw Harold coming down the hall, I walked past the nurses' station and joined him. "Thanks for coming."

"Anytime."

Chapter Forty-Four

After returning to my apartment, I asked Alexa to play classical music. I sat down in my recliner with a tall glass of water by my side. Good thing I wasn't a drinker. I knew instinctively that Missy had just said her last goodbye to me. She was the type of person who didn't want people hovering over her at the end. Losing her was already heavy on my heart, even though she wasn't physically gone.

The kiss was unexpected. Although, in the past, I'd felt zingers in Missy's presence, I'd never had the desire to have a sexual encounter with her. Hell, at my age, I didn't have the desire to have a sexual encounter with a man, either. So why was I thinking about it? Perhaps it was the excitement of the unfamiliar. I was also curious about why Missy had been attracted to me and how she intuitively felt that I'd respond. I recalled the note left on my door that read something like "You were the prettiest woman in the room signed M." Was that Missy? I should have asked her, not that it made any difference.

I sighed and picked up my embroidery. I was finishing the second receiving blanket for baby Marti. I told Alexa to turn off, located my audible book on my phone and pushed start. I'd done enough thinking for now.

Mid-morning the following week, Judy texted asking me to drop by after lunch. When I entered her office, she was all smiles. "It's good to see you, Martha. Have a seat."

"What's on your mind? It's usually me wanting to see you," I said.

Judy's smile abruptly disappeared. She looked nervous and seemed hesitant to speak. My curiosity started getting the best of me. "What?" I asked impatiently.

"How well do you know Audrey Metcalf?"

Judy certainly threw me a curveball with that question. "Not well. Harold and I had dinner with her and Bob Bell a few times. Audrey has become friendly with Ethyl and you know what I think about Ethyl. I believe she's convinced Audrey that I'm someone she shouldn't associate with. Also," I paused wondering if I should tell Judy my other thoughts. After all, I had no evidence.

"Yes?" Judy leaned forward.

"I probably shouldn't say this, but ever since I first met Audrey, I've had the feeling that she's a bad egg."

"In what way?"

Although I thought she would dismiss my claim, Judy seemed interested. "Something's off about her. My theory is she goes from place to place—I'm sure you know this isn't her first rental," I looked over at Judy and when she nodded yes, I resumed. "So, she goes from place to place latching on to wealthy men then she bilks them out of money or jewelry or something else before moving on to her next victim. Right now, she's with Bob at his lake house in the

Poconos. Doesn't it seem strange that she abruptly recovered from her ongoing Covid symptoms and was able to drive over two hours to Pennsylvania? I'm worried that she's going to try to get her hands on his property. I know that sounds outrageous but my intuition is usually right."

Judy folded her hands in front of her on the desk. "What I'm about to tell you needs to be kept strictly confidential. Do you understand?"

I nodded.

"Yesterday afternoon, just as I was leaving to go home, the front desk directed a gentleman to my office. His name was Jeffrey Metcalf and he was Audrey's husband—at least that's what he told me. He'd been unable to reach his wife for the last several days so he came here to see her and find out what was going on. He took the train from Brooklyn."

"Good grief! What did you tell him?"

"The truth. I told him she'd gone away for a few days with a friend. When he asked for the details, I told him he needed to speak with his wife. He asked me about her Covid symptoms and I told him they had presumably cleared up. I also told him that her rental agreement was ending soon."

"What did he say?"

"He gave me his card and asked that I get in touch with him as soon as his wife reappeared."

"Reappeared," I repeated. "Don't you think that's an odd term to use?"

"Yes."

I thought about the man's card. "Did Mr. Metcalf's card indicate a profession?"

"Yes. It indicated that he's a Realtor but there was no agency named."

"So, what are you going to do?" I asked.

"I'm going to notify Mr. Metcalf as soon as Audrey and Bob return to the Manor then I'm going to remind Audrey that our rental agreement with her ends on May 1st which is a little more than a week from now. If she wants to renew, the new lease will be for a year. I doubt if she'll agree to that, especially now that she knows that we know she has a husband stashed away somewhere. If she does make the decision to stay, then I'll have to take this up the ladder to the CEO."

"I knew it! I just knew it." Feeling guilty about my jubilation, I added, "I feel sorry for Bob. He seems like a really nice guy but even a successful, smart man can be duped when he's not exactly thinking with his head—if you know what I mean."

Judy gave me an I-know-what-you-mean look. "Text me if you see Audrey or Bob, will you?"

"Of course. Thanks for trusting me, Judy. You don't have to worry about this getting around. I'd never do that to Bob. He was one of my ambassador 'meet and greets' so I feel particularly responsible for his welfare."

"I know. That's why I asked you to come in."

When I got up to leave, Judy asked, "By the way, how's Missy? I heard she's not doing well."

"Not well at all."

"I'm sorry."

"Me too. I'll be in touch." I walked out the door and returned to my apartment.

As if my meeting with Judy didn't give me enough to think about, at dinner that night Harold told me that he'd received a text from Bob.

"Today?" I tried to sound nonchalant.

"Yes, why?"

"No reason. What did his text say?"

"That they're returning to the Manor tomorrow. He said he was bringing a jigsaw he found in his garage. He knows I've been wishing there was one in the shop. Nice of him to remember, don't you think?"

"Nice."

Harold looked at me then raised his eyebrows. "Spill it."

I tried hard to look innocent but Harold had my number. "My place. After dinner," I said.

"Sounds ominous." Harold shook his head. "You aren't up to more shenanigans, are you?"

"Who me?" I pointed to his plate. "Eat your chicken. It's getting cold."

After dinner, we skipped the music and walked straight to my apartment. Harold now kept my mini fridge supplied with beer and he had a bottle of wine in the cupboard. It seemed more practical than dashing around with a brown paper bag in his hand. He poured each of us a drink.

"Well?" he said kicking off our evening. I knew the mystery was driving him nuts.

I gave him a little poke which seemed to aggravate him even more. "I said I wouldn't say 'I told you so' but…"

"For Heaven's sake, Martha, what is it?"

"Audrey apparently has a husband. He was at the Manor yesterday looking for her because she'd gone silent the last few days. I imagine it was hard to have a secret conversation with her husband while she was in Bob's bed."

"And you know this how?"

I filled Harold in on the details of my conversation with Judy. "Let me know if you see Bob tomorrow, will you?"

"I suppose so. Are you or Judy going to tell him about the husband?"

"I'm certainly not going to. Audrey's lease is up next week. My guess is she'll leave as soon as she talks with Judy. Poof!" I threw up my hands. "She'll disappear. I'm sad for Bob though. I hope he hasn't fallen for her in a big way."

Harold sat back and took a sip of his wine. "Well, well, The Sleuth is right again. I must say, you do have a nose for sniffing out the bad guys. Congratulations. I've learned my lesson. I won't doubt your intuition again."

I gave him a dubious look. "We'll see how long that lasts."

It was Harold's turn to throw up his hands. "What? You don't believe me?"

I smiled coyly and finished my beer.

Late the next morning, Harold texted me that he'd seen Bob in the hall. I, in turn, texted Judy. I hadn't seen Audrey but that didn't mean she wasn't back.

At lunch, Harold came over and sat at my table. He didn't have a tray. "I've got news. You about finished?"

I wrapped my half-eaten sandwich in my napkin. "Your place or mine?"

"Mine."

We sat together at his table. "What?" I was dying to know his news. I suspected it had to do with Bob and Audrey.

"I spoke with Bob. Audrey brought him back to the Manor, packed the rest of her clothes, then she returned to his lake house. He told me she's going to live there until she finds other, more permanent, accommodations. She told him her rental agreement at the Manor was about to expire and she needed a place to live."

I shook my head. "And he agreed to this and allowed her to keep his car?"

"Yes and yes."

"Good grief! This is even worse than I thought. You're going to have to tell him to go talk to Judy, or I'll have Judy contact him."

Harold took my glass to the kitchen then returned with a cookie for each of us. "Text Judy. I want to stay out of this. He's going to need a friend, and I don't want him to think that I'm a snitch."

"Ok. Hand me my phone," I said, pointing to my sweater hanging over the back of the couch.

I texted Judy that Bob was back and she needed to talk with him pronto.

I added. *Ask him if he knows Audrey's whereabouts. Say you're worried because she hasn't returned. Harold and I would like to stay out of this.*

Long pause while Harold and I hovered over my phone. *I'll call him now. Thanks for the info.*

Chapter Forty-Five

The next day, with my curiosity getting the best of me, I dropped by Judy's office. When I put my head around the corner, she looked up. "Any news about you know who?" I asked.

Judy motioned for me to come in. After I closed the door and sat down, she leaned forward conspiratorially. "I told Bob about the husband's appearance, asked him for the address of the lake house, called the husband, then I suggested to Bob that he get Audrey to return his car and house keys ASAP."

"How did he take it?"

"More calmly than I thought he would. Perhaps deep down, he knew something was fishy. He said he'd report the car and house keys stolen if she refused to return them."

I sighed with relief. "That's good. I'm glad he's taking the whole thing seriously and not trying to protect his male ego. So is Audrey gone for good?"

Judy took a drink of soda from a can at her elbow. "It looks like it. Her apartment was furnished, but her personal items and clothes were gone. She won't get her deposit back unless she shows up and returns the key."

I got up from the chair. "Good riddance is what I say."

"Thanks for your help, Martha. Glad you found a good one in Harold."

I opened the door. "Me too. See you later."

"Martha," Judy called out, "don't forget your doctor's appointment tomorrow."

"Thanks for the reminder. I'll be there."

The next day, I met with Dr. Kinney. The week before, I'd taken various tests, and this visit was an opportunity to hear the results and get a diagnosis if there was one.

There was good news and bad. The good news was that I didn't have Alzheimer's, the bad news was that I had mild vascular dementia, which meant that certain parts of my brain were getting less blood flow than they needed. Because my case was mild, Kinney thought I'd be able to function in assisted living for at least a year or two longer without much difficulty. When I told him about my experiences of getting lost, he suggested that I ask for help as I traverse from place to place.

In all the excitement around Audrey and my doctor's visit, I'd almost forgotten about Susan's visit and our dinner at Brasserie 292. It was a good thing I'd already made reservations for dinner and the Manor's guest room. I texted Harold to remind him that the event was on Saturday. He was much less forgetful than I was, but he too was old. He confirmed that he'd pick me up at five-thirty so we could meet Susan and Michael and Uber together to the restaurant.

Although I knew the meal would be amazing, I was more interested in getting to know Michael and determining if this was a special occasion or not.

Michael was as dashing as I'd remembered: tall and slim with straight black hair, brown eyes, a tan, and a calm but friendly demeanor. A good match for Susan's hyper personality and suspicious nature.

They were a striking couple, and I knew they would make beautiful babies if it ever came to that. By the time we arrived at the restaurant, Harold and Michael were already engaged in a serious conversation about the pros and cons of a profession that kept a person moving from place to place. Susan seemed preoccupied and nervous.

After we were seated and our server asked for drink orders, Michael spoke up. "A bottle of Veuve Clicquot Ponsardin champagne for the table, please." The server slid away and Michael looked at Susan, then smiled at Harold and me. "We have something to celebrate." Before he could elaborate, the French champagne was ceremonially opened at the table and poured. Michael held up his glass. "To the future Mrs. Michael Moore," he touched his glass to Susan's. She smiled but was unaccountably quiet. Harold and I echoed the toast.

"Congratulations! I'm so happy for you." I said. "Have you set a wedding date?" It seemed as though they'd just met, but they were certainly old enough to know their own minds.

Susan finally spoke. "Thank you. Yes, next Fall. Probably late October." She reached into her small handbag, opened her wallet, pulled out a beautiful diamond ring, and slipped it on her finger. She looked at me. "I wanted to surprise you."

I took her hand. "What a lovely shape for a diamond. What's the name of the cut?" Susan pointed to the long, thin loaf of French bread sitting on a cutting board in the middle of the table. "It's a baguette cut, named for baguette bread because of its long, thin shape." She smiled shyly. "It's appropriate that we're all here don't you think?"

"And that the two of you met while eating a French meal on a cruise ship," I added.

"Yes," replied Susan. "And that."

The bride-to-be was finally smiling but I wondered why she had been nervous to tell me about their engagement. I also wondered if she'd told her parents. I looked at Harold and his expression reminded me that it wasn't any of my damned business. I focused on how delighted I was that they had come all the way to Poughkeepsie to give us the news in person. Pushing questions aside, I took a piece of the baguette, slathered on some butter, and sipped my bubbly.

In early spring I started having lunch with Laura. Although physically frail, she was as sharp as a tack, as my dad would say, and a delightful companion with interesting stories and a positive attitude. I still missed my five friends but I was grateful to have this lovely lady in my life.

In late May, I received a letter from Steve. The return address wasn't the prison so I assumed he was out. The letter said that he'd been released early due to good behavior, had secured a job as an auto mechanic, and was living in a half-way house for those recently released from prison. He sounded upbeat and reiterated about how much he appreciated my support. There was a postscript at the bottom asking if he might come for a visit sometime. He added his phone number.

That evening, I had Harold come by my apartment after dinner so I could show him Steve's letter. After he'd read it, I asked, "What do you think about his request to get together?"

"First of all, I want to say that you were right—again. He certainly sounds like he's rehabilitated and is willing to take on adult responsibilities. Have you told your son?" Harold folded the letter and passed it back to me.

I set it aside. "No, I haven't told him," I looked at Harold. "Believe it or not, most of the time, I don't want to be an 'I-told-you-so' kind of person which I will be if I talk to him. Besides, he's probably forgotten all about the young man." Moving on, I asked again, "So, do we meet him or not?"

"What if we meet him at a restaurant and treat him to dinner? It seems less risky. It's one thing to write stuff in a letter. Let's see what he's like up close and personal. He must have a means of transportation if he's willing to come here."

"I'll call or text him tomorrow. Let's invite him to join us at Sam's Place," I said then got up from the couch, giving Harold the clue that it was late.

Ignoring my body language, Harold stayed seated and asked, "Why there?"

"That's where I took the girls the night I got into trouble which led to the disciplinary meeting with Duly which led to getting to know you."

Harold shook his head. "Interesting how you like to connect the fragments of your life." He eased himself off the couch and walked to the door. "Sam's Place it is. I've never been there. Is it close by?"

I wondered if Harold was worried about venturing too far from the Manor. "Yes, it's close by."

"Just tell me when and what time. I'll look forward to continuing this adventure with you."

"Good night, Harold." I kissed him, and he headed to his apartment.

The next morning, I texted Steve. I figured that texting would automatically give him my phone number in case he needed to change our dinner plans.

Hi, I received your letter and was delighted to read all your good news! My friend, Harold, and I would like to take you to dinner on Saturday and hear more about your new life. If you're available, we'll meet you at Sam's Place on 5th street at six o'clock. Please let me know if this works for you. Martha

I finally received a return text about four o'clock.

I will be there. Thanks, Steve

The text was short but at least he didn't use substitutes for words like LOL and CU.

On Saturday, Harold and I took an Uber to Sam's Place. We left early so we'd be the first to arrive. When Harold scooted in the booth next to me, I was reminded of Missy. Something must have showed on my face because Harold asked, "What?"

"How did you get to be so perceptive?" I asked in return.

"What do you mean?"

Just then the server came by. Harold ordered a house red and I ordered a Corona Lite in a glass with a lime. When the server left, I continued. "Sometimes I feel like you can read my mind. You're very perceptive," I paused before I added, "especially for a man."

"I was trained to pay close attention to the people and circumstances around me. My hyper-perception is probably what kept me alive in combat." Harold narrowed his eyes at me, "Now, what did the look mean?"

"I was suddenly reminded of Missy for some reason," I said. There was no point in elaborating since my so-called romantic relationship with Missy was now water under the bridge.

Thankfully, Harold didn't dig deeper. He simply asked, "How's she doing?"

"To be honest, I don't know the latest. She's cut off all communication as she waits to die. I know that sounds dramatic but I think that's how she wants it and I'm respecting her wishes." I held out my hand. "The day you walked me back from her room, she gave me this ring. It was a gift from her mother long ago. She wanted me to have it in remembrance of her. It was her way of saying a final goodbye."

Harold took my hand and looked at the ring. "I was wondering about the ring. What a thoughtful gift."

My beer arrived and I took a sip. Not only was sitting on the same side of the booth bringing back memories, being at Sam's Place was also reminding me of all the friends I'd lost. It was, however, also reminding me of the good times we'd had. I held out my glass. "Cheers to us old fogies!"

Harold clinked his wine glass to my frosty beer mug. "To the last lap!"

Chapter Forty-Six

Steve arrived right on time. He was broader than I'd remembered and looked more like a man. He was neatly dressed in jeans and a clean t-shirt. He wore a blue New York Yankees baseball cap. I waved and he came over to our booth and sat down across from us.

"Nice to see you under better circumstances, Steve." I gestured toward Harold. "This is my friend, Harold Lancaster. Ever since you started writing me, he's been involved behind the scenes and he wanted to meet you."

Steve reached across the table to shake Harold's hand. "Nice to meet you Mr. Lancaster."

"Just call me Harold."

I added, "And you can call me Martha."

After Steve ordered a beer, Harold ordered a pepperoni and sausage pizza for the table. Since he was the one most concerned about Steve's reliability, I encouraged him to ask the questions. Steve graciously answered each of Harold's questions without showing any signs of animosity. After he told us about his job working in a local mechanic's shop and his housing, Harold asked him about his long-range plans.

"As soon as I save up some money, I'd like to get special training so I can work on 18-wheelers. I've heard there's more opportunity there and more money. Only problem is I need to save up for an apartment, too. I can only stay where I am for six months. It takes a bit to save up two months' rent plus a damage deposit. That's what the counselor at the housing office told me I'll need."

Harold cleared his throat, and I could tell a bigger question was coming. "Ever consider enlisting in the Army?"

Steve looked surprised. "I thought felons weren't allowed."

Harold nodded. "You're right but in some cases, waivers are available. You'd need a letter of recommendation and a few other things. If you could get in, they'd give you the diesel training you're looking for but you'd have to wait until you're no longer on probation and can show a good employment record."

Steve's eyes lit up. "Wow, I had no idea. My dad died in the Iraq War when I was about a year old and I've always wanted to follow in his footsteps. The only thing I own that I care about is his bronze star. I was able to salvage it before our house was repossessed and my mom took off."

"You must be very proud of your father," I said. Steve nodded, his face full of emotion.

Harold jumped in. "If you keep your nose clean and follow through with your current plans for the next twelve months or until your probation is up, I'll be glad to help you with the waiver if you decide you want to join up. I'm a retired Army guy myself."

"You'd do that for me?" Steve said with incredulity. I had the feeling no one had ever stood up for him or cared about his welfare before. I wondered about his mother but decided not to ask.

"Of course. You've had a rocky start in life, young man, but that doesn't mean it can't drastically change if you're willing to do the work," Harold said.

Everyone was quiet after the pizza arrived. It was surprisingly good.

Harold wiped his greasy fingers on a napkin. "How much longer are you on parole?"

When we learned that Steve would be on parole for the next three years, I wondered if Harold would live long enough to help the boy out. I pushed this thought aside. For Steve, just knowing he had someone in his corner was probably worth it, no matter the final outcome.

Early summer droned on, and I became increasingly aware of my mental decline especially as it related to walking to and from the places I normally traveled. Names also escaped me. My Post-it-notes helped in the name category and I frequently popped a Post-it in my purse before meeting someone whose name I was prone to forget.

To make sure I ended up in the dining room for lunch, I started meeting Laura at her apartment, which was only a few doors down from mine, so we could walk together. Harold picked me up for dinner. Because breakfast and my workout were the first thing in the morning, I seemed to navigate to and from those without much difficulty.

In July, I got a text from my granddaughter.

Are you available to talk, Gran?

Give me a couple of minutes.

My phone rang just as I got situated in my recliner.

"Hello?"

Two voices rang out. "We're moms!"

"Congratulations!" I said. "Tell me more."

"Marti was born day before yesterday," said Bobbie, "and everyone is fine. She's seven pounds, four ounces, and twenty-one inches long. She's as bald as can be and has big blue eyes."

"We already know that she's going to be feisty and adventurous just like her namesake," Barbara chimed in.

I chuckled into the phone. "When can I see her?"

"We'll try to come for your birthday in October." I think Bobbie replied. It was difficult to know who was talking.

"That would be wonderful. Send me pictures, will you?"

"Of course!" they answered in unison.

I heard crying in the background. "Gotta go. It's feeding time again. Bye."

"Goodbye girls. I love you all!"

"We love you too, Gran!"

When they hung up, I had to tell someone the good news, so I texted Harold.

I have a new great-grand and she's named after me! They're calling her Marti.

Congratulations! I can't wait to see the pictures.

Now that I knew everything was fine and the baby was indeed a girl, that afternoon I stitched *Marti* on the two receiving blankets that I'd embroidered earlier. I wrapped them in tissue paper and decided to ask Richard to mail them for me since he was coming to lunch later in the week. I also wrote a check to the girls. I didn't have a way to buy a card, so I simply wrote a note of congratulations and slipped it into an envelope with the check.

Although the days seemed long, the weeks sped by quickly and before I knew it, fall was in the air and the Manor was dressed up with fake yellow leaves and pumpkins. My birthday was around the corner, but I'd already told Richard I didn't want a big party. If the girls came with Marti, seeing them would be enough of a celebration.

At almost ninety-one, my energy was limited, but I still had a zest for life and I found satisfaction in my embroidery, my books, and my few friends. Laura and Harold kept me going with their stories of the past and their enthusiasm for the present. Lately, Harold kept busy making wooden boxes for Marcella and her friends to store their friendship bracelets in, and Laura was back to writing daily. She often shared her short stories with me.

I embroidered small pictures of flowers and framed them in oval frames. I sent these to my daughters, gave one to Laura and Judy, and left two with Harold to give to his daughter and granddaughter. Doing something creative and having a finished product that I could share with others was fulfilling in a way I'd never imagined.

That fall, I finally asked my son to take me out to lunch. I was tired of institutional food and, since I was no longer planning after-hours escapades, I needed the break. The change seemed to be good for him too and he talked animatedly about his new life as a single man. The house had sold and he'd bought a condo not far from the Manor. I was relieved to know I wouldn't have to move. He was considering dating again and he'd joined a dating site.

Susan and Michael were moving ahead with their wedding plans for late October, which was another reason I didn't want a big birthday celebration. The wedding was going to be in the city and I wondered if I'd have the energy for the trip.

When the wedding grew close, Susan's mother took me shopping for a dress to wear. On the way to the store, Maria questioned the couple's decision. "To me, the whole thing seems rushed. I can't imagine why they're in such a hurry to get married. Most couples their age live together for a few years first."

I wondered if she was jealous of their happiness or genuinely concerned. I wisely chose not to reply. Their wedding would be close to the one-year anniversary of their meeting on the ship. Having been there to see the look on Susan's face when she first told me about Michael, I thought that, at least for her, it was possibly a case of love at first sight.

The shopping trip was exhausting, but I was happy with the floor-length, smokey-gray, lace chiffon dress I'd purchased.

My wedding invitation included Harold. I was glad he was invited but I wondered if he'd agree to attend. Since getting a pacemaker, he seemed to be more at ease about his health but I didn't know if he'd want to venture as far as the city. At dinner that night, I read the invitation and showed him his name on the envelope. "I'd like to have you come with me if you feel up to it."

"I'd love to go," Harold said without hesitation.

"Terrific! It's a date," I said, genuinely happy to have him as my companion. Harold knew the current me better than my family did and I always felt safe when I was in his presence.

My son called to say he would pick us up at the Manor and drive us to the hotel in New York where the wedding and reception were to be held. Barbara, Bobbie, and little Marti were also coming with both of my daughters. Right after I'd received the wedding invitation, my granddaughter called to say they'd see me at the wedding rather than come to the Manor for my birthday.

I knew this would probably be the last time I'd see my family together in one place. Perhaps they'd assemble for my funeral but I didn't care about that one way or the other.

Chapter Forty-Seven

When I started having trouble making clothing selections for dinner, I asked Judy to stop by. She knocked and then joined me in the bedroom where I was standing in front of a closet full of clothes.

I motioned from one side to the other. "I'm fine choosing what to wear in the morning. All my workout clothes are on this side," I indicated the left side of the closet, "and all the t-shirts are mix and match with the leggings."

I pointed to my pants, blouses, sweaters, and dresses hanging to the right. "But by late afternoon, when I need to change into something for dinner, I'm overwhelmed with the choices and forget what goes with what. I thought we could pair them on one hanger. Will you help me?"

Judy looked at me with a sympathetic smile. "Of course." She pulled several hangers from the closet and laid them on the bed. "Let's start with these."

I'd narrowed my jewelry choices down to two sets so I could still make my own selections. I had a silver necklace and earrings set, a gold necklace and earrings set, my Swiftie bracelets, and my pin from Harold. I always wore the ring from Missy. Word had drifted over from skilled care that Missy was in a coma and not expected to live much longer. To me, she'd been gone since the day of my last visit.

Before she left, Judy asked if I had any Post-it-notes left. I brought them to her, she wrote the days of the week on them, and then attached one to each hangar. "This is so you can be confident that you're not wearing the same outfit day after day."

"What a great idea. Thanks for your help, Judy. What would I do without you?"

"Anything else?"

I gave her a hug. "Not yet."

That afternoon when I slipped into my dinner clothes, I felt confident knowing I wasn't pairing plaid with print or something else equally distasteful. I was also grateful to have one less thing to worry about.

Just before my birthday, I came down with a virus and had to stay in my apartment for a couple of days. The fever, headache, and cough took a lot out of me, and I hoped I'd rebound before the wedding and the special time with my family.

I requested no visitors because I didn't want to pass it on to anyone. Judy, however, checked on me each morning and afternoon, and someone from the night staff came by in the evening.

The day of the wedding was finally approaching, and I felt ready. Although I still tired easily, I had recovered from the virus. I had my grandmother-of-the-bride dress ready, and Judy had helped me set aside traveling clothes. Richard was to pick Harold and me up on the morning of the wedding and take us to the hotel, where overnight reservations had been made for us.

The wedding was at four o'clock so we'd have plenty of time to rest and change into our finery. The reception and dinner followed immediately after the wedding. Susan explained to me that the room where the wedding was to be held would be repurposed for the reception with an hour's delay for cocktails and hors d'oeuvres. She assured me that, if needed, this was a time I could put my feet up and take a short rest.

Richard dropped us off in front of the hotel and we were met by a bellman who took our luggage and our two clothing bags. I walked up to the young girl at the reservation desk and said, "I believe you have a room reserved for Martha Anderson."

She plucked on the computer then prepared two plastic key cards. When she handed them to me, she said, "Room 1642 has been reserved for Martha Anderson and Harold Lancaster. Here are your key cards. The elevator to your room is on the left."

I looked at Harold. When he raised his shoulders, I chose not to challenge the unexpected turn of events. I took the cards, thanked the young lady, then Harold and I followed the bellman to the bank of elevators.

Luckily, the room was close to the elevator, so there wasn't much walking involved. There was also no conversation. I opened the door to a room flooded with sunshine and featuring a king-sized bed. Harold must have noticed my expression because he immediately said, "Don't worry, Martha. I won't be up for any hanky-panky," he winked at me, "if you know what I mean." Then he turned, tipped the bellman, and closed the door behind us.

Always honest, Harold was clear about his intentions— or lack thereof. I gestured toward the bed. "It's a big bed. I'm sure we'll both be comfortable. In fact, I wouldn't mind taking a little nap after lunch."

We put our toiletries in the bathroom, hung our wedding clothes in the closet, and took the elevator downstairs for a light lunch. When we returned to our room, I took off my clothes, wrapped myself in my kimono, and laid down for a short nap. Harold did the same, minus the kimono. At three o'clock, we dressed in our best. Harold zipped up my dress and I straightened his tie. It all felt surprisingly natural.

When we approached the room reserved for the wedding, I immediately saw Ruth, Elizabeth, and Richard, Barbara and Bobbie, who was holding baby Marti. Rich and Samantha had two-year-old David in tow. Mother-of-the-bride, Maria, was close by speaking with a hotel employee.

I paused for a moment to take a mental picture. I hadn't seen all of my children and grands together since my late husband's funeral over eight years ago. Of course, the bride was missing but she would soon be the star of the show and then I'd add Michael to the family photo in my mind. I knew there'd be a multitude of actual photos taken, but I wanted a mental picture I could recall at any time.

As soon as they saw us, Bobbie and Barbara rushed over with Marti snugly wrapped in one of the receiving blankets I'd embroidered. She was indeed as bald as a cue ball, as my dad would say, but adorable with fat, rosy cheeks and tiny pink ears. When they placed her in my arms, she gave me a gummy smile.

My other great, David, was also adorable in a miniature tux with a tiny rosebud in the lapel. It was a special treat to see all three of my children together, though a bit jolting when I considered they were past middle-aged with graying hair and wrinkles.

The make-shift altar was adorned with baskets of fall flowers which reminded me of the flowers Harold brought me after my bout with Covid. Susan's maid-of-honor was a friend I didn't recognize. She was dressed in a dark shade of orange that I'd call russet and carried a bouquet of roses in various shades of orange and pink. The groomsman resembled Michael so much that I was sure they were brothers.

Susan was stunning in a simple white satin sheath dress that showed off her lovely figure. She carried a bouquet of orange roses with cascades of cymbidium orchids. Harold and I sat in the row with Maria and Richard who, I was happy to note, were behaving like adults.

It was a simple ceremony. When a few happy tears rolled down my cheeks, Harold handed me his handkerchief. I was glad to see Susan settled with a man she obviously adored. My dad would have predicted that she'd give him a run for his money but I felt assured that he was up to the challenge.

After the I-dos and the kiss, we left the room for cocktails and hors d'oeuvres in an adjacent space. Puff pastries with crab were passed around. When I took a bite, memories of the Captain's Dinner flashed into my mind and I momentarily wondered about Andre. I was surprised that I remembered his name considering I could barely remember the names of my children some days.

I looked over at Harold who was having an animated discussion with the groom's father. He wasn't as handsome or debonaire as Andre, but he was here and he was mine, at least as much as I wanted him to be.

A professional photographer took an abundance of photos, and Susan assured me that my Christmas gift would be an album. Although Harold held back, everyone in the family, including me, encouraged him to pose with the rest of us.

Dinner featured a selection of French entrees served family style. Whoever was paying for this party hadn't held back. There was good French wine and in lieu of a wedding cake, a croquembouche which was a tower of profiteroles or cream puffs, was on display. An ensemble of four musicians played music in the background while we ate. After dinner was cleared, more musicians arrived to provide music for dancing. When Susan encouraged us to join her and Michael on the floor, Harold surprised me with a very respectable two-step.

Our dance ended with applause and after we sat down, I had the feeling of overflowing abundance. I was full of hope for my family's future, full of love, full of pride, and full of gratitude for all I'd been given. And then, just as suddenly, I was tired. A hit-the-wall kind of tired like I'd felt the day Harold had rescued me in the hall between skilled care and assisted living. When Harold looked at me, I could tell that he'd noticed.

"Ready to turn in?" he asked. "It's your call."

I nodded. "I'm ready, Freddie."

Harold smiled. "A dad-ism, right?"

"How'd you guess?"

I got up and Harold took my hand. "I'd sure miss him if he wasn't around."

"Me too. Let's go say our goodbyes."

After many hugs, we slowly walked to our room. Harold helped me out of my dress and gave me first use of the bathroom. I removed my makeup and put on my nightie. Harold, in his boxers and t-shirt, went into the bathroom when I exited. The bed was soft and comfortable. Although the room was chilly, the puffy, white duvet felt warm and luxurious. Harold came to my side of the bed, leaned down and kissed me. "Good night, Martha."

He walked around to the other side, crawled in, and laid on his right facing the wall. I came up behind him, wrapped my left arm around his waist, and spooned into his s-shaped body. "Sleep tight and don't let the bedbugs bite," I whispered into his ear.

His belly vibrated with a silent chuckle. It was the perfect ending to a perfect day.

Martha's Dadisms

rascals
hit the hay
bellyaching
fit as a fiddle
sharp as a tack
cute as a button
bald as a cue ball
I'm ready, Freddie
dead as a doornail
neck-of-the-woods
built like a fire plug
drop dead gorgeous
scarce as hen's teeth
give him a run for his money
not the hill I wanted to die on
slicker than snot on a doorknob
a wet dog shaking off after a bath
you can't have your cake and eat it too
sleep tight and don't let the bed bugs bite
you couldn't swing a cat by the tail without hitting one

Acknowledgements

It may not take a village to publish a book but it certainly takes a circle of devoted people. I'd like to thank my editor and proof reader, Lynn Alexander, for her dedication, encouragement, and expertise. My cover and interior designer, Lance Buckley, always comes through and my critique group keeps me on my toes.

I also want to thank my three BETA readers: Claudia Johnson, Rebecca Johnson (not related), and Margaret Xanthopoulos for their insights and early preview of the book. Their positive responses gave me the courage to push on to publishing.

My years on the board of Friendship Village (now Encore Village of Schaumburg, IL), a large (1,000 population) continuing care organization and later, board chair of the parent company gave me insights into senior living. Thanks for the learning opportunities!

However, there's nothing like personal experience so I want to thank my friend, Donna Simons, who is a current independent living resident at a facility in Florida, for sharing snippets from her daily life. The line, "It's like being in junior high" came from Donna along with other stories and pithy sayings.

My late dad, Leon Horn, lived his final years in an assisted living apartment. Staff came by regularly for their mini-sodas and a chat. He undoubtedly shared his "dadisms" with them.

Perhaps I'll be "Martha" in a decade. If so, I hope I have her zest for life and sense of adventure. I also hope I have a cadre of friends with whom I can share my last hurrah.

About the Author

MERSHON NIESNER found her calling as an author later in life. Her first book, *Mom's Gone, Now What? Ten Steps to Help Daughters Move Forward After Mother Loss,* was published on her 75th birthday.

Her historical fiction books, *The Bootmaker's Wife* and *Angie, The Bee Lady,* were inspired by her great-grandparents who were Nebraska pioneers.

The inspiration for *It's (Mostly) Good To Be Martha* came to Mershon when she was a guest author at The Manor Book Club in Marco Island, Florida. The audience was made up of older ladies who were full of life and exuded enthusiasm. When they asked about her next project, she looked at them and was instantly inspired to write about Martha.

Watch for Book Two of the Martha series entitled *Murder (Maybe) At Martyn Manor.*

Mershon lives with her husband, Ken, in Naples, Florida. They have a blended family of six children, nineteen grandchildren, and eleven great-grands.

To receive Mershon's monthly newsletter, **Musings From Mershon**, email her at mershonniesner@gmail.com

Made in United States
Troutdale, OR
06/17/2025

32203167R00204